UNEXPECTED
arrivals

For my own unexpected arrival...

PROLOGUE

I STARED AT THE PAPER IN MY HANDS WONDERING WHAT THE FUCK I was reading. My eyes scanned the area around the mailbox and the perimeter of the house, but there was no one in sight. This had to be a joke. Any minute now, the cameras were going to come out from behind the other homes on our street, or a van would drive up and Ashton Kutcher would slide the door open, laughing hysterically at my melodramatic performance on the front porch. The longer I waited, the longer nothing happened. Kids continued to play in their yards, my neighbor still mowed his grass, and the occasional car still drove by without stopping.

The words on the page jumbled into a toxic mess my brain refused to comprehend.

Please consider this letter as a formal request to arrange a paternity test (DNA) for minor child Airy.

Airy—that was a name I hadn't heard in years. I'd gone out with Chelsea Airy once, and we'd been friends for a while after my dad's fiftieth birthday party. I hadn't heard so much as a peep from her since I'd gotten engaged. I'd reached out a handful of times, but she'd quit responding and fell off the face of the earth, and I hadn't thought about her since. There hadn't been a text, an email, a phone call, not even a Facebook message. She'd disappeared from my life as randomly as she'd stumbled into it.

Flipping the envelope over, I again read the return address and wondered who the hell sent this kind of information through the fucking mail. Clary, White, & Boyd—that's who.

"Mr. Carpenter, are you okay?"

The little girl from across the street pulled my thoughts back to the present, and my hand from my head when she tugged on my elbow. I realized I'd been standing in the same spot since I'd opened the letter and had yanked my hair by the roots since I'd begun reading.

"Oh, um. Yeah. Jamie, I'm fine."

"You look like my daddy after my mommy yells at him. Did Mrs. Carpenter yell at you?"

"Not yet, but I'm sure she will." I mumbled under my breath, "Right before she files for divorce."

"Maybe you should get her flowers. If it's really bad, my daddy buys my mommy things that sparkle. Maybe Mrs. Carpenter would like sparkles, too."

All the diamonds in the world wouldn't fix this—Cora could forgive a lot, but she'd never wanted children.

FIFTEEN YEARS EARLIER

JAMES

AFTER I SLAMMED MY LOCKER DOOR SHUT, I TURNED TO JOIN THE sea of people meandering the halls of Harbrook High. Another day in the life with kids I'd known since birth. Shuffling through the crowd, I made my way to second period without so much as lifting my head. The voices that said hello, and the familiar pats on the back never changed. Every day was just like the last. There were never new faces, and I'd grown bored with the old ones somewhere around junior high.

Until today.

I hovered over the desk I'd sat at since the year started, but instead of it being empty—waiting for my ass to grace its presence and warm the seat—there was a girl where nothing should have been. The light streaming through the window behind me cast my shadow over her tiny frame. I'd been prepared to kick her out, until she lifted her gaze and tossed my world on its side just before it sent me spinning.

The way her eyes caressed my body until she found my gaze, the soft pink glow on her cheeks, her long, dark hair falling over her shoulder to cover her breast...it all stole the air from my lungs. I'd never seen eyes so green or skin so smooth. There wasn't a flaw on her perfect face, and her lips—holy hell, her lips begged to be kissed.

When my heart resumed beating and my chest filled with air once again, I finally managed words. "Hey, I'm James." *Smooth, Carpenter, really fucking smooth.*

"Hi." She waved her delicate hand in greeting. "I'm Cora." Her name rolled off her tongue like a song, pure and angelic, but sultry and seductive.

Before I could ask her to switch seats with me or decide to sit next to her, an unwelcomed interruption barreled into my shoulder. "Carp, looks like your ass is relocating to the back."

My head jerked to the side to find my best friend, Neil Samson, with a wicked grin plastered on his face. He was moments away from embarrassing the shit out of me if I stood here like a lost puppy a second longer. I allowed him to move me as he proceeded to his normal hiding place in the last row, but then my eyes held hers until they were forced away.

"What the hell was that, man? You act like you've never seen a new kid in class." Neil's voice carried around the room. "And since when are you into nerdy-chic chicks, anyhow?"

Backhanding him across the chest, I found a seat as close to Cora as possible. "Dude, shut the hell up. What's your problem?"

He held up his hands in surrender. "Nothing. Chill out."

Mrs. Johnson stood in front of the board, anticipating the sound of the bell to start teaching. This had been my least favorite class all year. I sucked at chemistry and struggled to maintain a *C* in order to keep my spot on the basketball team, but my desire to skip this period all changed in one introduction.

"Why go for the brainiac who looks like a loud noise would make her jump? I wouldn't be surprised if she was afraid of her own shadow." Clearly, Neil didn't see what I saw when Cora came into view.

There was nothing nerdy about her; quiet maybe, but that was quite possibly the fact that she was the new kid in town. She might be a star athlete, smart, and gorgeous, too. Neither of us knew a damn thing about her, but I planned to find out everything I could.

All through class, my focus stayed trained on her, wondering what she was like and where she'd come from. No one showed up here who hadn't been born in the county limits, ever. People either grew up in this town or they retired here. Geneva Key was home to more money than Fort Knox and fewer and fewer younger generations. Those of us who grew up in this blip of a community left the first chance we got, and I didn't know a soul who'd escaped and came back. There was no way to earn a living on this island—either people owned property that had been handed down through family lineage with hefty trust funds, or they'd found the tiny town after making their millions elsewhere and decided to call Geneva Key home.

I was part of that first group, as were most of the kids in this school. My parents ran organizations I couldn't tell anyone the first thing about, but none of them were located on the island, and most of their work involved international traveling. At least that was the story I was told when they'd left me with nanny after nanny growing up, and then alone when I'd hit an age that I started getting busy with the hired help. The idea of their fourteen-year-old son having sex with the au pair was more than they could handle. And if they hadn't caught us, I never would have complained. There's something to be said about an older woman teaching a teen the ways of the world...or the bedroom. And Sofia had done just that—prepared me to be a man.

I'd been so lost in my thoughts—that had veered off on a rabbit trail about my au pair—I'd missed the opportunity to find out how the raven-haired beauty had landed in our beach cocoon. My plan was to be at her desk when the bell rang and escort her to next period, maybe ask a few questions along the way, but that didn't happen. And my attempt to find her in the halls proved futile—not that the five minutes between periods offered me much chance to learn anything of substance.

When lunch rolled around, I strolled into the cafeteria with my horde of friends in tow. The basketball team was a tightly knit group of guys, and we owned this school and this town. I'd managed to make captain my junior year, and they were like my flock. I loved every one of them and had since pre-school. Today, my sights were set on something far more attractive than tall guys who belched too much and had a tendency to smell like they'd just finished a grueling practice.

There she sat, alone, at a table against the far wall in the corner. She'd chosen a spot away from the bustling of teenagers in favor of a quiet nook. Even if she hadn't been sitting by herself, the tray in front of her would have given her away as a newbie. No one who'd been here any length of time ate food made in the cafeteria.

I turned to Neil, who'd almost run into me when I'd stopped to admire her. "I'll catch you guys later."

His head moved with mine to the girl with a book in her hand and her food untouched. "Seriously, Carp, do not get sucked into whatever *that* is."

"Thanks, Dad, but I think I'll be all right." I didn't wait for his reply or bother listening to the grumblings of my teammates as we parted company.

With each hello directed at me or invitation to join a crowd I'd never sit with, I just threw my hand in the air or gave them the James Carpenter award-winning smile the ladies all loved to see and kept moving.

I didn't bother asking if the seat in front of her was taken; it wasn't. And by the looks of things, I didn't have to worry about anyone trying to move in on the fresh meat. My backpack slid down my arm and onto the table as I sat across from her. She watched me silently while I retrieved my lunch from inside my book bag, but I acted like I didn't see her until I was ready to face her. I could feel the stares from around the lunchroom, and when I glanced up, I saw girls who'd spent years trying to get my attention gawking with their mouths slightly ajar, taking in the sight.

"I guess no one told you not to buy lunch?" I scoffed at the sight of the gray hamburger on an even duller-looking bun. I speculated those were fries next to it, but I wouldn't have bet money on that guess.

"Not much of a choice. I didn't have a lot of time to prepare for a new school." Even the sadness in her words didn't take away from the smile in her voice.

"Unexpected move?"

Her head bobbed slowly.

"Where are you from?"

"White Plains." She took a sip from the bottle of water in front of her. "New York."

"Why the hell would you leave New York for Geneva Key?" My teeth sank into the bright-red apple I'd missed eating between classes.

"I didn't have much of a choice." Her head cocked to the side when she'd repeated herself, and she studied me for just the briefest of seconds.

I wouldn't be surprised if she were memorizing the crystal-blue eyes watching her or the way my brown hair sat perfectly messy on top of my head, or possibly, the way the muscles in my jaw tensed as I chewed. Girls had found far less interesting things to adore about me.

Cora returned her attention to her book and dismissed me as quickly as she'd answered.

Unsure of what to do with a girl who didn't fawn all over me, I tried again. "Your parents move here for some odd reason?"

"No."

Her response wasn't cold, more like vacant. I couldn't help but notice people had resumed their meals and no longer gave us any attention.

"So you wanna tell me what brought you here?" It came off more agitated than I intended. I wasn't irritated with her, just the situation. She clearly wasn't aware of what opportunity sat in front of her.

Cora closed her book and pushed her tray aside to set the novel down. I didn't recognize the title, nor did I particularly care. I was more interested in why this gorgeous girl was sitting alone in an unfamiliar town not wanting anything to do with anyone around her.

"My parents were killed in a plane crash last week. My grandparents brought me home with them after the funeral. We got here last night."

Holy shit.

That was not on my radar.

I stopped chewing and stared at her. The way her emerald-green eyes dulled made my heart clench painfully. Words weren't going to ease her pain, and neither was my cocky attitude. With the half-eaten apple in one hand, I reached across the table with the other. My fingers rested on hers before curling in with the slightest bit of a squeeze. She fought against the tears that filled her aching eyes, but one escaped against her valiant effort. Mindlessly, I set the fruit down and wiped the lone tear from her cheek with my thumb.

"You want some of my peanut butter and jelly?" I could have slapped myself. She was orphaned less than a week ago, and somehow, I believed half of my sandwich would ease that pain.

She chuckled the tiniest bit, and the tears cascaded down her beautiful face. The loss radiated in her eyes, but God, I'd give every last cent in my trust fund to keep her smiling.

"Captain of the basketball team eats PB and J for lunch? And you said the school food was bad." It wasn't as funny as it sounded coming from her lips.

"My reputation supersedes me."

"Yeah, something like that." She'd suddenly become shy. Her eyes cast down, and the corners of her mouth fell flat.

"Sorry, I'm a tad arrogant at times. You'll have to excuse that. It's just part of my charm." I bent over, craning my neck to coax her into meeting my gaze. "So tell me, Cora, have you ever been to the beach in December?"

My chest tightened, hoping she'd take the bait, desperate to find a way to spend time with her. I'd never had the instant attraction to anyone that I felt for her. It might have been nothing, yet it might have been everything. Unless she was willing to let me in, there was zero chance we'd find out.

"I've never been to the beach at all."

"Do you have plans after school?" My pulse raced with anticipation.

"Don't you have basketball practice or weights to lift or some other equally macho thing to do?"

"Yeah, but I'm done by five. I can stop by your house and pick you up."

"You don't know where I live."

I wondered if *she* knew, although now wasn't the time to ask such an insensitive question. "Just tell me who your grandparents are. I've lived here all my life. I'm sure I know them."

"Chase. Gwendolyn and Owen Chase."

If I'd been drinking anything, it would have ended up all over her light-pink shirt that cupped her perfect breasts like it was made to showcase them. "Seriously?" Chase as in the financial company —that Chase. They made everyone else on the island look like paupers.

She shrugged as if it were insignificant.

"You don't seem impressed."

"Why would I be? I don't know them any better than I know you. In fact, I might know you better at this point. We've certainly had more conversation."

"So why did you come live with them if you're not close?"

"I don't have any other family, and they wouldn't let me stay with friends for a year and a half while I finished high school. They didn't think it was appropriate for a seventeen-year-old to be gallivanting around New York unescorted." That last part was clearly a repetition of a sentiment they'd communicated to her, probably more than once in the last week.

Again, she'd rendered me speechless, which was a difficult task. Before I could figure out something to say, Neil came strolling up to the table.

"Carp, you coming?"

Any other time, that would have been my escape. I would have been pissed it'd taken him twenty minutes to come to my rescue, except this girl was different. "Nah, man. I'm good here. I'll catch you after school."

"It's okay, James. You can go. I'll be fine." No one at this school called me James; however, the way my name floated past her lips made me want to drop the surname and be like Madonna or Prince.

"Yeah, *James*. You can go." Neil scowled at me like I'd offended him by turning down his invitation.

I looked back at the dark-haired beauty still seated in front of me. Her green eyes had dimmed again, and I hated leaving her. The pressures of high school sucked. Even though I normally called the shots, I gave in this time—my friends had been my lifeline since we were all in diapers.

"I'll come by when I get out of practice, okay? Say five thirty or so." I grabbed my uneaten lunch, stuffed it into my backpack, and waited for her reply with Neil standing over my shoulder. Never in my life had I felt the need to sucker punch him, until now. I was having a hard time holding back today.

She glanced up at Neil and then to me. The tiny nod she gave me only served to cause my fist to ball at my side. My best friend wasn't acting any differently than either of us always did, but it crushed me to hurt her in the process. I didn't stop it. I got up and hoped I could make it up to her after school.

When we were out of earshot, I punched him in the arm so hard it almost knocked him off balance. "What the fuck, Neil?"

"You can't be serious about her? She'll never fit in with our friends."

"Then maybe it's time to find new friends. Jesus. You were such a dick."

"She called you James. Is she your mom?"

"Hey, asshole. That's what I told her my name was. Hard for her to know differently when she's been in the school all of four hours, and the town about eight more than that."

"Who cares?"

I stopped in my tracks. Neil halted in front of me. I'd only had a handful of defining moments in my seventeen years, times where one instant changed my life, and this was one. "Dude, both of her parents died last week. Cut her some fucking slack."

"Ahh, a charity lay. I get it, Carp."

And just like that, the fist that had been balled at my side since I'd gotten up from my seat landed on his right cheek. The fight erupted faster than I realized what had happened. I saw red, and my best friend met my right hook. When we were finally separated, I glanced back to the corner I'd last seen Cora, but she was gone. And my vantage point from the principal's office didn't offer me another glimpse of her before the final bell.

Thankfully, Neil and I had only been given detention and weren't suspended, but that hadn't sat well with the coach. Even though the administration had been lenient, Coach Howard was not. He didn't hesitate to bench us both until after Christmas break.

***

It was almost six by the time I pulled up to the Chase mansion. The lights burned brightly throughout, but there were no cars in the driveway. I didn't have her phone number, so I hadn't been able to let her know I was running late. When I knocked on the door, it took ages for someone to finally answer it. I'd been expecting hired help, so it came as a shock when Cora greeted me.

"Hey." She had yet to meet my eyes, and instead, stared at my feet.

I lifted her chin and noticed the red rim beneath her lashes and the bloodshot look around her irises. "I'm sorry I'm late. I didn't have your number to call."

"It's okay." She swiped her tongue along her lips, and I traced its movement until it disappeared back into her mouth.

"No, it's not." Running my hand through my hair, I tugged on the roots in frustration. "I got in trouble at school and then with the team. I came as soon as they let me out. I haven't even been home."

"I know. I saw."

Fuck. I'd hoped she'd left the cafeteria when I'd gotten up, and she'd missed the shitshow between Neil and me. "It's not a big deal."

"Look, I appreciate you trying to be nice, but I don't want to come between you and your friends."

I chose to ignore that comment. "Are you ready?"

Her eyes grew wide, and she glanced around and then back at me. "For what?"

"The beach." I didn't wait for her to turn me down. "Do you need to tell your grandparents you're leaving?"

"They're not here. No one is."

I stopped myself from asking the obvious. There was no way in hell this girl should be alone after what she'd been through in the last week, but who was I to judge? Maybe they'd gone to the store —although, that thought made me laugh. I doubted the Chases did any of their own shopping.

Instead, I snatched her hand. She pulled back just enough to grab the handle and close the door behind her. The Chase property sat directly on the beach. We just had to walk around the massive home to the back and out to the sand. The sky had grown dusky, although a slight bit of color still clung to the horizon just above the water. It would be dark soon, but there wasn't a cloud in the sky, and the moon was full.

We both left our shoes behind her house and embarked on the evening. Cora didn't try to talk, and neither did I. I was perfectly content holding her tiny hand in mine, wandering the shoreline. I'd walk all the way up the Gulf Coast if she'd stay with me. When the sun had set completely, and the moonlight was all that lit the path, I finally took the chance on a conversation.

"Where was everyone tonight?"

"My grandparents left this morning for Prague. They'll be back in a couple weeks."

"What about the staff? I doubt they leave that place unattended."

"Most went with them, I think. Honestly, James, I'm not sure. When I got up this morning, there was a driver waiting to take me to school, a stack of cash and a credit card on the counter, and their itinerary."

I squeezed her hand, wondering just how lonely she truly was. The rest of us lived the same sort of life: drivers, cooks, maids, and allowances to tide us over while our parents ran around the world doing God knew what, leaving us to raise ourselves. I just couldn't understand anyone doing it after such an upheaval in her life.

"So you're alone in that enormous house?"

"It's not so bad. At least this way I don't have to talk to anyone. I don't have to pretend everything is okay. If I need to yell or cry or laugh uncontrollably, there's no one to stop me." She didn't let go of my hand. Instead, her grasp became a little tighter with that statement, as though she were afraid she might drift away if she let go.

"Have you eaten dinner?" I knew she hadn't eaten lunch, and from the sounds of it, there had been no breakfast, either.

"I'm not hungry. I'm doing good not to be a blubbering mess."

Cora offered me a pitiful excuse for a smile, or maybe it was a grimace—either way, it was to pacify my need to comfort her.

"Were you close to your parents?" It was a tough topic I had to tread lightly around. If I pushed too hard, she might break down, and my hope was to get her to open up and share something she loved with me.

Her lips tilted up and then parted into the most stunning smile I'd ever had the pleasure of witnessing. The happiness reached all the way to her eyes, and even in the darkness of the night, I could see the vivid green almost glowing with love.

"They were my best friends. We were very close." She hesitated before saying anything else, and I waited. "I was supposed to be with them on that flight. I'd begged to stay home to see Coldplay in Manhattan. They'd reluctantly agreed to leave me alone for the first time. Well, as alone as a teenage girl can get with people always in the house."

I'd heard of things like this before, where fate intervened, although I'd never known anyone who'd been on the receiving end of it.

"I think my mom knew—well, not *knew*. Like a premonition that something was going to go wrong. I just think she thought it was going to happen to me. She left her assistant, Faith, behind to escort my friends and me to the concert. Faith got the call on our way home. She tried to keep it together until after we'd dropped everyone else off, except I could see it in her eyes, written all over her face. Even though she worked for my mom, she loved her, too. They were super close. When she finally broke the news, her soul shattered with mine. I think leaving her was worse than leaving my friends and my house and my school. She's been around as long as I can remember."

"Did she live with you guys?"

"Practically. Faith tried to get temporary custody of me, but she didn't have the money to fight my grandparents, and since my parents' will hadn't specified who got custody, I went with my next of kin. So here I am."

"Jesus. That's awful. Have you talked to her?"

"Not since the funeral. It's wrong; I should want to reach out to her, return her calls. It's just that she's a painful reminder of all I had to leave behind."

"I'm glad you're here with me." It was stupid, but I didn't have a clue what else to say. I'd never lost anyone close to me, and I wasn't close to my parents and probably never would be.

She stopped with her feet at the edge of the shore and let the water roll over her toes and up to her ankles. The glow of the moon highlighted her natural beauty and made her appear almost angelic. When she stared up at me, I couldn't stop myself from pulling her in. I needed to protect her, to comfort her, to ease her pain. Yet all I had to offer was a hug. Cora came willingly, wrapping her arms around my waist, her head resting on my chest. She was tiny in comparison, and somehow, I hoped that the difference in our size offered her reassurance.

For the second time that day, I'd experienced another one of those moments, one that would alter the course of my life. With Cora in my arms and the ocean kissing our feet, my heart fell, our souls collided, and I'd found the love of my life. At seventeen and a junior in high school, serendipity—no, fate—had delivered the missing piece of my rib in the form of Cora Chase.

2

JAMES

THERE WERE DEFINITE BENEFITS TO HAVING CLOUT, NOT ONLY IN school, but in Geneva Key in general. Once I'd decided Cora Chase owned my soul that night on the beach, it had taken a matter of days for the student body at Harbrook to fall for her as well. She'd even captivated my best friend once he'd spent time with her and got over the changes. Cora was magnetic, and she had a personality that drew people in once she let down her guard.

Cora had only been in school two weeks before we were out for Christmas break, and in that time, it was no secret that the five-foot-three-inch Yankee had me wrapped around her little finger. And by the time we returned after the new year, we were a solid couple everyone stopped to admire and tried to befriend. She joined the track team in the spring and shined like the star I'd known she was from the moment I'd met her. The other students quickly figured out she was a force to be reckoned with in the classroom as well. This girl had it all. And there wasn't a soul on campus who didn't either envy me for having her or wish they were her. A year ago, that would have fed my ego, yet a few weeks with Cora and that part of me dissipated.

I wanted to be better for her, she needed a soft place to land, and I was determined I would be that security in her life. In order to do so, my pride had to take a back seat to her needs. Neil had been the only person who continued to keep his distance. All he saw was her changing me, although he didn't recognize what she did was make me a better person. Cora dulled my hard edges. She loved the things about me no one else saw: the way I listened when she talked, my ability to be silent when she needed company, my need to show her how special she truly was. It didn't seem like much at the time, but for a girl who'd just lost both of her parents and had a tumultuous relationship with her new guardians, it was huge.

For the first time in my life, I breathed for someone else. My heart pumped to fuel my body to make her day better. She gave the same in return. There was nothing about our relationship that was one-sided. As soon as Neil recognized that and realized Cora wasn't going anywhere, he got on board and fell for her just as hard as everyone else who ever came into contact with her. Despite the tragedy she'd faced, Cora had a smile that won over rooms. She was friends with people in the band, on the varsity track team, and in the debate club. Her acceptance had no limits, and truth be told, she made Harbrook a better place to be.

Our senior year, I found myself sitting with people at lunch that I'd gone to school with for a decade and didn't know their names. That was Cora's style—she never wanted anyone to be excluded. Everything about her was beautiful—inside and out.

"Have you decided on a college, Carp?" Jordan was one of the many people Cora had made friends with when she first got to Geneva Key, and they'd become close since.

This was a sore subject between Cora and me, and I hated for people to ask about it when the two of us were together. "The University of Kentucky and the University of North Carolina both offered me a basketball scholarship."

Cora, Jordan, Neil, and I all sat together during study hall. Having finished our homework, we had nothing better to do than chit chat. Unfortunately, this topic occupied the minds of most seniors in Geneva Key—we all wanted out. Cora hadn't applied to the same schools I had, and we now had to make the choice of one following the other or try the long-distance thing.

"Are you going to take one of them?" Jordan kept digging, though her curiosity was innocent.

"I'm not sure. They're both good schools with great basketball teams."

"Except he can't live without Cora within arm's reach." Neil's sarcasm grated on my nerves, and I shot him a glare to demonstrate just how irritated I was.

The bell rang before the discussion could get heated. Neil knew I wouldn't put up with his shit where Cora was concerned. She was my world, and if I had to give up a scholarship, then I would. I didn't need it anyhow. My parents had plenty of money and didn't give a shit where I went to college as long as I went.

I kissed my girlfriend goodbye with a quick peck on the lips and parted ways, then Neil and I headed to our next class together.

"You're too young to be making decisions based on a girl, Carp."

"Says the guy who has never gotten laid." I rolled my eyes without looking at him.

"Dude, do you have any idea how much pussy you will be abandoning if you two go to school together? I get this is great in Geneva Key where there are no options, but you're a fool if you let that girl dictate your life."

I stopped and stared at him like he'd lost his damn mind.

"Don't look at me like that. I'd say that to any guy about any girl. If she's it, she'll still be it after college when you've had a chance to enjoy freedom."

"What the fuck are you talking about, Neil? It's not like I have parents breathing down my back, or hell, even a chaperone. I certainly wasn't a fucking virgin when I started sleeping with her. You don't get the connection because you've never felt it. I don't have a desire to be away from her."

"That'll change." His matter-of-fact tone pissed me off.

"No, dude, it won't. I don't care if my dick never meets the warmth of another pussy. She's it for me."

"You're an idiot."

Neil was once again saved by the bell signaling the start of our next class. By the time the period was over, my anger had calmed and he'd forgotten about the conversation entirely. And when I saw the inky hair and bright smile of the girl I loved, I no longer cared.

I stopped at her locker while she exchanged books. Cora closed the metal door, and instantly, her hands met my hips, her body pulled into mine. She stared up through the fourteen-inch height difference and waited for my lips to touch hers. This was her MO— she did it every time she saw me. I probably should have been embarrassed by her affection and my need to reciprocate it, but I never was. I loved showing the world who I belonged to, and I refused to ever let distance stand between us.

I escorted her to our last class of the day. After, I knew what was coming. I couldn't avoid the conversation. We neared a time we'd both have to make decisions, and it couldn't be put off any longer.

"You coming over?" she asked like it was really a question. Her refusal to assume my time belonged to her only served to keep me interested.

"Of course. Anyone going to be there?"

"Is anyone ever there?" Her chest heaved in frustration.

Cora had made a life in Geneva Key, even though she felt slighted by her grandparents. She never came out and said she would have been better off with her mom's friend Faith in White

Plains after her parents passed away, but I knew she thought it. Losing that relationship had almost been as hard as losing her parents. Her grandparents had insisted she live with them, the only problem was that they only *maintained* a residence in Geneva Key; they didn't actually *live* there. All they'd done was ensure she was alone without any adult supervision—not that she'd needed it—or guidance, which she craved.

She hadn't shared a lot about Gwendolyn and Owen Chase with me. Her father had written his parents off when Cora was just a baby, and whatever had happened in the family left an indifferent taste in Cora's mouth. Her grandmother tried to connect with Cora, but Cora remained loyal to her father and the legacy he'd left behind. She was never rude—she just wasn't inviting.

I wrapped my arm around her shoulder and pulled her to my chest to kiss the top of her head. While she missed having adults around, it didn't bother me in the least. "I'll follow you home. I don't have any homework, so I'm free for the night."

"Good, me too." She released me, took my hand, and together, we left Harbrook.

I expected her to launch into a persuasive speech about school in the fall, but to my surprise, when we got to her house, she just led me to her room.

Cora dropped her backpack by the dresser and turned to me. Her tiny hand fisted my shirt and pulled me in before closing the door behind us. Her lips turned up in a coquettish grin that drove me wild, and I knew instantly what she was after. She didn't waste any time. Long fingers wrapped themselves around the hem of my T-shirt and started to lift. She wasn't tall enough to get it over my head, though all she had to do was start the ball rolling, and I'd take over. I reached between my shoulder blades and tugged the shirt off. With each inch of skin I exposed, her hands roamed further.

The warmth of her touch sent chills up my arms and down my

back. She knew what she did to me, and I think she secretly enjoyed being able to bring a man twice her size to his knees. Her soft lips peppered kisses all over my torso, teasing me with a hint of tongue. Cora normally took her time, enjoyed foreplay, stretched things out, yet today, she was more interested in getting down to business. The button on my jeans came undone, and the zipper broke through the silence of her bedroom as it was lowered. She hooked her hands into the waistband of my boxer briefs and slid them, along with my jeans, down to my ankles.

All it took to excite me was a glance from Cora—it never failed to surprise her that I was fully erect by the time my clothes came off. Fuck, she was gorgeous, and she was mine. There wasn't a guy on the planet who wouldn't be sporting a chub the size of Texas at the mere thought of sinking into her. She didn't wait for me to help her with her clothes. As soon as mine were removed, she shimmied out of her own. I never tired of staring at her lean form. Cora had the body of a runner. She was petite and not overly endowed, although every inch of what she had was perfect, and I loved it. Her curves leaned in at just the right places, and her swells rounded in opposition. Even as thin as she was, there wasn't a hard edge to her.

She took my hand, led me to her bed, and encouraged me to sit on the edge. As little as she was, she had an uncanny ability to lead me in any direction she wished to go. Once I'd settled, Cora climbed into my lap and hooked her arms around my neck. Our height difference made it difficult for her to get much leverage with me standing, but in this position, we were equals. Just before she lowered herself onto my dick, her lips met mine, and her tongue invited my mouth to open for her. She deepened the connection in both places at the same time, and her heat captured me as she sank down.

My hands gripped her tight ass, kneading the firm flesh as she rolled her hips and lifted herself up and down. I spread my knees to allow for deeper penetration and couldn't help the moan that escaped from deep within. When our lips parted, her head fell back, and her long hair tickled the tops of my thighs. Nothing ever felt as right as becoming one with Cora Chase. Heaven found Earth in those moments and shed light on even the darkest of times. We worked in tandem, her giving, me taking until her face was crimson from exertion, and I knew her thighs burned from the workout. The way she clenched her muscles inside left me a slave to her touch.

Wrapping my arms around her waist, I rolled her over onto the mattress, allowing her to rest while I took her to a place I never wanted to share with anyone else. I cocked one knee up under her thigh and lifted myself slightly onto the other for better leverage and made love to the most beautiful girl I'd ever encountered. When her heat intensified from within, she was close, and I drove longer and deeper. Each plunge took her closer to the place of ecstasy we both strived to reach. Her back arched, she gasped and held her breath, and I kissed the tender spot beneath her ear that sent her into orbit… just before I whispered, "I love you, sweetheart."

And we came apart, together.

Those last few rolls of our hips were my favorite part of the entire experience. Only the sounds of ragged breaths lingered in the air followed by the explosions of color behind my eyelids. It was my own personal nirvana.

I touched my forehead to hers briefly before rolling off to her side and tucking her frame next to me. I'd be the laughing stock of the school if anyone ever got wind of how much I enjoyed just being with her after sex. There was something peaceful in those moments I hadn't experienced any other time in my life.

She peered up at me with eyes so green Crayola would be envious, and a sated smile graced her lips. We didn't normally talk much after sex, but I could see words lingering on her tongue. Cora had something to say, and she'd used her body to prime me for the blow.

I pulled back slightly in anticipation of hearing something that would rock my world and prayed it wasn't anything that would destroy us.

"I got into UK and UNC."

My mouth hung open in shock, unsure I'd heard what I thought I had. Cora and I had gone round and round about colleges, yet never in a million years did I think she'd take the initiative to apply to one of the schools I'd gotten a scholarship to. "What?"

She propped her head on her hand, and that just-fucked look morphed into love. "I applied over the holidays. I didn't say anything in case I didn't get accepted. I wasn't sure since I'd waited so late to send in my applications. But I got both letters in the mail this week."

There were so many thoughts running through my head that she'd left me speechless.

The tips of her fingers traced soft circles on my chest while Cora refused to meet my eyes. "So all you have to do is decide whether it's going to be Kentucky or North Carolina." She paused and took a deep breath. "And if you want me there with you."

I'd never witnessed this side of my girlfriend—the one that was unsure, insecure.

With little effort, I raised my arm lifting her at the same time to move her on top of me. She immediately adjusted and pushed herself up to straddle my waist. I grinned at the pink tinge still kissing her cheeks and the glow that us being together had left on her skin.

"There's no question whether I want you with me. The question is, what changed your mind?"

She shrugged, and I couldn't help but laugh at how timid she suddenly appeared. "You're my only family, James. UK and UNC are great schools, and I just need an education. It doesn't matter where it's from. And you've got fantastic opportunities at both, so I didn't want you to feel like you had to choose between basketball and me." She cast her gaze down to my sternum in uncertainty.

I loved that in the year we'd been together, Cora had never taken to calling me Carp. She was the only person in the school, including teachers, who used my first name. "Babe, there's no way I could go anywhere without you." I lifted her chin with my fingers to force her to see the truth in my eyes. "I gave you my heart on the shore of Geneva Key. I have no plans to take it back."

She couldn't fight the smile that tugged at her lips and met her eyes. "So where's it going to be? Mid-west or the South?"

"Your grandparents don't care where you go?" I shouldn't have asked. As soon as the words came out of my mouth, they were a reminder that her parents weren't around to bounce ideas off of and talk things to death. I'd filled in the best I could, though sadly, we were teenagers living adult lives without much influence. "Forget that. Where do you want to go?"

She worried her bottom lip with her teeth while she contemplated her answer. And with wide eyes, she said, "North Carolina."

And just like that, we became Tar Heels.

***

"You two are going to the same college?" Neil didn't try to hide his agitation at my declaration while we jogged around the island.

"Why are you so surprised? I'm going to one of the best schools in the country, and it also happens to have a kick-ass basketball program."

"You're also toting a serious amount of baggage with you. I don't get it. It's like you can't breathe without her filling your damn lungs with oxygen." He'd picked up the pace, making defending myself more difficult—not that I should have to.

"Why do you care?" My heart pounded like a bass drum at a rock concert. Each beat crashed in my chest more forcefully than the last.

"Just hate seeing you throw your life away on a high school girlfriend."

"Jesus, are you my father or my best friend? You love Cora. Where's this coming from?"

"Forget it, dude. Do what makes you happy."

I stopped and dropped my hands to my knees. We'd taken to a pace that left us nearly sprinting on the sand. I couldn't keep up and focus on the conversation at hand. Surprisingly, Neil remained with me. "Are you jealous?"

"Of a chick? Hell no."

My stare met his, and it was easy to see he wasn't lying. He wasn't jealous, he was hurt. "Then what gives?"

He gave me a half-assed shrug. "I guess I just thought we'd always play college ball together. But ever since you met Cora, basketball has played second string to a female. That was never you. It was never hoes before bros."

"Neil, we aren't ten anymore. I didn't choose for Cora to walk into my life, but I'll be damn sure I don't let her walk out."

"So you're willing to walk away from a friend of eighteen years, instead?"

"I'm not walking away from you. Just because we don't go to the same college doesn't mean we won't be friends." Damn, I needed a tampon and a Hallmark movie. Neil could bring the fucking chocolate.

"I guess we'll see, huh?"

"Georgia Tech and UNC are like four hours apart. It won't be like walking down the street as a kid, but it certainly doesn't require a plane ticket to get there."

He stood with his hands on his hips, watching me pant like a bitch trying to regain normal breathing function. "We've still got two miles. Are you done being a pussy?"

I didn't have anything else to say to my best friend to get him past this mental block he had going on. There weren't words that would erase his trepidation, and I wondered where his sudden need for security came from. He'd never been clingy, and now, he could have given Saran Wrap a run for its money. Our friendship had always been effortless, even after I'd met Cora. Abruptly, in the last couple of weeks, he'd gone from being a carefree playboy to an uptight asshat.

"You're the one who needs some fucking Midol."

He grinned back at me with a cocky smirk and slapped me on the chest. "Let's go."

Something weighed on Neil's mind, and without going all emo on him, I had no idea how to get him to confide in me. It was more than Cora joining me at UNC. Though I didn't have a clue just how much more until I tried one more time when we got back to my house, right before he got into his car.

"Neil, man, you going to tell me what the hell's been up your ass the last couple weeks? I know it doesn't have a damn thing to do with my girlfriend."

He removed his sweaty shirt, tossed it through the open car door, and then leaned against the side of the vehicle. "You don't want to hear me bitch and moan."

"You're right, but I'm doing that anyhow, so it might as well be about what's really bothering you instead of the cheap shots you keep taking at Cora."

He wiped his hand down his face and took a deep breath. "My parents filed for bankruptcy."

My jaw dropped. Like legit, came unhinged and hung open, leaving me completely mortified.

"Apparently, my dad has somewhat of a gambling problem."

"Holy fuck, what the hell was he betting on to have lost millions? And why the fuck didn't your mom put a stop to that shit?"

He rolled his eyes in my direction to glare at me. "Clearly, she wasn't aware his business trips to Vegas were poker tournaments where he lost his ass and kept betting trying to recoup the deficit."

"There's no way he lost everything playing poker." I couldn't hide the shock in my voice.

Neil's parents not only came from a large fortune, they'd also made a vast sum with the invention of some rubber-mesh material used by NASA. There should be money for five generations after Neil.

"Unless they're lying and something else happened, that's the story I was told."

"Is that why your sister came home?"

Natalie was six years older than her brother and married right after she graduated from college. Another trust fund relationship in the books—thank you, Geneva Key. She'd shown up a couple weeks ago, about the same time Neil started whining all the time. I hadn't put the two together. I assumed her marriage hadn't worked, not that she'd come home to bail her parents out.

"Yeah. She's trying to help them determine the best way through of all this. Although, her husband is over my parents' crap and told her she needs to come home. That left them with no other option except to tell me the truth."

"At least their house is paid for, so they don't have to worry about losing that."

He raised his eyebrows as if to say, "Not quite."

"Seriously? This is like the worst game of Monopoly ever played."

"Yep. My sister's husband—the lawyer—advised them to sell it to try to get out from under the debt and the second mortgage. If they're lucky, they'll break even, though that does nothing for their future."

"What about school?" College was probably the last thing on his radar. It seemed to be a huge issue the last few days so I couldn't help but wonder where his head was in regard to his future.

"I didn't get a scholarship. My parents can't pay for it."

"So that's it? You're just going to stay in Geneva Key?" It was hard to imagine my best friend's life was crumbling around him while the world just kept spinning. And if he stayed here, he'd get sucked into the black hole that ate the youth in this town.

"You're kidding, right? My family can't stay here."

"What are they going to do?"

"No clue what *they're* going to do, but I'm moving to Syracuse after graduation. Natalie and Nathan offered to pay my tuition, as long as I'm far away from Mom and Dad."

"When the hell were you going to tell me?" I didn't have a right to be angry. I sounded like a jilted girlfriend.

Neil had some heavy shit weighing on him, but damn, he'd raked me over the coals about Cora, and all this time, he was hiding a monumental secret.

"I kept thinking something would happen and they'd find a way to send me to Georgia. And then last night, Natalie told me she needed a decision. So I took the only opportunity I had." His expression held nothing other than defeat.

I wanted to be positive and tell him how great it was that his sister had come through, though knowing Natalie, there were strings attached, and Neil would owe her more than he could ever repay… and it wasn't going to be a monetary sum. "What's the catch?"

"Apparently, I'm going to law school."

And there it was. Neil was a bright guy—however, he'd never shown any interest in becoming a lawyer. "And I guess that means you'll owe Nathan's firm several years of service after graduation?"

"Yep. So goodbye, basketball."

There was no point in trying to tell him he could do both. Neil was good, but I wasn't sure he could walk onto Syracuse's team much less do that and maintain the GPA his sister would require to keep footing the bill. She had him by the balls, and that was how she liked to keep the men in her life.

"Have you considered taking out loans for Tech?" No kid should be saddled with that kind of debt, but it beat the alternative.

"I've already tried. I didn't qualify for any type of assistance this year because of my parents' income last year. Funny how that works. The government doesn't care if you're broke now; they only care that your family wasn't broke—at least on paper—twelve months ago. So that would mean figuring out what to do for a year before I could reapply. And then I'd be two semesters behind everyone else."

"I'm getting an apartment. Live with me. Get a job for a year. Dude, your sister doesn't need to own your life for the next decade."

"Your girl won't go for that." He tried to dismiss my offer by sliding into the driver's seat of his sedan. The dumbass didn't realize his window was down.

"Cora and I aren't going to live together, Neil. She's going to be in the dorms. At least think about it before rejecting the idea. Call Natalie and tell her to hold off for a week."

Even though he bobbed his head as if he agreed to what I asked of him, I could tell by the look on his face he'd resigned himself to his fate.

"One week. Seriously, Neil."

"Talk to Cora. If she doesn't have any objections, I'll consider it."

"I'll talk to her, but I can already tell you she won't care. She considers you a friend."

He started the car and put a baseball hat over his sweaty hair. "Let me know what she says." He lifted his head as the only acknowledgment that he was leaving and backed out of my driveway.

An hour later, I hung up the phone with Cora. Her heart was going to get her in trouble one of these days. She not only believed it was a good idea for Neil to come to North Carolina, she also wanted to pay for his tuition out of the money her parents had left her. There was no way he'd ever agree to that, yet I adored her even more for trying to do it. She loved Neil because I loved him, and she couldn't bear to see anyone suffer or go without, so for her, what Neil's parents had done was unforgivable.

When I called Neil, it took less than fifteen minutes to convince him to tell his sister to piss off, and all of three seconds for him to refuse Cora's offer. But I had managed to get him to move to North Carolina, and somehow, I'd help him figure out the rest before the semester started.

3

JAMES

THERE WERE SEVERAL BENEFITS TO HAVING MONEY—NOT THAT I
had any, but my parents did. Their absence proved to work in my
favor when I asked about leaving for Chapel Hill earlier than
expected. Sadly, they were excited by my ambition and desire to get
a head start on college. I failed to mention that Cora and Neil would
be joining me, and they didn't question my need for a two-bedroom
apartment versus one. Everything fell into place like the stars were
aligned by celestial forces.

Life was perfect for those four years. Neil worked the first year
we were there in order to establish residency and gain in-state
tuition while Cora and I attended classes and did the whole
freshman thing. Life in Chapel Hill so far surpassed anything I'd
ever imagined it would be. And being on the UNC basketball team
made Harbrook seem pitiful in comparison. I couldn't go anywhere
and not be recognized. As a starting freshman forward, I was the
talk of the town, and ESPN loved to grace the screen with my face.
I'd never anticipated the attention I'd get from the student body
much less the girls on campus and off. My affection never left the
dark-haired angel who'd owned my heart since that night on the
beach.

Maybe I was pussy-whipped, or love-struck, or maybe she was just my destiny, but nothing was ever going to come between us. I counted down the days until graduation—even though it was three years away—to be able to propose to her and legally make her mine. Waiting that long was a risk, but I refused to be responsible for her not chasing her dreams as aggressively as I pursued my own. She supported me in everything I did, and I made sure to do the same—marriage might have derailed that, and we were still young. I had to remind myself daily that if we were meant to be that would still be true at the end of our senior year.

Like a girl with a juvenile crush, I dreamed about the day she'd take my last name. Cora was aware of how I felt even if I didn't shout it from the rooftops.

"Why don't you move in here after exams?" I twirled a piece of her hair as she lay on my shoulder. The feel of her warm skin pressed against mine was euphoric. Even though it was a chick thing to say, I enjoyed the afterglow of sex with Cora almost as much as I did the actual act.

"With you and Neil?" Her voice was groggy, and she was tired. This was the best time to get her to concede to my wishes. Sleep tugging at her lessened her will to fight.

"Yeah. You're here all the time anyhow. It seems silly for you to pay for an apartment as a storage unit."

"I'm not sure Neil would be all that excited about your plan."

Neil and I had talked about it at length. The two of them had become incredibly close over the last year, and he'd grown to love her like a sister. She was his confidant as much as she was my own. I couldn't have asked for a better outcome between the two and never would have suspected this was where we'd be after that fight in the lunchroom our junior year of high school. Yet here we were, and Neil knew how much I loved Cora.

"Actually, he was the one who suggested it."

"Hmm. I'm not sure how your parents would feel about you

shacking up with me." Her playful tone told me she was at least considering my proposition.

"Probably the same way your grandparents would. Somehow, it would get leaked to the press, and the paparazzi would be looking for the money shot to splash all over the tabloids and ruin their good names." I did my best Perez Hilton impression to exaggerate their archaic thoughts.

Her finger traced circles on my skin, and she nuzzled into me.

"Have you talked to them recently?" I wasn't brave enough to inquire about them when she was awake.

"My grandmother sent me a couple emails. They're more like newsletters than personal contact. I can't figure out why she bothers. If she showed half as much interest in me as she does fundraising, our relationship would be completely different." She refused to admit how she wished they were close, though I knew the truth. What I didn't know was why Cora never accepted the olive branches her grandmother tried to extend.

I was losing her attention by the sleepy response she'd given me regarding Gwendolyn Chase, except she hadn't answered my original question. "Will you think about it? Moving in. Neil and I could move your stuff in a day."

Cora didn't answer with words. Instead, she kissed my jaw and cuddled down into the crook of my side where she loved to sleep, and I loved to hold her.

When I woke the next morning, the bed was empty, and I could hear voices in the kitchen. After throwing on some basketball shorts, I made my way toward the scent of freshly-brewed coffee to find Cora and Neil huddled around the kitchen table chatting.

Before I could even consider what had them in a verbal uproar this early in the morning, I had to have caffeine. Just the smell brought life to my tired limbs. One sip awakened my senses and the second brought me to functioning as a human. Joining them at the table, I lifted Cora and took her seat before easing her onto my lap. "What are you guys talking about?"

"Cora moving in." Neil smiled at her as though they had some secret I wasn't privy to.

"As in Cora agreed? Or you two are debating it without me?" I snickered. They wouldn't be up to anything that would hurt me. Not once had I felt a single twinge of jealousy where Cora was concerned—she hadn't given me any reason to.

"Yep." She popped the *P* with a grin that overtook her cheeks and resonated in her eyes.

"So Neil can convince you, but I can't?" I feigned hurt, throwing my hand across my forehead in exasperation.

She playfully swatted my chest. "No, silly. I just needed to make sure everybody felt the same way."

Cora had worried for over two years about intruding on my friendship with Neil. What she hadn't considered was that she was now just as much his friend as she was my girlfriend.

"When are we moving you?" I no longer needed the coffee to start my day. It wasn't that this would change much because it wouldn't. Other than having her stuff here, our days would remain the same. I couldn't remember the last time she'd stayed at her apartment. "I'll go put on tennis shoes so we can get started."

"Down, boy," she teased. "I just figured I'd start leaving stuff here as it showed up. There's no need to go racing into the night to move furniture we don't need."

I hadn't thought about what we would do with her stuff. I didn't think she had an emotional attachment to any of it. She'd bought it when we moved here after deciding against the dorms—the smell of teenage spirit drove her away—and since she was never at her place, there was little chance she'd grown committed to it.

"What do you want to do with it?"

She shrugged. "Not get rid of it. I guess just put it in storage. I spent a lot of money and won't get it back if I try to sell it. Eventually, I'll need it for a house."

Cora winked at me and set the butterflies in flight in my stomach. Even after being together over two years, those bright-green eyes never failed to erupt the flame that burned in my heart for her like she'd just doused it in gasoline.

Neil sat there looking perfectly content, as though nothing made him happier than seeing the two of us together. He'd struggled a lot this year. The financial change had been difficult for him, although the emotional pain he endured from his family's absence had taken a greater toll. I thought that was why he and Cora had become so close. While his parents hadn't died, they might as well have. They were so engrossed in their own bullshit that the moment he was no longer in their home, they'd completely let him slip away. Add to that, Natalie had basically given him an ultimatum to either move to New York and go to Syracuse, or she was cutting him out as well. And she remained true to her word. All he had left was the two of us by the time we had arrived in North Carolina.

There was no doubt in my mind that once he started school in the fall and hopefully earned a place on the basketball team, I'd watch him come to life again. Seeing him this way now made the corners of my mouth lift in a goofy grin.

***

"I'm late."

"What do you mean, you're late?" The words slipped past my lips in a much harsher tone than I'd intended.

"I mean, I should have started my period four days ago, and it hasn't come. I'm late." The fear in my girlfriend's eyes was more crushing than the thought of her being pregnant our sophomore year in college.

"Maybe it's just stress." I'd heard stress could change the body's chemistry, surely it could change a woman's monthly cycle.

"I'm on the Pill, James. It should be like clockwork."

"Exactly, you're on the Pill. So there's no way you could be pregnant." I wanted to believe those words, but even as a guy, I wasn't stupid enough to believe anything was foolproof except abstinence. And we were far from celibate.

She stared at me in disbelief. "You're not really that naïve, right?" Her clipped tone gave me more insight into her trepidation than the fear in her eyes.

I took her into my arms, pulling her onto my lap, and sat on the bed. Her thin arms wrapped around my midsection, and her head met the hollow of my neck. When I kissed the top of her head, she relaxed into my embrace.

"I get that the timing would be horrible, but is having a child with me the end of the world?" We'd never had a conversation about kids, and I wasn't excited about having it now. It was a reality we might have to face sooner rather than later, and we had to discuss where she stood.

Her shoulders rose as she inhaled deeply. When she finally spoke, her words were an insecure whisper. "James, I don't want children."

I pressed my cheek against the top of her head and smiled against her scalp. "I'm not gung-ho on having them right now, either. But if that's what happens, we can make the best of it."

She pulled back so I could see her face. The tears streaming down her cheeks nearly broke me.

"Whoa, don't cry, Cora. We'll get through this. Regardless of what happens, I promise I'll be right by your side. It's not like I'm going to be a dead-beat dad or anything." I tried to joke and lighten the situation to no avail.

"I don't mean I don't want kids now. I mean *ever*."

The expression on my face fell, as did my heart. I couldn't imagine this beautiful creature never bringing life into the world. I'd had dreams about what our children would look like. A boy and a girl. They were amazing in my mind, and there had never been a part of me that hadn't believed they would be part of our lives in the future.

My hand brushed her dark hair from her face, and I tucked it behind her ear. "Why?" Thankfully, the word had come out soft and sincere, and not flabbergasted and dumbfounded. I couldn't understand why a woman wouldn't desire children, especially not one as smart and beautiful as Cora. Maybe that was my sheltered, conservative upbringing, but I'd take a flogging from any feminist for believing it.

"My career after college is my focus. I want to enjoy being married and not have to worry about a little human who needs constant attention. I'm selfish. I'm not interested in sharing my time with anyone other than you."

I stared at her in disbelief. One part of my heart soared thinking she refused to take time away from me, while the other crashed in destruction thinking we wouldn't have a family outside of the two of us. And then it hit me like a ton of bricks—if she were pregnant, and she didn't want kids, that would either mean abortion or adoption. Neither of which I could handle.

She shook her head and closed her eyes. "No child deserves to be an orphan, James. I refuse to ever let my children go through that."

And there was the ugly, bitter truth. Her selfishness derived from the loss of the two people she'd loved the most and lost. Her heartache our junior year had been palpable. I'd never met them, yet they'd changed my life by giving me Cora, who I never would have encountered had they not passed away.

Cradling her face in my hands, I softly kissed her lips. "Sweetheart, that isn't likely to happen."

"It could. And I refuse to chance it. There's nothing you can say to change my mind on the subject. I just hope it's not a deal breaker for you."

Now wasn't the time to discuss whether or not this was a

defining moment in our relationship. I would never leave Cora; we could always get a dog. "Maybe we should just get a test instead of worrying about something that might not be a looming threat."

She was normally the rational one. Finding myself in the situation to keep her calm was oddly rewarding given the circumstances. I relished the chances she gave me to be her knight in crumpled tinfoil.

After an hour of back and forth about her not being ready to find out if we'd completely derailed our lives, she finally conceded. I trudged down to the drugstore and left her at home nearly comatose. Maybe it was the shock of the possibility, but she wasn't in the state of mind to go out in public.

When I came back into our bedroom, I found the love of my life curled up in a ball on our bed, covered by her favorite blanket. Her bloodshot eyes had dried, and the tears no longer lingered, yet the pain in her features had me praying this was a false alarm. I knew in my heart I could never pick between my child and Cora, and if she took that decision away from me, I'd never forgive her.

"Come on." I held my hand out to her. I couldn't let her do this alone. I didn't care how awkward it would be with me watching her pee on a stick. I'd hold it between her legs if that was the level of support she needed.

My heart pounded, and the rest of the world was mute. The air around us became a vacuum that sucked up everything other than the stress of what we were about to do. She followed me into the bathroom, and I shut the door behind her. The crinkle of the plastic bag bounced off the walls. I could hear each breath the two of us took—they were ragged and labored. Once I had the box open, I handed her the test and read the instructions out loud. Before I could turn around, she had already peed on the stick and pulled her pants up. She handed it to me, I capped it, and then she tucked her tiny frame into my side for protection. Even though I didn't have any control over what showed up in that window, she found comfort in my embrace, and I willingly gave it to her.

I watched intently as the color crept up beneath the plastic, while Cora had closed her eyes and buried her face in my chest. It seemed I held my breath through the wait, and then I kept waiting and waiting. The second line never came. Glancing at my watch, I realized we'd been standing here for six minutes, and the test took three. We'd dodged the bullet, but now there was a bigger issue that hung in the air. And it wasn't one I was sure I could let go.

Time and distance from what could have been a life-altering mistake seemed to ease the confusion over children. At twenty years old, I wasn't interested in considering kids, and I honestly believed —when we graduated, had careers, were married and settled—Cora would change her mind. We didn't discuss it again, and subconsciously, I thought that was intentional on both our parts.

***

"Hey, Carp. That was a great game." Tiffany was a cheerleader I'd tried my best to avoid. She was a nice girl, except ever since she'd broken up with her boyfriend, Todd—also our team captain— she'd been making a play for me.

"Thanks." I tried to shake it off and keep moving toward the locker room. I wasn't comfortable with her forwardness, especially when Cora wasn't nearby. She was like my wingman, and everyone on campus knew we were a package deal...including Tiffany. That in itself pissed me off. There was nothing I found less attractive than a woman who went after a man in a relationship with someone else. Don't get me wrong, I thought men who did the same were equally repulsive.

"A bunch of us are going to The Grid in a bit...you coming?"

I swore she knew Cora wasn't here. She always walked a fine line, but anytime she got near me and I was alone, she pushed far harder than friendly flirting. I politely declined the invitation, and just as the words had left my mouth, Coach congratulated me on the game. My face lit up at his praise, and I stuck my hand out to grasp his. The moment I extended my arm, Tiffany took the opportunity to steal an embrace, and the courtside photographer got the shot that would send my world into a tailspin with Cora.

The next morning when the student paper came out, there it was on the front page. I cringed at the sight. There was no way I could keep Cora from getting her hands on it. I suddenly felt empathy for all those celebrities who appeared to be in compromising positions with people other than their partners. I hadn't done anything wrong —in fact, I'd done everything right. But it sure as hell didn't look like it from the likes of that image. Tiffany was tucked into my side, the way Cora always was, and even though the smile on my face didn't have anything to do with the girl on my arm, Coach appeared to be part of the secret the three of us shared.

I'd managed to make it to my senior year without a scandal or negative press. I hadn't even so much as had a blip on the public radar. When the team was out doing stuff that made it into the news, I was never involved, and neither was Neil. Sometime during the start of our junior year, he'd met Hannah, and his heart belonged to her. She and Cora became fast friends, and the four of us were always together. We didn't do the party scene, and for the most part, we were all low-key. Neil and I had to study to maintain our GPA and stay on the team. Several of the other guys were looking at being picked up by the NBA, though neither of us had our sights set on pro ball. I was less than a year away from proposing to Cora and starting our life together...one I'd been waiting for since high school.

I knew when I saw her face, someone had been so gracious as to provide her with her very own copy of *The Daily Tar Heel*. She glared at me and turned in the opposite direction. My feet carried me as fast as they could.

"Cora!" I hollered across the courtyard.

She heard me, and her pace slowed when her shoulders dropped, yet she didn't stop or turn around. My long legs took me across the yard, and I caught up to her in a few strides. I swept my arms around her in an embrace from behind, unwilling to let her walk away.

"Sweetheart, it isn't what you're thinking."

"Really? So Tiffany McDowell wasn't wrapped around you at the game last night?"

I couldn't help the quirky grin that lifted the corner of my mouth. Nothing riled Cora, ever. Seeing her jealous over Tiffany was cute. Only because she had nothing to be jealous about. I had less interest in anything romantic with Tiffany than I did with Neil —actually, Neil would be preferable.

"Are you seriously laughing at me, James?"

"Cora, I have zero interest in other women."

She finally relaxed in my arms and turned toward me. Her hands snaked behind my back, and her cheek rested on my chest. "Do you have any idea how bad it looks? I feel like people are laughing at me."

"I'm sorry. I can't imagine how you feel. But I tried to tell you about it last night, and you were already asleep. Then you left at the crack of dawn this morning. I didn't want you to be blindsided."

"What happened?" Her voice was pitiful spoken against my chest.

I let out a heavy exhale. Cora had seen Tiffany in action before. I wasn't the only guy in the locker room she'd done this sort of thing with—I was just the only one with a girlfriend. And even if I hadn't had one, no one on that team would ever date her. She was off-limits—it was bro-code.

"She came up to me after the game. I was still on the floor before we all went back to the locker room. That's when Tiffany asked if I was going to The Grid after everyone got changed. I told her no. As soon as I declined, Coach walked up and told me how well I'd played. I reached out to shake his hand, and Tiffany must have seen the photographer trying to get the shot between the coach and his player. She literally clung to me like a damn octopus, Cora —like that Ursula chick in *The Little Mermaid*." I hoped she didn't question my knowledge of the purple hag.

"I want to be mad at you. I look like an ass to everyone on campus, even though I know how she is."

"If you look at my face, you'll see my expression is directed at Coach, and my left arm is limp at my side—not embracing her the way I always do you."

"I don't care to look at it. I just want to be pissed off for a while. And maybe make you wander around school doting on me and turning your nose up at the likes of Tiffany. You should probably carry my books, too. Oh, and I might have drawn a few mustaches on papers left in the student center."

"On me? Why?" I pushed her back to see her expression.

"No! On Tiffany. Don't worry, I used a light blue Sharpie to keep with school spirit." Her laughter filled the air around us, and I quickly became aware of people staring in our direction.

Seconds after we seemed to have moved past the uncomfortable photograph, Tiffany wandered up as though she'd been waiting for the perfect moment to destroy my day…more than she already had.

"Hey, Carp. Did you see our picture on the front page this morning?" It was like she was oblivious to the fact that Cora was stuck to my side. Hell, Cora could have had her hands down my pants and her tongue in my mouth, and it wouldn't have deterred Tiffany.

"Not cool, Tiffany. Do you have any idea how many problems you've caused?" I hadn't run into Todd yet, though I was sure I'd have a pissing contest on my hands with him, as well.

She flipped her hair over her shoulder and adjusted the books in her arms. "Oh, calm down. It was just a victory picture." Tiffany turned her attention toward Cora, yet she continued to speak to me. "If anyone has an issue with it, maybe they should have been there or not be so insecure. Confidence is so much more attractive." Her eyes flitted to mine. "Right, Carp?"

"What are you trying to pull, Tiffany? You're not endearing yourself to anyone on the team. All this is going to do is make people angry. Not only have I had to explain your actions to Cora, I'm sure I'll also have to face Todd this afternoon in practice. Not a great way to build team morale."

"You guys are too uptight." She hit my arm playfully while Cora and I stared at her like she'd lost her ever-loving mind. "See you on the court." She didn't even bother saying goodbye to Cora, and for some reason that pissed me off as much as what she'd done the night before.

As we watched her saunter across the commons, I had no idea what to say. She'd done me a favor by giving me the chance to deny what it appeared had happened, and she hadn't countered that it had been anything more. Although, at the same time, I felt the tension ebbing off Cora, and that made me want to hit the bitch—Tiffany, that is.

I leaned down to take Cora's mouth, distracting her from the heinous beast that had just left us, before breaking away and to lighten the situation. "Maybe we should go buy a pack of light-blue Sharpies and get all the guys together to do some more artwork on Tiffany's cover shot."

She looked up at me with humor in her eyes, and then we set off to the bookstore and tagged every copy of the paper we could find. Throughout the day, we noticed people had joined our plight in disfiguring Tiffany's image and laughed with each new rendition we found. There were some really talented artists on campus.

4

JAMES

OTHER THAN KIDS, THE ONE THING CORA AND I HAD AVOIDED LIKE the plague was our plans after graduation. Neil and I had talked openly about buying a small financial firm and joining their team once we had our diplomas in hand, but Cora planned to go to grad school—although she hadn't said where.

"We're going to have to talk about it at some point, Cora." I tried to reason with her when she walked in on Neil and me discussing businesses to consider. He politely excused himself, leaving the two of us alone.

"Why ruin the end of our senior year when we don't have to, James?" She flitted about the kitchen putting away the groceries she'd bought. I loved the way she hummed a song I'd never heard trying to placate me into denial. It was endearing even though ineffective.

"It doesn't have to ruin anything." I followed behind her in a perfectly choreographed dance, taking items from her to put them in places she couldn't reach in an effortless display of teamwork—we worked together like peanut butter and bananas. She was the flip to my flop. The basket to my ball. The nut to my sack.

She stopped and turned unexpectedly, nearly knocking me over.

"Don't make life decisions based on my whims. You and Neil clearly have a plan outlined, which I think is fantastic. I never believed he'd manage to graduate with us—he's worked hard to pull this out. Regardless of what happens, or where either of us ends up, we'll figure it out."

"If you'd tell me what schools you are considering then we can look at investment firms in that area so we can all stay together." My tone had taken on a plea that verged on whining, and I neared a point I wanted to put myself in timeout.

"You are aware we aren't a ménage, right?" Her laughter filled the small space.

I pressed her against the counter with my hips, swaying slightly. "Brother husbands—like sister wives in reverse. You into that kind of thing?" Cora was about as modest as they came; the mere question was laughable.

"You know me, the Porn Queen looking for my next poke." Her eyes rolled, though I couldn't help but think of her on video.

"Let's make you my private royalty." I waggled my eyebrows.

And she blew me off with silly laugher. "You could hang a crown from Neil's—"

"Don't you dare finish that sentence." No matter what the situation, the two of us found a way to make it fun.

Part of our avoidance of this topic was neither of us knew how to approach the truth that we might separate. Even if for only a short time, in the grand scheme of things, two years was nothing compared to eternity—regardless, she wasn't willing to face the possibility.

Her small hands snuck under my shirt and roamed my chest while she tilted her head up to stare into my eyes. She'd gone from distant to playful to erotic in less than three minutes, and under her touch, I was a goner. As much as I craved taking her right there on the counter, I had to back away and pry her delicate fingers from my skin.

Her lip stuck out, and she pouted in my direction. The problem was, Cora always knew my hand, and she always held the ace of hearts. When I refused to return her affection until we'd had some semblance of a conversation, she took matters into her own hands. And Cora played dirty. She had a wicked poker face and could totally count cards if necessary—she flat out cheated. Her brows rose as if to question my resolve, just before she lifted her shirt over her head.

"What are you doing? Neil could come back in." I turned between my half-dressed girlfriend and the front door. "Put your shirt back on, Cora."

Her coy smile toyed with me.

"Fine, if you're interested in playing this game, then let's move to the bedroom."

She gently shook her head in refusal, reached behind her back, and unclasped her bra. I tried to grab the straps before they slipped down her arms, although she evaded my reach and shot it across the room. It hung from a lamp beside the couch, and I couldn't get past her to retrieve it.

"Cora…" My tone held a warning—and zero weight.

"James…" she mimicked, mocking me.

"Can you be serious for just a minute?"

"Depends, can you drop this and enjoy your girlfriend? Or do we really need to get Neil involved? I've heard he's hung like a—"

"Don't go there." The rumor mills on this campus were insane. I had no desire to think about the size of Neil's junk, and Cora sure as hell didn't need to be pondering his endowment.

"How about here?" Her hand snuck beneath the waistline of her shorts. "Is this a safe place?"

I growled in response.

She knew I'd give in and not get answers. I was tempted to call her bluff and text my best friend to have him come home. I snickered at the thought of how quickly she would use me as a shield if he walked in the door, or how fast she'd duck behind the counter or try to make an escape to our room. I didn't want to do it, there was no way in hell I wanted anyone seeing parts of her she reserved for me, but desperate times called for desperate measures.

"What are you doing?" Her voice was sultry and seductive.

"Dialing Neil."

She called my bluff, and the hand that was down her pants now assisted the other in removing them completely, along with her underwear. There she stood in all her naked glory in our kitchen with her clothes—minus the bra still hanging from the lamp—in a pile on the floor. "You wouldn't do that."

Before I could actually hit send, the front door swung open and in strolled Neil with Hannah right behind him. It all happened so fast. I had gotten too far away from her to actually provide any barrier or coverage, and Neil's sights landed on her breasts before dipping down to her neatly trimmed landing strip just above her goods.

"Oh, shit. Dude, I had no idea. I thought you two were talking."

Hannah slammed the door closed to keep outsiders from seeing in, while I watched the scene unfold, and Neil stared at Cora's baby maker like a prepubescent teen.

"Cora, oh my God. Where are your clothes?" Hannah squealed in hysterical laughter.

In no other situation would anyone find humor in this, but I couldn't help it. She'd created this by refusing to talk and making jokes about threesomes, and here she had her very own gangbang in the making. When the world started spinning again and time resumed ticking, she ducked behind me and used her toe in an attempt to pull each scrap of fabric close enough to grab without further exposing herself...like everyone in the room didn't now know what color her drapes were.

My stomach hurt from laughing so hard, and when I bent over to ease the ache, she squawked for me to stand up while she redressed.

47

Hannah and I couldn't control ourselves, and Neil was the color of a ripe tomato, yet he still hadn't moved. We all should have been mortified, unfortunately, this was far too amusing to let go.

"I thought you two were going to *talk*. What the fuck happened?" Neil sounded like his balls had rescinded, which only further spurred me on.

"I tried, dude. This"—I waved my hands at my half-dressed girlfriend—"is what I'm dealing with. It's always sex with this one. I'm starting to think she's only after my body." That comment earned me a playful swipe to the back of the head.

Before I could make the situation any worse, Cora had managed to get dressed—minus the bra—and took her spot next to me. When she tucked her dark hair behind her ear and righted herself as if she hadn't just been caught naked in the kitchen, I burst out laughing again. I couldn't stop, and Hannah's giggles just kept me going.

Cora finally glared at me, shutting me down. That was, until her bra came soaring past my face. I wasn't sure who'd shot it back to her, Hannah or Neil—they both looked guilty.

"You three are impossible." She huffed out a loud breath, and I noticed how rosy her cheeks had become when she stepped around me and plopped down at the breakfast table.

When I tried to hug and comfort her, she pushed me off with a fake frown.

Neil sat down, followed by Hannah and myself. "Time for a family pow-wow."

Cora thought it was adorable that Neil tried to have communal rap sessions between the four of us. Personally, I thought he was a dork who'd lost his cool factor between Geneva Key and Chapel Hill, and we'd never managed to find it again. That first year we were here, he'd become the old man to our youthful antics. When we added Hannah to the mix, it was all downhill. She was the perfect complement to his anal-retentive ways. Yet somehow, together, we all worked flawlessly.

"Cora…" Neil tried to be the voice of reason while Hannah and I continued to giggle like school girls. "You need to give us some idea of what school you plan to attend, so we can make plans with you."

I didn't give her the chance to respond before adding, "We're only like six weeks from graduation. You've applied to grad schools. Just tell us which ones you've heard from." I had tried this before and gotten nowhere.

She stared at us like a mute.

"Don't make me tell them, Cora." Hannah hated to betray her friend; however, she also wanted me to be happy, and without Cora in my life daily, I wouldn't be. That, in turn, would make Neil unhappy, which led back to her. It was the circle of life, the days of our lives, as the world turned.

Cora's shoulders slumped. There was a reason she'd kept this a secret, although, I had no idea what it was until she opened her mouth. "The top two possibilities are both on the West Coast."

And the Financial District was northeast.

She intentionally waited as long as she could so she wouldn't have to break the news to me that what she wanted was on the opposite side of the country from what we'd been planning for. Her eyes filled with tears. "It's like my parents dying all over again."

Her words crushed me. She'd told me countless times that we were her only family. She'd welcomed Hannah like a sister, and she adored Neil. The truth was, we were all tightly knit. During our sophomore year, her grandfather had passed away from cancer, leaving her grandmother—whom she never spoke to—as her only living relative. I felt sorry for Gwendolyn. She was lost without Owen and often tried to connect with Cora, but Cora was unable to forgive whatever grudge her dad had passed down as a family heirloom.

Neil hadn't said more than about ten words to his parents since he'd left Geneva Key and hadn't spoken to Natalie at all. And I only went home at Christmas. I still talked to my parents, although Geneva Key seemed like a lifetime ago, and we'd all forged our own way here. Granted it had been with our parents' money—except Neil who'd worked his ass off—nevertheless, the fact still remained…she'd be alone.

"Oh, honey, don't say that." Hannah grabbed her hand across the table and held it tightly with her own. "We can figure something out; we just need to talk about it. Right, guys?"

There was no reason to break up the Breakfast Club; we'd just have to find a way around detention.

***

The compromise ended up with Cora picking Cornell Tech in the heart of New York City to pursue an engineering degree. She'd taken math and science classes, but I didn't believe that was what she'd intended to do on the other side of the country. It had been a possible path she'd tossed around, yet unlike everything else she did, this was the one thing she'd never had a firm grasp on. Cora had floundered with career choices, and in all honesty, I believed her desire to go to grad school stemmed from her inability to pick a direction. If she continued with school, it bought her more time to be indecisive.

Even with her concession, she didn't seem the least bit upset with her choice. Hannah had decided to go to culinary school at The Michelin Institute on Long Island. She and Neil were getting their own place, and Cora and I were going in search of one ourselves. Neil had become a miser since his parents lost their fortunes—he'd give Scrooge a bad name. Somehow, he'd managed to pay for college as he went, helped with rent and utilities, and squandered away money to keep them afloat. I prayed to God he hadn't taken after his old man and started gambling—albeit, if he had, he was clearly better at it than the previous generation. I wasn't sure how long he could manage, but I assumed he would figure it out. Either way, I was ecstatic we had a plan and multiple businesses to look at investing in.

Graduation came and went with little fanfare. The four of us walked in the ceremony, although since my parents had been out of the country, and Cora's grandmother hadn't been invited, that only left Hannah's parents. They had invited us all out to dinner, and we enjoyed an evening with them. At the end of the day, it was just that —the end of the day. One that simply marked the end of one chapter of our lives and the start of another.

And the following week, the four of us took off on the road trip of a lifetime meandering our way up the East Coast and into New York. The trip included every stop we could find from the capital to the largest ball of yarn and the tiniest rocking chair. If there was a place of interest, we pulled over. We weren't in a hurry to get anywhere and had a blast on the open road—even when Neil got lost in a corn maze and scared in the World's Largest House of Mirrors. I had no idea a grown man could have such an aversion to clowns. It had taken us well over an hour to retrieve him from the tangled web of reflections. Although our strangest stop had been one closest to home at the Cryptozoology & Paranormal Museum. We'd gotten thrown out for making fun of the Bigfoot and Loch Ness paraphernalia. Apparently, there were people who believed the displays were scientific artifacts.

"Oh look, The Awakening!" Cora cooed as if she'd just uncovered some fantastical exhibit we had to see.

"Isn't that a Robin Williams movie?" Hannah asked from the back seat.

"This is a sculpture that comes out of the sand. It's a giant hand."

"And why do we need to see a huge hand?" Neil jabbed at Cora.

"For the same reason you insisted on seeing proof of Bigfoot, you oaf." She turned to me in the driver's seat for the final call.

"Come on, we've stopped at way stupider things." Cora wagged her eyebrows and bounced in the seat next to me.

"Fair's fair, guys."

The groans from the back seat weren't really in opposition. Cora was right; we had stopped at some inane places, and every one of them, even the most basic, had ended up being fun because we made them that way.

It hadn't taken Cora long to bound out of the car and down the beach toward the sculpture. It was more than a big hand—it was an entire man trapped in the sand as though he were grasping for life while being sucked down. It was magnificent in itself, but the photo ops were even better. We'd gotten there late in the afternoon as most of the kids and their parents were leaving, and soon, Cora hung upside down, suspended from a finger, while Hannah had jumped into the palm of the hand. People probably thought the four of us were drunk when Neil and I started making inappropriate gestures to the dude's mouth but whatever—it made for good Facebook fun before we called it a night and hung out in D.C.

Thus far, we'd turned an eight-hour drive into three days with zero desire to hurry along. "Anyone down for The Tattoo Museum in Baltimore tomorrow?" We all sat in the hotel room on our iPads searching for places to stop the following day. "They do tattoos and piercings."

Neil high-fived me expressing his vote. However, the girls weren't as easy to convince. "You two realize if we stop, we'll end up spending the entire day there and only make it forty-five minutes farther than we are right now?" Hannah seemed to think she made a valid point, yet Neil and I just shrugged and started looking for designs to get inked.

"I could go for a piercing."

My head whipped toward Cora, leaving me dumbfounded by her pronouncement. I gave her the stink eye and forgot anyone else was in the room. "Yeah? How about your nipples? Or better yet, your clit."

She threw a pillow at me. "How about I'll pierce whatever you do?"

I shrugged. "I'll get my nipples pierced."

She didn't say I had to keep them; she just said I had to have it done. I could endure a little pain to see bars through her perfect peaks that would give me something to suck on while I teased her. Fuck, yes. That I could do.

"Deal. You get yours done, and I'll do mine. Still want that clit ring?" The humor in her voice left me wondering if she was playing or not.

"Hate to tell you, girly, your man doesn't have a clit." Hannah giggled thinking Cora had misunderstood.

"No, but he does have a penis. And from what I've read, a Prince Albert is quite the treat."

Before I could object, she and Hannah had launched into a discussion of their own. "So you'd let someone stick a needle through your clit if Carp got a ring in his dick?"

"Hell, yes. In the long run, it'd be worth the pain."

"I'm not piercing my dick, Cora. Forget it," I interjected.

"I'll pierce mine." Neil was a moron.

"You realize you can't have sex for like six weeks while that shit heals. And have you ever seen pictures of what that looks like infected?" Nope, nope, nope. Not me. Dick rot was a hard limit.

"I'm not going for six weeks without sex, Neil. Not going to happen." Hannah laughed at her boyfriend.

"Cora, I think you and I got mix matched."

"Eww, gross, Neil." Cora had as much sexual attraction to Neil as I did Hannah. We were like family, and the two of them were like siblings to each of us. The notion itself was repulsive.

He hadn't even realized what he'd said when the pillow came flying at the side of his head, nearly knocking him over.

"Can you not think about Cora's vagina and your penis in unison?" Hannah couldn't get the words out without cackling.

The next day, we got to the museum an hour before it opened, hoping to beat the rush. We bypassed the actual history of tattooing in favor of the tattoo parlor itself. All four of us managed to get in, although we spent the entire day sitting around waiting between people who had appointments and those who'd gotten there before we had.

I had no idea what Neil and Hannah were up to when they headed back together to get matching tattoos. They went before Cora and me, and then reappeared approximately two minutes later both having been permanently branded.

"So what'd you get?" Cora bounced in her seat with excitement and anticipation.

Hannah came over to where we were sitting and started to unbutton her pants.

"Whoa, what are you doing?" I shielded my face from accidentally viewing her lady bits.

She just rolled her eyes and pulled down the right side of her jeans to expose Neil's name in black with a red heart for the E. I glowered at the inscription and then stared at my best friend.

"I thought you two were getting matching tattoos?"

Before I realized what he was doing, he revealed her name in the same spot with the same black writing and prissy hearts for *A*s. Where she had one heart, he had two.

Leave it to Cora to point out just how redneck she believed the mark of the beast was. "You got each other's names tattooed on you? Please tell me you got married before we left Chapel Hill and you just forgot to mention it." Her face was priceless. She was mortified, and there was no denying it in her expression.

Luckily, Hannah was too enamored with their little hearts to notice, and all Neil cared about was Hannah's happiness. Dumbasses.

"Cora Chase?" The girl behind the counter called her name.

She grabbed my hand and pulled me with her behind the curtain. I'd promised to go first, and at the time, I hadn't really thought Cora would follow through, yet here we were with needles on trays and barbells and antibiotic ointment, and a woman I didn't know encouraging me to take off my clothes.

Suck it up, Carp. Your girl isn't the least bit concerned or scared...stop being a fucking pussy. The mental pep talk did little for me, and even less when we were joined by another member of the staff. The *man* was poised to pierce Cora's nipples at the same time the ginger did mine.

I was so caught up in watching how he handled her peaks that I hadn't paid the least bit of attention to what the girl in front of me was doing to my own...until she stabbed a needle through the center and left it there. I jerked and almost backhanded the bitch without warning. Jesus, she must have a death wish. As close as I'd come to knocking her out, my attention raced back to Cora who now had a matching silver spike through her pink nipple that was erotic as fuck. While I was gasping for breath, trying to regain my composure, she was perfectly serene and chattering away with the dude in latex gloves. And then the next needle slid through. Holy fuck, this woman sucked at warnings.

Cora licked her lips, sucking the bottom one between her teeth. I'd seen her do it a thousand times just before I sank my dick into her warm center, though seeing her do it now made me realize she liked the pain. And that was hot as fuck. Until the redhead in front of me tugged on the needles to replace them with barbells. I winced, and from the other seat, Cora laughed at my discomfort. Just before she winked. Fuck, I wanted to take her off that chair and have my way with her. I didn't even care if Johnny and June here watched.

"No saliva on the piercings for six weeks or until fully healed." The guy directed his comment toward me.

"Dude, she's the nipple sucker." I pointed back at my girlfriend whose mouth hung open.

"Yeah, does she bite, too?" The banter with the piercing peeps had gone too far when the girl appeared aroused by the thought of Cora biting my tits.

The laughter died instantly on my lips, which they all thought was a joke. Whatever. I needed my girl to get her boobs covered and us to get the hell out of Dodge before someone tried to ram a rod through my cock just to see what kind of rise they'd get out of me. Fuckers.

The fabric from my T-shirt rubbed my sensitive piercings in the oddest of ways. It was almost sexually arousing at first but then quickly turned to irritation. I wondered if putting Band-Aids across them would ease the sensation, yet when I mentioned it, Cora laughed. She didn't have to worry about it, she had a bra keeping hers from feeling what mine did. Since she thought it was so funny, I stopped in the middle of the museum and tugged my shirt over my head.

I didn't brag about how I looked—I'd left that shit behind in high school—but I was well-aware women stopped to stare. Being on the basketball team kept me in top physical condition, my muscles were well-toned, and I maintained a healthy tan playing skins in the park. Add the new piercings, and it was a sight the ladies wouldn't resist.

Cora didn't insist I put my shirt on. Instead, she came to my front, put her hands on my biceps and ran them up to my shoulders. Standing on her tiptoes, she secured her fingers behind my neck and jumped up to wrap her legs around my waist in a daring show of ownership. Not only did she ride my waist with my hands firmly on her ass, but she made love to my mouth as though no one was watching...or everyone, depending on how I looked at it. When the catcalls and the whistles started, she jumped back down, having proved her point.

I was hers.

And she was mine.

There was no way in hell there was a woman around who hadn't seen her claim me. It took everything I had not to throw her into the back seat, rip her clothes off, and fuck her like we were in high school again. Sadly, I think had I been gung-ho, Hannah and Neil would have taken the front and gone at it themselves. We'd gotten entirely too close over the last few days. Sharing hotel rooms and tiny spaces, we'd given up having any privacy and just tried to enjoy our partners quietly. Although, I hoped they tried to block out the noises as much as I did the two of them. God knew, I didn't want Neil and Hannah getting off to the sounds of Cora and me.

The moment we found a hotel and checked in, both couples forgot about the other in favor of each other.

***

By the time we finally made it to New York, we needed a day in the hotel to recoup before embarking on housing and businesses. The plan had been for Cora and Hannah to enroll in courses for the fall while Neil and I looked at a handful of companies. Until we saw where the physical locations of these places were, it didn't make sense to find a place to live and end up two hours away because we hadn't planned well.

The girls hadn't been on their own longer than an hour before Cora called, hysterical about Hannah refusing to get on the subway. Cora had grown up in White Plains, so where being in the city wasn't unfamiliar to her, Hannah was a small-town girl from Idaho. I swore it was the lost state. No one was from Idaho. Other than potatoes, I couldn't think of a single thing Idaho had. Whatever it was hadn't prepared Hannah for the city.

"James, she won't go back down the stairwell to the subway."

"Why? What happened?"

She didn't have any phobias I was aware of.

"Some guy peed on her shoe." Even though Cora was exasperated, I could hear the giggle in her tone. She thought Hannah was ridiculous, even if she hadn't come out and said it.

The laugh that erupted from my mouth startled Neil who was already worried about his girlfriend being without him. He'd traveled the world before his parents' bankruptcy. Hannah had not, and he only let her go because Cora was familiar with the city.

"What's going on?"

He was worse than any girl. I shooed him off.

"Sweetheart, just take a cab. She'll learn and get used to being in a new place. And keep her away from men with their fly open."

I spent the next ten minutes calming Neil's ass down. Jesus. He acted like Hannah had never made it a day on her own. She might have been sheltered, but she was a survivor, resilient.

We had an appointment with a business broker in Midtown, and the girls were going to have to figure this stuff out on their own. My concern wasn't Cora. She could pacify Hannah by taking a cab—hell, she could afford to take them all over Manhattan if she chose to. The person who couldn't afford that luxury was Hannah, and if she were smart, she'd use Cora's knowledge as a resource while it was available to her.

My mind was swimming by the time we got back to the hotel. The girls hadn't returned, but after the urination incident, they were only approached by a handful of other people asking for money or creeping Hannah out. All while Cora laughed at her naïveté. I had to give my girl credit—while she found humor in Hannah's behavior, she was patient and grateful for her friendship. Those two had the kindest hearts of anyone I'd ever met. They made perfect friends.

"Neil, do you realize we have weeks' worth of financial information and company history on three businesses that might potentially be ours?" It was mind-boggling. And even more so, that we were doing this without the help of our parents. Although, we weren't dumb enough to sign anything without having a lawyer look at it.

This trip was for exploration. We had three viable options in front of us and now had locations to begin looking at housing.

"Do you think we're making the right decision?" He'd gone back and forth. Not because he thought we were making a poor choice but because he stood to lose everything. And he was afraid Hannah had put her faith in him to provide for her while she went to culinary school.

"Dream big. You never thought you'd graduate from UNC without tons of debt. You didn't believe you'd walk onto the basketball team. You did both...*and* you managed to do it while saving money and maintaining a job."

"Yeah, thanks to you and Cora."

"Cora and I didn't go to work for you, or practices, games, or classes. We didn't manage your money or your homework. Take credit for what you did, man. It's fucking impressive. I'm not at all worried about our success. You shouldn't be, either."

I knew that was easier for me to say. If the business bombed out or we sucked as investors or financial planners, I had the resources to start over again. Neil didn't have any mulligans.

Before he could respond, the hotel door burst open. I didn't think I'd ever seen something so cute in all my life. Cora was decked out in Cornell Tech garb, and Hannah had on a chef's jacket and a big hat on her head. Their arms were loaded down with bags, but it was obvious it wasn't all from the schools.

I kissed Cora and took her things. "Where all did you two go?"

They glanced at each other and giggled. It appeared wherever they'd been, they had fun. I'd been worried this morning by the subway incident.

"Shopping," they said in unison.

"How did your meeting go? Any businesses worth considering?" Cora's enthusiasm made me happy. No matter what I did, she always supported me with her whole heart.

Neil and I started chattering away about all we'd learned and the information we had to go over in the next couple of days. Even though it was daunting, we had to go through all of it before we could move ahead with any of the ventures. And even if we identified one we wanted to proceed with, we would have to review it with an attorney. And the only attorney I knew was the one my parents used in Geneva Key—one of the few professions able to survive on the island.

I dreaded telling them anything about what we were doing. Not that I thought they'd be against the idea, because I didn't. I just wasn't interested in their advice or opinions. They'd been absent most of my life, and I'd be damned if they started involving themselves now.

5

JAMES

MOVING TO LONG ISLAND HAD BEEN LIKE RELOCATING TO A different planet. I wasn't a stranger to wealthy people—Geneva Key and Chapel Hill had been full of them—but everything about this place was foreign from the way they talked to how people dressed. It took me weeks to get to the point that I could understand the dialect—not because the words were all that different, it was the speed at which people spat them at me. And yes, they spat.

Once we'd settled in—after realizing that even with the monetary resources Cora and I both had, without spending millions, our housing options were limited…and small—life started to take shape. Between the four of us, it made more sense to share an apartment until we were all solidly on our feet. With the girls in school and Neil depending on the business for income, it made sense to live like *Friends* when the going rate for a two-bedroom space was three grand. And in the long run, it left Neil and me without guilt choking us with all the long nights because Cora and Hannah were together and not alone in a strange city.

My phone rang, and I glanced up to see it vibrating on my desk. Cora's smiling face stared back at me. "Hey, sweetheart."

"Are you and Neil having an affair?"

Her question caught me off guard and immediately put me on the defensive. The two of us had been working a lot of really long days since we'd bought Reynolds Wealth Management, but I'd never thought she'd believe I could violate her trust. "What?" I shoved back in my chair and stood abruptly, as if she could somehow see my outrage. "How could you think I'd be with another woman?"

"Did Neil have a sex change?" She'd lost me. "Because the last time Hannah checked, he was definitely a dude. I just never knew you were into men."

I rolled my eyes and sat back down. "So now you two are contriving fairy tales about Neil and me having a sordid affair over stocks, bonds, and dollar signs?"

"Meh. I've heard of stranger kinks. Maybe you're one of those weirdos who likes the smell of dirty money."

"Or maybe I like to be able to deposit them into my bank account to keep your pretty little head covered at night while we sleep."

"Which is all we do these days." Her tone was playful, even though she was right. We'd turned into an old married couple who scheduled sex for weekends only. "Since I have this rocking body, and Hannah's fairly easy on the eyes herself, we figured the two of you have to have something going on."

I grinned as I leaned back in my seat. One of the best things about Cora was her ability to tell me something bothered her without lobbing grenades or screaming. She never left me feeling maligned or attacked—I wanted to be the best I could be for both of us. "We tried, except he's a little hairy for my tastes. Have you seen his back? Gross," I added in my best valley-girl voice.

"Maybe you should suggest waxing…everywhere."

And…she'd crossed the line. "Okay, that took it too far. I won't be able to erase the visual you just created of my best friend in precarious positions…hairless. Thank you for that." My laughter filled the line, and the sound of hers made my heart ache.

"James?" Her soft voice was tinged with longing.

"Yeah, babe?"

"I miss you."

For years, we'd spent all our free time together. Yeah, Neil was my best friend, and we'd been together as friends since birth, but Cora was my soulmate, which ran deeper than any relationship I had outside of that. And I had neglected her in recent months while chasing the almighty dollar.

"I miss you, too. Why don't you get dressed, and I'll come home? Let's go spend a night in the city."

She didn't hesitate or bother mentioning it was already after seven. Tomorrow might suck, but tonight didn't have to. "Be careful. Love you."

She disconnected the call, and the screen went dark. I didn't clean up my office after logging out of my computer. It would all still be here tomorrow, and there was never a guarantee the person I loved would.

"Neil, I'm heading home," I called down the hall to my partner's office.

"Did you just get the same pitiful phone call from Cora that I got from Hannah?"

I made my way toward him only to find him slipping his arms into his sports coat and turning off the lights. "More or less. I'm heading home to take Cora out. What do you guys have planned?"

"That actually works well. We're going to stay home. Shoot me a text when you're on your way back so I can make sure you don't walk in on anything."

"Dude, gross. Common areas are off limits for that shit. We all agreed."

"I'm fucking with you, Carp. Get a grip." He smacked me across the chest.

Neither of us wanted to bother with public transportation and hadn't driven because traffic on Long Island wasn't much better than in Manhattan, so we opted for a cab home to our girls.

It was a good thing Hannah had never been a temptation for me. While Cora was dressed to go out, Hannah was dressed to stay in…with Neil. I almost reconsidered wasting time on the streets of New York when I could have Cora naked in our bedroom instead—almost. Cora needed to get out and do something. While I was gone all day, she spent her time cooped up in a classroom or in our living room doing homework. She'd found something she loved, but Cora wasn't a homebody. She didn't have to be painting the town red, but she loved culture and art and music.

Cora started talking the moment I walked in the door. "I found a band playing at a warehouse club just outside the city. Five-dollar cover charge. Hurry, go change. They hit the stage at eight, although I'm sure they're playing all night."

She followed me to the bedroom, encouraging me to make things quick. She was excited and bouncing on her toes.

"Do I want to know what seedy part of town we're going to that only charges a five-dollar cover? Or worse, do I need to bring earplugs to drown out the band that doesn't warrant a higher entry fee?"

"Who cares if the band sucks or the place is located in a skeevy part of town? We're going out. Together. That's all that matters. And even if the music blows, I can either grind my body against yours on the dance floor all hot and sweaty or sway to romantic ballads and listen to your heartbeat."

I tossed my shirt over her head. "You're a real romantic at heart, Cora."

"Or we could get wild and crazy and see how far we can get before someone interrupts or throws us out."

Publicly making out with Cora was always a huge turn-on.

She'd figured out years ago that I had a bit of a voyeur in me, yet we'd only tiptoed around the idea—never really given it any merit.

"Don't play games."

She dropped her tight ass down on our bed and pressed her knees together with her hands, leaving her arms extended. "Totally not playing, James. We're in New York. Anything goes, and no one cares. We can make tonight whatever we want it to be." She'd gone from innocent love goddess to sexy siren with just the way she shifted her brows. The arches were high as she posed her statement like a question.

I grabbed her wrist and pulled her to me. "Don't toy with me, woman."

She smacked me on the ass and winked. And silently dared me to follow. Which I did like a puppy on a leash. That woman could lead me into the fiery depths of hell carrying a gallon of gasoline, and I wouldn't question her motivation.

***

"Thank God for GPS. We would never have found this place. The outskirts of town—try Timbuctoo." The club was nondescript from the exterior—the owners hadn't believed in curb appeal, that was for sure.

"Obscure can be good, right?" She hopped out of the car before I had a chance to answer.

Hand in hand, we went to the back of the line. The place was packed. The club was well run, or the band was a local favorite— either way, something brought customers in droves. While we waited, we determined it wasn't the band that had people flocking to the place.

"James, the music is horrible. We don't have to stay." Suddenly, Cora looked around at the crowd surrounding us as if she were turned off.

"We're already here. We might as well see what's going on inside. If we don't like it, we can leave, right?" It hadn't dawned on me until Cora's eyes darted from person to person that we were slightly out of place. However, no one besides us seemed to notice or care.

We paid the cover, and a bouncer opened the heavy, metal door to allow us entrance. The noise from the band was like a frontal assault. It could be felt like a wave of heat crashing through the open door. It was bad, but the light show already had me intrigued, and with each step we took, something else caught my eye. Whoever had designed the club clearly aimed to appease the visual —the aesthetics were artistic, and it didn't take me long to realize why.

After making our way to the bar, where the line went surprisingly fast, I ordered while Cora moved to the beat of the music. Her fingers were tucked into the pockets of my jeans to prevent accidental separation, and it allowed her to sway without paying attention to me.

The bartender slid the shots across the counter, and staring me straight in the eye, asked, "You want any E with that?"

"Excuse me?" I couldn't have heard him correctly. I swung my head to the people flanking my sides wondering if they'd witness what I just did.

"E? You want any? It's twenty a pill."

I didn't have a clue what to say so I tried to play it cool. "Nah, we just got here. I'll be back." I was in the fucking Twilight Zone.

Cora tossed her shot back as quickly as I'd handed it to her. I ordered two more thinking both of us needed to loosen up and let go. Ever since leaving Chapel Hill, our lives had been filled with stress like we'd never witnessed before. Owning and running a business was far different than going to college and pretending like I had the knowledge I needed to succeed. And while I believed Cora would be successful as an engineer, she had to work her ass off at Cornell. Couple that with not having time for the one thing the two of us loved—each other—and it was a recipe for a stress-filled disaster.

I'd never done any drugs, not even smoked pot. And to my knowledge, neither had Cora. Yet here in this warehouse, where the night was endless, the music put a pulse in my body, and the lights were art, I thought it was time to live a little.

"You want to do what?" Cora wasn't quite as easy to convince as I had been. "James, are you insane?"

"It's not like I think we should make a habit of it. I just thought it would be fun for one night."

"You have to work tomorrow." I could tell by the expression on her face that she'd shrieked that last part. The music was loud, so I hadn't actually heard the inflection in her tone.

"And you have school, what's your point?" I took her hands and kissed her knuckles. "We always play it safe. For once, how about we let go?"

God, I could be the star of the next Oxygen movie against peer pressure.

She laughed and threw her hands in the air. "What the hell, why not?" Two shots had apparently liberated her more than I'd thought they would.

Turning back to the dealer behind the bar, I purchased two blue pills with a picture stamped on them. "Smurfs," he said with a grin as though that should mean something to me. "House special."

I jerked my head up in acknowledgment, trying not to appear ignorant. Everyone else here seemed to be having a phenomenal time. Cora opened her mouth, and I dropped the tablet on her tongue. Then I handed her a shot before mirroring her actions. Together, we swallowed the pills with the liquor and made our way to the dance floor.

"Promise you won't let go?"

"Why would I?" Her question caught me off guard.

"I just don't know what to expect. I need to be certain you'll be with me through whatever happens."

The right side of my mouth tipped up in a quirky grin. With my eyebrows raised, I caught her eyes and then scanned the crowd. "By the looks of it, you can expect a good time. And I promise, I won't let you go."

She finally saw what I'd been staring at since we walked through the entrance. Everyone here was in love—with the music, the beat, the lights, the bar, the drugs. One thing or another had them all captivated and *very* friendly.

I hadn't noticed the sensation creep up on me: the warmth, the heightened tingles brought on by human contact, the halos around everything that glowed. It wasn't until Cora pressed tightly against my front, reached up and pulled my head down, that it occurred to me just how intoxicated I was. Her lips were like heaven, though her tongue immediately sent sparks to my dick. It was slow and methodical, the build increasing the desire I had pressed against her. The sexual urge was nothing compared to the spiritual connection. Our bodies were fused at the mouth, and our unity was like a religion.

With each song that played, the music got better, and we got closer to the darker perimeter of the dance floor. Our hands roamed each other and anyone near us in an all-out gropefest. I'd never liked strangers touching me, though here, even the random dude brushing up against me as he took a spot against the wall was euphoric. Strategically placed shadows provided hiding places for club goers to enjoy themselves. I couldn't speak for Cora—and she hadn't said a word—but I'd never felt so alive in the dark. My fingers ran under her blouse and beneath her bra while hers dipped into my jeans to find my length. There, with hundreds of people surrounding us, we explored the other like we had in the privacy of our bedroom so many times, yet every bit of skin felt different than before.

We inched into a corner. With her back to the wall, I shielded her from prying eyes—not that anyone paid the slightest bit of attention to what we were doing. There was a riser that ran the edge of the room that was maybe six inches high and just wide enough for one person to stand on, and it put Cora at the perfect height for me to take advantage of her. The moment she released the zipper of my jeans, I dropped my hands from the sides of her head to her ass. She freed my dick, while my shirt covered her working it. In a twist of determination I doubted I could ever duplicate, I eased her panties to the side and held them there while I kneaded her ass. She made no attempt to stop me when I took her mouth with mine and then situated myself between her legs. She finally let go after lining the head up with her heated entrance. Cora allowed me to support her weight in my hands until she'd wrapped her legs around my waist and forced me deep inside her pussy.

I was so focused on the pleasure she brought, I forgot about the fact that I was fucking my girlfriend against a wall in a packed club. My hips moved with the undertones of the music. What we were doing was more than intercourse, it was beautiful and something everyone should experience. Her head remained tucked into the crook of my neck, the moisture from her breathing tickled my skin, and when she spoke in a deep groan, I thought I'd rip her apart with my thrusts. They only served to drive her higher, almost to another dimension. And the longer it went, the further away an orgasm became. Unlike having sex sober, I wasn't chasing the peak—I was basking in the climb.

My jaw clenched, and my muscles ached. Cora hadn't had the inability to climax and had rung that little bell twice while I made love to her against the wall. It was primal and animalistic, but at the heart of human existence, what we were made to do—except maybe not in a club. I didn't have any idea how long we'd been here or what time it was, but I was ready to go home. My high had plateaued, and while I still enjoyed it, I'd rather be wrapped up in my bed with my girl without the possibility of someone watching me fuck her like we were stars in an adult video.

Even that desire hadn't stopped my continual pursuit of her pussy. And this place was like Vegas—there were no windows and no clocks—meaning tomorrow could have come and gone. My mouth was desperate for water, but I was clueless on how to break free from the bond between us to get it. It seemed the instant my mind had wandered from what I was feeling to what I desired, my pace slowed, and all I could imagine was how good cool liquid would feel running down my throat.

"Babe, as good as this is and as much as I don't want to stop, I need to get out of here." I breathed the words onto her glistening skin as though they were seductive.

Instead of climbing off my cock, she leaned her head back against the wall and rode me like a horse until her eyes rolled back and her jaw dropped, mimicking the *O* she was after. When her insides finally stopped pulsing, and her hips quit moving, she lifted her lids and met my eyes with an intoxicated grin. Her pupils were so big, I could barely see the color of her irises, yet the glow on her face was breathtaking. The rosy hue that highlighted her cheekbones, the sheen of perspiration, the way the corners of her mouth tilted up—if I weren't careful, I'd get lost inside her again.

As if she'd heard my thoughts, her legs slipped down mine and our physical connection was lost. She shimmied her skirt back down to cover her ass, and I zipped up my pants, yet I left my shirt untucked to hide my still-raging erection. I was surprised my dick wasn't raw. I took Cora's hand to lead her outside, and once the dancing lasers illuminated her face, I realized smudged mascara lined her eyes. I laughed at how rough she appeared in contrast to her normally well-put-together self.

"You look like a linebacker." I chuckled with my pronouncement.

Cora didn't see the humor in my comment. The grimace on her

face only spurred me on. If I hadn't cared whether she took off to the bathroom alone, I would have continued ribbing her, but I wasn't about to let her out of my sight in this place.

"Your makeup is smeared. I wasn't talking about your size." I licked my thumb and tried to wipe the black mess from under her lashes.

She broke out into laughter and swatted at my hand. "That's disgusting, James."

I leaned down to whisper in her ear as we continued walking. "And fucking you against a wall at a rave wasn't?" It had to be the drugs talking. I didn't speak that way to Cora—she had never shown any interest in dirty talk. Even though we had fucked like rabbits, the language stayed PG.

Her feet stopped moving, and Cora turned into me. Grabbing a fist full of my shirt, her small hand pulled me down so we were eye to eye. "Keep it up, and you'll be fucking me on the hood of your car in a parking lot."

Growled.

I growled at her smutty words dancing in my head. I doubted she heard the animalistic noise over the thump of the bass and the beat of the drums, though there was no mistaking the hungry look in her eyes.

"Come on, let's get you home."

Cora chuckled as she attempted to remove the black smudges beneath her eyes without a mirror. The cool fall breeze felt amazing when it hit me outside the club. The air was chilly, yet coupled with the perspiration covering my skin, it was refreshing and sobering.

The two of us giggled about nothing while making our way through the cars. And had I not been coming off the best high of my entire life—even better than state championship wins and college basketball games—I probably would have noticed the cop sitting at the end of the street. And had I noticed him, I likely wouldn't have gotten behind the wheel of a car, and I *definitely* wouldn't have rolled through the stop sign next to his vehicle.

***

"You care to tell me how you got arrested for driving while intoxicated?" I couldn't tell if Neil was truly pissed, or if he thought the situation was absurd.

"Does it matter, jackass? Just come get me."

"Yeah, see I'm not sure how you think I'm going to do that in the middle of a workday when my partner didn't show up this morning."

"Neil, this shit isn't funny. I used my call to get in touch with your stupid ass because I was afraid Cora wouldn't hear her phone. I don't care if you have to close the place down, come bail me out."

"Where am I going to get bail money, Carp?"

"Try the fucking bank. There's plenty in the business account. I'll replace whatever you have to use tomorrow."

"They haven't told you what they set bail at?"

"Dude, no one's told me shit other than I was under arrest. Don't make me call a fucking lawyer."

"Calm down. I'll send Hannah after you. She should be out of class at this point. We'll figure it out."

"Thanks, man."

"Hey, Carp?"

"Yeah?"

"Don't be surprised when Hannah tries to get you into rehab. She flipped out on Cora last night. Funniest shit I've seen in a long time. Nothing like a sober chick talking to a girl who's still blitzed about falling off a wagon she'd never been on."

"I hate you." I didn't hate him, but he and Hannah would have a field day with this shit. Neither Cora nor I had ever been in any kind of trouble—figured we'd go for the gusto.

Thankfully, the cop had been lenient with Cora, probably because she was cute as fuck and flirted just a little. There'd been no point in trying to deny I was messed up when the guy had me get out of the car. All he had to do was look at my pupils and notice there was no color surrounding them because they were enormous. And taking into account where I'd just pulled out from, the picture was easy to paint. I'd asked him to take me and let Cora call Hannah to come pick her up. He'd agreed yet didn't wait around for her ride to show. We'd left with me in the back of the cruiser before she got there. Luckily, I'd seen Hannah and Neil pulling up just as we left, so she hadn't spent any time alone. She also wasn't now facing criminal charges.

I didn't have a clue what time it was—they'd taken my phone and watch when they checked me into this luxury resort equipped with three walls, twenty-seven bars, and my very own semi-private bathroom. The crowd in this place was restless, and if I closed my eyes and hummed, I could pretend it was a party, and the temporary tattoos on my fingertips were my stamp to get back in the door.

"Carpenter," a deep voice bellowed from down the corridor of cells.

I stood and walked to the door, holding the bars like every cliché action flick I'd ever seen. I almost stuck my head in to get a better look, and then thought better of it. Instead, I waited for the guy to find me. "Yeah."

He flicked his head at me and stood in front of the door. "C74." The latch clicked, and he pulled the door to the side. "You're out."

I didn't ask any questions, and it wasn't like I needed to gather my things from my suite. My feet moved as fast as the cop let me go without running the guy over in an unnecessary jailbreak or an attempted assault on an officer.

The guy never introduced himself or spoke to me after informing me I was being set free, so when we got to a desk and he just pointed, I took that as instruction and sat my happy ass down. An hour or so later—I'd counted to sixty, sixty times using the Mississippi method—the latest member of the clan of mutes handed me a plastic bag with my crap in it and let me out the door. They'd released me on my own recognizance; however, I had a court date in thirty days—assuming Hannah didn't have me in rehab before then.

I'd expected to find Neil's girlfriend waiting on me outside, but to my relief, Neil was there in slacks and a dress shirt.

With his hands in his pockets and a shit-eating grin on his face, he said, "It's amazing what you can find out about someone in jail under the Freedom of Information Act, yet you can't even get so much as a confirmation someone is in a hospital who's protected by HIPAA." He shook his head as if this was fascinating information I should look into further.

"I'm not the least bit surprised criminals have no rights while the ill are sheltered. So what'd it cost you?"

"Nothing. They said they were letting you out on your signature and told me you'd be ready in about an hour. That part was a lie—it was more like an hour and a half. And I figured since I busted you out for free, I could spare thirty minutes."

I clapped him on the shoulder, grateful he was here in place of his girl—I loved her, but no one needed to be lectured about their time in the pokey while hung over. "Thanks. How's Cora?"

"She was a little rattled last night, so I sent her a message on my way here to tell her you'd be home, and she seemed okay."

"Thank God she didn't get caught up in this shit. You taking me home?"

"Nope. I've got work to do, and now I'm almost two hours behind. So you're coming in. Close your door and no one will see just how bad you look...or smell. Jesus. Better yet, take a whore bath in the sink before you step foot in the office. You reek of sex, sweat, and stale alcohol. Please tell me the first was not acquired during your stay at Casa de Custody."

I just glared at him and got in the car. Neil tried to talk it up on the ride to the office, but I wasn't interested in mindless chatter. My head hurt, I stunk, filth covered my body, and all I wanted to do was go home to shower.

Instead, I got to serve another sentence at the office until Neil deemed it time to retire for the evening. When I reminded him of my impounded car, he assured me Cora and Hannah had retrieved it sometime today.

After I finally stumbled through the door, I realized my girl had been anticipating just how bad off I'd be. She coaxed me into a warm bath—I now understood Chandler's love for them in *Friends* —then offered me my favorite sweats and two aspirin. I expected a lecture, instead, she curled up in bed with me and turned on the television. I was out before she'd found a channel to stick with, and when I woke in the morning, she was right where she always was— by my side with her head on my chest.

God, I loved this woman.

She never failed me. I couldn't imagine life without her. And I realized at that moment, with her soft breath blowing against my skin, it was time to make it official. We'd talked about engagement, we'd flirted with the issue—although with her going to grad school I hadn't pushed. But, now it was time.

6

JAMES

As much as I wanted to run out to purchase a ring and secure its place on Cora's finger, that task didn't prove to be as seamless as I believed it would be. I'm not sure what I thought it would cost, but I hadn't anticipated choosing between a diamond and a down payment on a home. She was worth every penny, but it had to be the perfect ring to invest that kind of money. And thus far, it felt like I'd been to every jewelry store in town and left empty handed. At the end of the day, I couldn't tell anyone what I had in mind—I just knew I hadn't found it.

Cora hadn't made an issue out of getting engaged; in fact, neither of us had even mentioned it since we'd left Chapel Hill. We both assumed we'd be together forever...her parents weren't around, and our only family already shared an apartment with us. So while the notion was always at the forefront of my mind, everyday life took precedent over conquering that goal.

I'd missed the chance at Christmas, and in what seemed to be the blink of an eye, Cora was dealing with exams at the end of her first year of grad school. All she talked about was engineering and class. Every bit of free time we had was spent driving to places around the city or the state to enhance her knowledge. Her excitement fueled my own, even though her desire wasn't in marriage or starting a family—she was chasing a career. And I respected that.

"Oh my God, where's James?"

I was in our bedroom when I heard Cora burst into the house like her ass was on fire. Her voice had been filled with excitement and not panic, so I wasn't surprised when she came racing down the hall and launched herself onto the bed next to me. When she finished bouncing from her weight hitting the mattress, she crawled across me, straddled my hips, and placed her palms against my chest to sit up.

"You're not going to believe what happened, today!"

Her enthusiasm was as contagious as her grin. My hands naturally gravitated toward her hips. She leaned over to grab the remote and turned off the television before giving me any insight to what had her flushed with anticipation.

"Dr. Parker got me an internship for the summer at Halifax."

"The engineering firm in Manhattan?" The company was enormous and recognized worldwide for their modern design. They focused on commercial property, and their buildings were like works of art in a city skyline.

"Yes! And even better, it's for Drake Halifax—one of the managing partners. I'm dying. I still can't believe it's real."

I leaned forward and took her face in my hands. Smiling against her lips, I murmured, "I'm proud of you, sweetheart."

"There were over two thousand grad students considered from all over the country. I have no idea how I managed to land it over all those other people, but who cares, right?"

"You don't have to interview for it or anything?" Not that I thought anyone would have beaten her out for the spot if they'd met her in person.

"I kind of already did. Part of our final was the presentation I've been working on. They were streamed on the school's website, and I guess he saw it. I don't know. Even if it's a divine twist of fate, I don't care. It's freaking Halifax!"

She hopped off me as quickly as she'd found me. "What am I going to wear for my first day? Do you think I should go shopping? I don't really have the clothes for a professional work environment. This guy could be the key to my future after graduation, James."

Everything seemed to be falling into place. Cora had been apprehensive about coming to New York to begin with, but if she could firmly believe this was where she was meant to be, there wouldn't be any remaining questions about our moving forward. Not that there were now, but she'd followed me from Geneva Key to Chapel Hill and then New York. I needed her to find something in those decisions that made them right.

"Why don't we go shopping this weekend? When do you start?"

"Monday." She rifled through the closet, the hangers sliding on the bar as she sifted through her wardrobe. "Really?" She peeked her head out. "You'd do that?"

"Absolutely."

***

It was funny how everyone else's life was falling into place, and mine suddenly seemed to spiral out of control. I'd all but forgotten about the incident earlier this fall. I'd hired an attorney in hopes of getting out of the DWI charges, and he'd assured me he'd take care of it. For what I paid him, I allowed him to carry the weight of that stress and hadn't thought about it since.

"James Carpenter," I announced when I answered the phone in my office.

"James. Scott Brawley."

"Hey." I wasn't interested in the pleasantries of conversation when I paid this guy by the quarter of an hour. He needed to get to the point in the next fourteen minutes.

"Got a couple options for you." He acted like I was buying a car, not my background check. Being in the financial industry, my record needed to stay squeaky clean—any mark could cause a backlash for the company.

"Lay it on me."

"No one wants to bother taking this to court, which plays in our favor."

"I'm listening." I wondered if lawyers took courses on how to run down the clock without ever saying anything of substance in order to pass the bar.

"One hundred and sixty hours of community service and pretrial intervention. After that, you can pay to have the charge expunged from your record. Or, a ten-thousand-dollar fine and PTI."

"Are you fucking kidding me? You consider those options? I've paid you close to that and could have gotten the exact same results six months ago."

"I'm sure you're frustrated, but the state could take your license, and if they chose to be hardasses, jail time could be tacked on. So while the options might not look like much, they provide you with an opportunity to keep the incident off the record."

There was no way I had time to work off weeks' worth of community service. "I guess the fine."

"I'll send you the paperwork. You'll need to get the payment to the court by the end of the month."

"Yeah, thanks."

After we hung up, I glanced at the clock and groaned in frustration, wondering how that handful of words had taken seventeen minutes of Scott's time. I was hemorrhaging money as it was—his bill only added to the shitstorm. I'd had to dump a sizeable sum into the business, I'd finally broken down and bought a diamond—even though I didn't have a setting to put it in—Cora and I were covering more than our half of the expenses at the apartment, and now the state demanded a mint.

For the first time in all the years we'd been together, I didn't feel like I could talk to Cora about my anxiety. Not because she wouldn't have listened…I just didn't think it was fair to burden her with the financial state of the business while she was on the high of a lifetime at Halifax. She was heading to Paris with Drake in a couple days and had been dancing around the apartment since she'd started the internship. I loved her too much to bring her down.

That left me with Neil to confide in, yet he was already aware of the financial constraints and that I was pouring money into a business that he couldn't match. He was only taking enough of a salary to survive, which was how Cora and I had ended up supplementing the household expenses.

Cora thought it was Hannah who wasn't coming through on the rent, not Neil. When she mentioned Hannah's tuition costs, I let her believe that was the issue because Hannah didn't have a trust fund, and I didn't want my friend to feel any worse than he already did.

I'd known that by taking over a business, we ran the risk of a downturn before an upslope, yet the value of an established name with existing clients had been more appealing than a startup in an already overpopulated market. I believed in what we were doing, and I had faith in Neil as a partner—we just had to turn things around to remove a layer of gloom looming over us. We talked about it in terms of the business and what to do there, and the rest was left unspoken. I saw the shareholder loans on the books—Neil was keeping track of what I put in versus him, and I would get it all back. I just had to make it 'til then.

"Hey, James. How was work?" Cora met me at the door and kissed my lips.

Either I'd gotten really good at disguising my mood, or she'd totally lost her ability to read me.

"Long. Glad to be home. You?"

And my day continued downhill.

"Great actually." She held something back.

"But?"

"Drake got a lead on another prospect in Paris, so we're leaving earlier than planned." Her meek grimace said more than her words.

I set my stuff down and took off my tie. It had been the week from hell, and the only thing that had gotten me through it was the thought of spending the weekend wrapped up in Cora. If they left any earlier than Monday, it would cut into that time.

Her lips thinned just before she tugged her bottom one into her mouth. "In the morning."

Part of me wanted to explode, although that wouldn't change the circumstances or her departure; it would only diminish the few hours I had before she went halfway around the world with a man she admired and the ladies chased.

"Wow. That's soon."

"Yeah," she whined, and then her mouth turned down into a pitifully cute pout. "Please don't be upset."

"I'm not upset." Lie. "It's a great opportunity."

As much as I wanted to act like things were okay and yammer on about her trip, I didn't have it in me. Exhaustion took over just after she set the alarm in the bedroom and told me *Drake* was picking her up in the morning so I didn't have to drive her to the airport. Hopefully, when she came back in two weeks, I'd be in a better headspace, and she would have had the trip of a lifetime.

When she returned fourteen days later, she dropped another bomb I wasn't expecting. Drake Halifax offered her a paid position under him that would start when the fall semester did. She would get course credit for her work with them and still finish her master's degree on time, so in her mind—and I guess logically—it was the best of both worlds. Except the days of her managing her own schedule had gone completely out the window with her acceptance.

"What did you tell him?" I was a tad put off that he'd made this proposal in the City of Love, but that was just me being a jealous prick.

81

"I told him I needed to discuss it with you, and I'd give him an answer on Monday."

"Does that mean it's actually open for discussion?"

"Sure. Although I can't think of a single reason you'd object."

"It's a huge time commitment. You'll have a job on top of a demanding curriculum."

Cora wrapped her arms around my neck and cooed in my direction while smiling and staring into my eyes. "Aww. You're worried about me?"

I rolled my eyes and pulled her arms from my body. "You need to think it through and not make a decision about how glorious the job would be based on spending two weeks with the guy in Paris."

Obviously, her decision had been made long before she'd ever brought up the topic.

***

When relationships shift, the person being left behind starts to notice the nuances of how things have changed. And the subtle differences ate away at me with regard to Cora. I'd always been her number one, we'd done everything together, made every decision as a couple—or so I'd thought. When I looked back on the two major ones, she'd followed me both times. It hadn't been about what was best for her; I hadn't considered what she'd needed—just how it would have impacted me not to have her around.

Cora now had a life I wasn't involved in. Between work and school, she'd become just as busy as I was, and coupled with my schedule, we almost never saw each other. When we did find a few moments alone, all I heard about was how wonderful Drake Halifax was and all the plans he had for her career—none of which were in New York.

"He's considering me for a new office, James." She squealed with delight.

"Drake?"

The way she rolled her eyes reminded me of a child who thought I'd said something dumb. "Of course. Who else?"

"That's awesome. How soon is he talking?"

"I'm not sure. I mean, I haven't even finished my degree."

"Yeah, but that's only a few months away. Is he thinking right after graduation, or does he have a plan to groom you into a position."

Cora continued folding laundry while she talked, and I put them away as she went. Luckily, it provided me the opportunity to shield my expression.

"Oh, there would be other people in the office. But it would be a huge stepping stone."

"I'm sure it can't be as great as having *the* legendary Drake Halifax mentoring you." I was sure he was a great asset to her career, though something about him bothered me. It might have been the green-eyed monster that lingered on my shoulder, constantly telling me to watch my back.

I lurched forward when a pillow hit me from behind.

"What was that for?" I turned sharply to see a smile on her face and the glimmer in her eyes.

"You're jealous."

"Am not. If he can further your career, that's great." I didn't believe a word of any of that.

"He's taking me to a benefit with him next weekend. James, do you have any idea how big this could all be for me? This man produces greats. And for whatever reason, he chose me."

It made me a dick to think he'd chosen her for her physical assets and not those that could benefit his company. Drake was notoriously single, and while he didn't do it often, when he did take a female under his care, he took them all the way under. I'd read the stories and seen the reports. I'd even listened to the female who'd accused him of inappropriate behavior in exchange for that one-on-

83

one attention—right before she'd agreed to a hefty out-of-court settlement along with an air-tight non-disclosure.

This guy was trouble in my world whether Cora saw it or not. He took far too much interest in her for it to be so casual. Picking her up, escorting her places, taking her to fancy dinners in the name of charity. It was all great, but in my opinion, he should have been taking a date, not my girlfriend.

In my mental tirade, I'd slid right over the fact that she'd said next weekend. "Cora, we're supposed to go with Hannah and Neil to see Elton John next weekend."

She stopped what she was doing and came back to me. Putting her hands on my hips, she stared up with her neck craned. "James, I can't turn my boss down."

Normally, I would have caved, but I'd spent a fortune on these tickets and had been looking forward to an actual date with my girl-friend. Penciling time onto the calendar had gotten old. "Yes, you absolutely can. I can't believe you didn't realize you already had plans."

Her lips met the side of my neck, the one that made me weak with her touch. Although, this time, I pulled away. I wasn't letting this one go so easily.

"Don't be that way. We can go see Elton John another time."

"Oh yeah? Like when? It's not like he tours annually, Cora."

I hated fighting with her, but I was holding firm. She was going to have to pick. I wasn't giving her an out and letting it go. I'd done it countless times since she'd gotten back from Paris. At some point, I had to stand up and hold my ground.

"James, it's a concert. This is my future."

"I remember when *I* was your future," I grumbled the words under my breath as I turned away, not realizing I'd said them loudly enough to be heard.

Her hand snagged my belt loop. "What?"

"Nothing, Cora. If that's what you want to do then so be it. I realized months ago how little you care about how your decisions affect us." It was a low blow—one I shouldn't have taken.

Her face dropped and what had been excitement that lifted her cheeks earlier now weighed heavy in her expression. "That's not fair."

"The truth's not always nice, but the truth is still the truth." I just couldn't stop myself. Even though I was saying things that would elicit an argument, the filter on my mouth seemed to be on sabbatical. And it dawned on me that not only was I trying to goad her into a fight, it felt good to have her direct *any* emotion toward me—even if it were negative. We'd been on autopilot for so long, I'd forgotten what passion felt like.

"How about this for the truth? I've never been with anyone else, James. No one. You're it. And when we met, I was in a vulnerable place that you happened to land right in the middle of. Losing my parents wasn't all I lost that year…I lost myself."

I stared at her taking deep breaths as my heart thundered in my chest, and the air I sucked in whistled past my slightly parted lips. My eyes narrowed while I wondered where she was going with this.

Her hands dropped to her sides in tightly balled fists that turned her knuckles white, and her jaw clenched just before she swallowed hard, and then she opened her mouth to speak. "I lost the fire I had inside me, the do or die, the stop at nothing, the leap-and-soar mentality—all of which were who I was at the core before I left that concert. Never would I have followed some guy to college, much less back to New York—"

The whistling stopped and my lungs burned with the breath I held. There was no way I'd let her pin her decisions on me. "You made a choice, Cora."

"You're absolutely right. I did. I made a choice to go to Chapel Hill. And another to follow you here. And now I'm making a choice to follow *my* dream."

"No one says you have to choose. I'm just wondering when we

get back on the same path. When the *us* becomes as important as the *when*. When we decide that we have to have the happily ever after we've promised each other."

"We're not even engaged, James. It's pretty hard to keep making life plans based on a fairy tale that I seemed to have conjured up in my head."

"You wanted to wait until after graduation!" I hollered in her face, somehow making my lack of moving forward her fault. I had the stone, I had just never found the ring. Maybe that was just some twist of fate that was destined to keep us apart. Or maybe it was me stalling. Or maybe it was me not being certain this was right. It seemed no matter which way we turned, another obstacle moved in front of us. I couldn't dodge them all, and she'd quit trying.

"Undergrad, James. That was almost two years ago. We're twenty-four years old, and we've been together since we were seventeen. At what point do you know it's right? Because if you haven't figured it out by now, then maybe there's nothing to figure out."

I jerked my head back, not believing what she said. "Is that what all this is about? The fact that I haven't proposed, yet?"

Her chin dropped to her chest, and a melancholy sigh escaped her lips. I waited in silence, unsure of how to proceed. The words we were dancing around were heavy and life changing. And something I never thought the two of us would consider.

"That's just it, James. There never should have been a timeline. When it was right, it should have just been right. Don't you think?" The resignation in her voice, the loss of fight…it sent up bigger red flags than the words out of her mouth.

I stomped over to my dresser and pulled out the top drawer. Digging through the socks and boxers, I found the velvet box. But when I presented it to her, it had the opposite effect I'd assumed it would. Instead of the smile returning to her pouty lips, or the glimmer dancing in her eyes, I'd sealed my fate.

"What's this?"

"The diamond I bought months ago to put in your ring." I knew where this was about to lead, and no matter how hard I tried to think of words to draw us away from it, my mind went blank.

"What happened to the ring?"

"I couldn't decide on one. And then I decided to have one made."

"Hard for a jeweler to make a ring when you have the stone in a box in your underwear drawer." Her voice was soft and defeated. When she handed me the box back, her teeth worried her bottom lip —she was about to throw my life completely off course.

"We've both had a lot going on, Cora." I was desperate for her to see how much I loved her, to feel the depth of my emotion in the way I looked at her. Except when I met her stare, all I saw was sadness.

"Exactly. If it had been a priority, you would have made it happen."

She sat down on the edge of the bed, and I took a seat next to her. I didn't want to be the one to speak next. Words would be messy, and I wasn't sure I could handle anything she had to say.

"I'll always love you, James. Maybe our lives are just going in different directions. Maybe we need to follow our own paths to see where they take us. One where you're not inhibited by having a shadow, and one where I'm free to follow a path I might have to walk alone."

I slowly bobbed my head, unsure of how to get her to reconsider without pleading. "This doesn't sound like it's open for discussion any more than the benefit Drake is taking you to next weekend."

"Don't you need to breathe? Just a little? Try things out—spend time in a new city as a single, adult male?"

"No, Cora. I don't. Since you walked into my life, I haven't had any desire to live a day without you. I dropped the ball on the ring, but that didn't mean you weren't and haven't been my top priority. I guess I always thought everything I was doing, I did for us—our future."

She inhaled through her nose and released the breath through her mouth. "Maybe the best thing for our future is to spend some time apart."

And that was it, she'd chosen him over me.

7

PART TWO

JAMES

I HADN'T HEARD FROM HER SINCE THE DAY SHE'D LEFT. MY GOAL had been to give her time to miss me and realize she'd made a mistake. However, as the days turned into weeks without any communication, my willpower waned, and I thought my sanity would follow shortly behind.

Two shots of tequila turned into four at a bar down the street from our house. I'd become quite the regular in an attempt to avoid my apartment, my best friend and his perfect romance, and the room I'd shared with the only woman I'd ever loved. And after the fifth shot, the drunk dialing started to take shape, and the closer I came to resembling a blubbering idiot than James Carpenter.

"Don't do it, dude."

I had my phone in my hand, studying it as though it were the holy grail and held the secrets of life. Instead of staring at the screen, daring myself to dial her number, I peered up at Rex, the bartender who'd listened to more of my personal hell in the last few weeks than a priest heard confessions.

"Let her go. Don't call her. Especially not when the liquor is thinking for you. That's almost as bad as letting your pants do the talking." He wiped the bar off, but before I could respond, he got called away to help another lonely sap living his dreams out of a bottle.

Me: I hope you're doing okay.

I hit send before my shrink behind the bar could advise against it again. It was harmless. It wasn't a phone call, and she didn't have to respond. She could read it and know I was thinking of her without actually replying.

Cora: I hope you're okay, too.

The message came through like she'd had her phone in her hand waiting for me to reach out. I hadn't expected it, and certainly not so soon. I hadn't thought this through. Now that I had her attention, I didn't have another move lined up. I'd opened a door without any plan for what to do on the other side.

Me: How's work?

There was something that riled every woman into a lively discussion. I rolled my eyes at my own stupid question. This was painful even for me, and I'd started it.

Cora: Great. I graduate in a couple weeks, and then I'm off to France.

Me: Another rendezvous with Drake?

Cora: No, I'm relocating to train in a new office Halifax is opening in Paris. I'm moving.

And five shots turned into ten before Rex cut me off and poured me a cup of coffee.

I'd lost her.

I hadn't fought when it mattered, and now I was too late. She'd seized the opportunity in front of her.

When she was in Manhattan, the possibility of fixing us was still real. With her halfway around the world, there was little point. I didn't bother responding. And when I finally dragged my drunk-ass home, I vowed to start living tomorrow as though Cora Chase had never existed.

She'd chosen her path, and now I'd blaze mine.

***

I quickly realized that in the two years we'd lived in New York, I hadn't managed to make a single friend I could hang out with. The four of us had been perfectly content to hang out together like we always had. The girls had met people at school, but they only saw them between classes. Neil and I hadn't ventured outside of the office, and the only other people we worked with were women. That would have been a recipe for disaster, and it was one I'd never considered out of respect for Cora. However, now that I had time on my hands and my best friend was still in a committed relationship, being the third wheel wasn't all that appealing—not to mention, Hannah was like a damn parrot who repeated everything she heard.

I hadn't dated anyone other than Cora since I was a teenager. I didn't have a clue how to meet people in a city this size, and I didn't have a wingman to work the social scene. Regardless of the fact I'd never lacked for confidence, this town was daunting when flying solo.

"Are you going out after work?" Neil sounded like a broken record. Every day it was more of the same. He didn't understand why I wasn't hanging out at home the way I always had.

"Yeah, just going into the city to see what I can find."

"What are you looking for?"

I shrugged as I cleared my desk and then shut down my computer. "Something different."

"Different than Cora?"

"Different than life."

"Maybe you should give yourself some time to process the end of a long-term relationship, Carp. You don't have to be with someone to be happy."

"I'm not trying to find a wife, Neil. But sitting around the apartment I shared with her while watching you and Hannah make googly eyes at each other doesn't do much for my self-esteem or my mental clarity. Do you realize we haven't made any friends in two years?"

"No, we've been trying to salvage an unhealthy business. That's what being an adult is."

There was no way in hell Neil was going to give *me* the responsibility speech. "The role of an adult is not foreign to me. And I'm not waving off my responsibility or doing anything stupid. I'm simply trying to meet some people."

He held up his hands in surrender. "Okay. I'm not trying to push. Just know that you don't have to go racing into the sunset. You're allowed time to grieve, and Hannah and I are around to help you—if you'll let us."

"Should I get you some Midol? Maybe some chocolate? Give me a break, Neil. I'm not grieving. I just broke up with my girlfriend and realized I haven't made any friends."

"Fair enough."

I closed my door after he left and proceeded to shed the suit and tie for a more casual look. And then I headed to Manhattan. The great thing about New York was that there was always someone up, and there was always something open—if I wanted cookies delivered at two in the morning, there were people who'd make it happen. If I wanted to chug beer until midnight on a Tuesday there were places for that, too. Yet finding one that fit me was like trying to find Cinderella after the ball.

Every night I went somewhere different: I liked the brew but wasn't interested in the patrons, or the place was dead, or the bartender sucked. I had yet to make a repeat stop at any of my destinations and hadn't found a single person—male or female—to connect with. I spent money faster than I could withdraw it and got nowhere in the process.

Until I found Sideways Shots. I wasn't sure how I'd even ended up here. It wasn't my intended destination for the evening, yet here I stood just the same. Everything about this place was different than those I'd visited in the last couple weeks. Located off a side street on a corner, the heavy, metal sign hung like a banner calling to me. Lit from above, the blue glow of the neon against the hammered steel seemed a tad funk, a little modern, and right up my alley.

The inside didn't disappoint. The house band that could be heard from the street played an eclectic mix of rock and alternative original music, and the people inside appeared to be a white-collar crowd—who I guessed to be late twenties to mid-thirties. While it wasn't packed, there was a steady stream in and out the door, and most of them were friendly.

"Hey, what can I get for you?" A saucy brunette stared me straight in the eyes with one slightly closed, hinting at something I wasn't sure was there. Her glance begged me to ask for her phone number, but then I realized this was how she brought in tips—that little glimmer would catch any straight man's attention. And if it didn't, her cleavage would.

"New Castle. Draft if you have it."

She grinned and winked before turning around. The brunette delivered my beer and then passed four other people to take the order of a guy who could be my brother. While the men serving drinks dealt with the ladies, the other two females each had their own set of male customers. I watched with piqued interest as I downed my cold brew.

When I finished my first pint, the brunette raised her brows at me—she was waiting on someone else, yet I had her attention. I gave her a nod, and she delivered another chilled glass, just like the last. There was no "hi," no "bye," no "thank you very much" or "I'd love to suck your dick"—she just dropped off my drink and then turned to the newest person in the queue. When the crowd waned, she came by to ask if I wanted another glass.

"Yeah, thanks."

When she returned a minute later, she leaned forward with her elbows propped on the bar and her chin in her hands. "You're new here. How'd you find us?"

"Just trying some places out."

"New to New York or just the social scene?"

"Social scene."

"I'm Bridgette. Glad you wandered in."

"James. My friends call me Carp."

She got called away to do her job, and an unassuming woman slid onto the barstool next to me. I'd been sitting at the corner slightly turned to watch the crowd, so noticing her wasn't difficult. The girl was cute, with short, red hair most women couldn't have pulled off. Actually, she looked like she should be with the band and not at the bar. Her fitted shirt, tight jeans, and combat boots were better suited for rock-grunge than happy hour.

"I'm Collette." She stuck her hand out in an introduction, completely throwing me off.

"Carp. Nice to meet you."

"I haven't seen you here before." She paused to get the attention of one of the males behind the counter, who simply nodded as if he knew what she wanted without asking. Then she turned her bright eyes back to me. "First time?"

"Yeah. You a regular?" I didn't think I'd ever get used to the difference in women in New York versus those in the South. I welcomed the more forward approach—it took off some of the pressure.

She laughed. "You could say that."

Bridgette returned with a smile that could light up the room, although it wasn't directed at me. "Hey, Letty. What the hell are you doing here?"

"Turns out I have no life outside these walls."

"You need anything?"

"No, Eric got it. Thanks."

"You work here?" I asked when she turned her attention back to

94

me. It was the only plausible explanation based on the conversation.

"Yep, been here since we opened."

Letty—as she preferred to be called—turned out to be the owner of Sideways Shots. She was smart and driven, and her employees seemed to adore her. I was impressed—and she was available.

The great thing about Letty wasn't her tight ass or her outgoing personality—it was the fact that she wasn't interested in anything other than playing the field. And that night, she let me play *her* in the loft above the bar that must have cost a fortune.

The place was silent even though I'd expected to hear the thump of the band beneath us. The industrial feel and the openness of the room left me exposed—more in a voyeur way than one that was uncomfortable. There was nowhere to go for privacy other than the bathroom, and the windows that lined the wall spanned from floor to ceiling. I didn't have a clue if there were other occupied units that could peer in through the glass, and honestly, I didn't care. This girl had been all kinds of upfront about what she liked and how she liked to have it.

And she wasn't playing. She waltzed over to her nightstand and opened the drawer. From inside, she pulled out a string of condoms, promptly tore one off, and then tossed the others to the side. As soon as she threw the foil wrapper at me, she lifted her shirt over her head and then shed the rest of her clothing...all while I stood there and enjoyed the show.

"You going to join me, or are you just going to watch?" Letty cocked one eyebrow and gave me a come-hither smirk that brought my dick to life.

She didn't have to ask twice. In seconds, my clothes were on the floor, my jimmy in its Johnson, and we were fucking like rabbits on every available surface. It was great, meaningless sex—and exactly what I needed to find some mental clarity.

I finally put my clothes back on around three in the morning. When I told her I needed to get home, we exchanged numbers, and she let me out. There was no kiss goodbye—in fact, there'd been no kiss at all. There were no promised expectations—just two consenting adults having a good time.

I'd gone back the next night, and the night after that, until I'd become a regular amongst all the other regulars. Letty and I fucked around when the urge struck, and she'd introduced me to other people who frequented her establishment and encouraged me to have fun with them as well. Our only agreed upon stipulations were: no falling for the other and always use protection. There wasn't a hint of jealousy between either of us, and no expectations—even though I never took her up on the offer. One fuck buddy sufficed.

However, my high came crashing to an abysmal low when I missed a phone call and subsequently several texts late at night because I'd been fucking Letty six ways from Sunday. I hadn't seen them until I'd gotten dressed, and by the time I'd read each one, it had been hours since they'd stopped coming in.

Cora: How's life treating you?

Cora: I realize it's late on a Friday night. You're probably asleep since you didn't answer my call. Or maybe you're mad at me.

Cora: I wish I'd listened to you. You were right.

Cora: I hate this place. I just want to be home.

Cora: Please don't hate me, James.

Cora: I miss you.

The last message was like a dagger to the heart. I missed her too, but she lived on another continent. She'd made that choice with no regard for what it would do to us. Although, as much as I'd like to freeze her out, I loved her—I'd always love her.

I glanced at the clock and did the math. I thought Paris was six hours ahead which would mean it was mid-morning. She'd been up late, yet knowing Cora, she still wouldn't have slept in.

Me: Hey. Sorry I missed your call. I was out with a friend. You okay?

While I waited for her response, I reread the messages she'd sent and wondered what she meant by "you were right." I could only pray she wasn't referring to Drake. If he'd hurt her or tried to touch her…I wouldn't be able to keep from pummeling him. She wasn't mine by definition, though she'd always be mine in heart.

By the time I got home, she still hadn't replied. I didn't want to call and wake her up or keep sending her messages if she wasn't able to talk, yet the sudden flurry of communication had me worried and desperate to hear her voice. I'd managed to push my loneliness aside when I met Letty, even if it was superficial. Cora had just torn the Band-Aid off a wound I'd been neglecting.

***

I didn't get another message from Cora for several days, and I had refused to let myself reach out to her. In the meantime, I buried myself in work, and then Letty. I'd never met a woman like this— perfectly comfortable in who she was and no expectations other than a good time. I gladly provided her with what she asked for, and I loved being with a woman who just wanted to hang out, dance, drink, and fuck—without jealousy or the promise of another day.

Hannah, on the other hand, didn't like much of anything I did these days—sadly for her, she didn't get a vote. I knew she still talked to Cora, mainly because she didn't try to hide it—not that I expected her to. Hannah failed to recognize that Cora left me; I didn't leave Cora—so I wasn't sure why Hannah expected me to sit at home and pine away for a girl who'd moved to the City of Love without her soulmate. Yet Hannah's growing disapproval of my life created a chasm between my best friend and me. I would never ask him to choose between the two of us. I knew what his choice would be, and I wasn't ready to lose twice in a matter of months. My ego just couldn't take it.

Our lease was ending, and they'd chosen to stay and keep the place. Business had taken a drastic upward swing, Neil had repaid the money he'd borrowed, and I'd found another apartment down the road. Soon enough, our lives would be separated—Hannah's and mine. She would only have the information Neil gave her and not be able to witness it with her own eyes. I'd still see my best friend every day at work, and I could continue living as a single man in New York City. Because that's what I was…even if Hannah refused to accept it.

I kept missing Cora's texts. It was like she intentionally sent them in the middle of the night when I wouldn't be awake—or hell, maybe Hannah had told her the hours I kept, and she tried to interrupt my escapades. All I knew was anytime I tried to respond to her messages, I got nothing in return…even if it'd only been five minutes since she'd sent it. Somehow, she was allowed to contact me, yet I couldn't reach her.

Although tonight, she'd crossed a line I refused to ignore.

I'd been balls deep in Letty when I heard my phone ding. I wasn't such an ass that I'd pulled out and gone to see who it was—I already knew. It was the same person who routinely texted this time of night—and then failed to respond. I made sure to get Letty to scream before trashing the condom and getting dressed.

The second Letty's door closed behind me, I pulled my phone from my pocket.

Cora: I love you.

That was it. There was no way in hell she could send those three little words and not answer the damn phone. I didn't care what time it was or what she was doing. If she had time to text that sentiment, then she could talk. However, she didn't pick up on the first try, or even the second.

Me: If you think I'm letting that go, you've apparently forgotten who I am. Answer the fucking phone, Cora.

I was pissed. These games were sucking the life out of me and keeping me from moving on. True, I was happy sticking my dick in a gorgeous woman, but I'd never feel the comfort of another pussy if it meant there was any possibility of getting Cora back.

She sent my third call to voicemail.

Me: Are you kidding me with this shit? Call me. Now.

Cora: I can't talk right now. I just needed you to know I was thinking about you.

Me: If you can't talk, why are you texting?

Cora: I'm in a meeting.

Me: That's hardly fair. Why is it you can reach out to me then don't answer when I reciprocate?

Cora: I'm responding now.

Me: You know what I mean.

Cora: Can I call you tonight?

Me: Tonight for me or tonight for you?

Like it mattered. If she cared to talk at noon or three or midnight, I'd stop what I was doing to answer.

Cora: A few hours. When I'm out of work.

Me: Sure.

Cora: I do miss you, James.

I didn't respond. I wasn't willing to go down that road until I heard her voice and knew what was really going on.

Several hours later, my phone rang and the woman I'd loved my entire adult life lit up the screen. God, I wanted to stare at her image, except I had to answer to actually speak to her. I hadn't allowed myself to wallow in pictures of her or of us since she'd left. I tucked them all away in a box, and after I'd moved, I hadn't brought any of them back out. They were safely stored in my closet —nothing was in plain view.

"Hello?" That one word came off harsher than intended.

"Hey, James." Her voice softened my resolve. I hadn't wanted to let her back into that place she'd occupied for so long...the one I'd shut off, though the sound of my name on her lips had me ready to surrender.

I waited for her to speak, leaving us in silence, I finally asked, "So what happened?"

The sigh that echoed through the speaker broke my heart. "This has just all been too much."

"So come home."

"I don't have a home there anymore. Plus, I signed a two-year contract. I'm here until it's over."

"You always have a home here." I hadn't meant to say the words. I'd thought them, and they'd escaped at the same time. "And why did you sign a two-year agreement?"

"Those were the terms of the job."

"Is it iron-clad?"

"I don't think they can force me to stay, but if I break it, I'll never work for another large firm as an engineer. So, yeah, I'd say it's pretty iron-clad."

"You going to tell me what happened?"

"I don't know. There's not really much to tell. I just think I should have taken more time before I jumped to make so many life-changing decisions so quickly."

"Have you met anyone there? You're not lonely, are you?" I wasn't asking about guys when the first part had come out, but then I wondered if she had and whether or not I cared to know. "Do you at least like your co-workers?" Maybe if I kept speaking, the questions would morph into something that was more obscure than finite and prying.

For the first time in ages, Cora started talking—like we had in high school and college. Once the gate had been opened, the information came flooding through. Yet none of it pertained to Drake Halifax or any situation he'd been a part of. I learned all about her job, the people she worked with, how frustrated she was by her limited French —she believed the ability to communicate in the native tongue was the difference between being treated like a tourist and a citizen. Cora loved the food and the clothes and the culture—but missed the States.

I couldn't tell her much about my life other than the business had finally turned around, I'd moved out—which she was already aware of—and I'd made friends with Eric and Cason. I mentioned the other girls at the bar, although I did so in a much less familiar context. She didn't need to know I'd been intimate with anyone else any more than she'd willingly admitted she'd been with Drake Halifax and now regretted it. We both had secrets that would only serve to hurt the other, and we skirted the issue.

I'd been so thrilled to hear from her, I'd forgotten about being at work and ignored my line ringing and cell phone dinging and emails arriving...until Neil showed up in my doorway with an irritated glower on his face.

"You going to work today or shoot the shit with one of your latest harlots?" He'd said it loud enough that Cora heard every word before I could cover the receiver.

I could have ripped his tongue out. "I'm on the phone with Cora."

His eyes went wide just before a sheepish grin engulfed his features.

"Hey, Cora. I'm going to need to go, but it was great talking to you. Don't be a stranger, okay?"

"Yeah, sure, James."

I heard the hurt in her voice, even though she didn't verbalize it. Just before she hung up, I stopped her. "Hey, Cora?"

"Yeah?" I hated the sadness that lingered in that one word.

"I miss you, too."

"Goodbye, James."

***

After another long day, I packed up my office and headed to Sideways Shots. I needed the distraction, and home was a lonely place these days. My phone buzzed in my pocket, pulling me away before I sat at the bar. I rolled my eyes and groaned at the sight of my mom's face appearing on the screen, her name flashing like a warning sign. As I answered the call, I turned around and walked out to the sidewalk to hear her better.

"Hi, Mom."

"Son, that's hardly any greeting for your mother. You could pretend to be a little enthusiastic."

No one was around to see the finger gun I'd put to my temple and motioned pulling the trigger. It was melodramatic and probably insensitive to some group out there, but she grated on my nerves. And this pacified my desire to be disrespectful to her.

"What's up?" I ignored her need for me to stroke her already inflated ego.

"Your father's fiftieth birthday party is just a few weeks away, son. You're planning to come home, right?"

"I hadn't thought about it."

"This is a big one, so you should be here. We're having a whole weekend of activities. I expect you to attend."

"Mom, you act like I don't have a business to run and a life of my own that is nowhere near Geneva Key."

"That may be true, but you have plenty of time to make arrangements. Neil can watch your little shop while you're gone for a couple days."

And she wondered why she never heard from me.

"Plus, your father has some business he'd like to discuss with you. So you really should plan a couple days before or after to spend some time with him."

Amazing. The woman hadn't so much as even sent me a text on *my* birthday, yet she expected me to drop what I was doing to come racing home to celebrate with her and my dad. As usual, she didn't give me time to object or even say no.

"I'll email you all the details. Have your secretary contact Sheila to make arrangements on your father's calendar for the other. I don't get involved in that sort of thing."

No, she just used my dad's assistant as her own personal slave. I hoped to God my dad paid Sheila well; she was a saint for having stayed with him so long.

"Kiss, kiss, son. I'll see you in a few weeks."

"Bye." She'd already disconnected, so my word fell on a dead screen.

That woman had the ability to send me to the depths of hell just by the sound of her voice. She never cared about anything I was doing the way she did my dad—they were two little selfish peas in a narcissistic pod.

She'd managed to thoroughly ruin my evening. I hated playing her games almost as much as I hated being her puppet. Neither she nor my dad gave a shit about seeing me, considering they hadn't once come to New York since I'd moved here three years ago—at least, not to visit me. The invitation was for appearances only, and my attendance was expected. Their friends and business associates would have a lot to say about the heir to the Carpenter throne not showing up, even though not one of them gave a damn about me.

This was who I was, what I'd been born into. I could say no, I could refuse to go, but in the long run, it wouldn't prove anything, and it wouldn't solve any problems. It would only serve to create more that my parents refused to see. They believed they were top notch. I'd been successful, gone to a good college, played basketball for an elite team, now owned my own financial business in New York—and they took credit for all of it because they'd funded my childhood. It was the same gift every parent gave their offspring, yet somehow, it equated to *their* success where I was concerned. It didn't matter that I could count on one hand the number of weeks per year they'd been home while I was in high school, and on the other, the number of days I'd seen them since I'd graduated.

I hoped to God that never was my measure of success in anyone's life—much less my son's.

***

STEPHIE WALLS

"So you're really going back to Geneva?" Neil was dumb-founded I hadn't found a way to get out of my dad's birthday week.

"I don't have a choice. It's just a few days. Plus, he wants to talk business. I have no idea what that means, but if there's even a remote chance that benefits us, then it's a sacrifice I'm willing to make."

He scoffed. "Right. Like your dad is going to serve you help on a silver platter."

"Yeah, that was about how it grabbed me. If I have to go, I can hope something positive will come out of it, right?"

"Sure. Just don't get disappointed, and keep your guard up. He's cutthroat and won't hesitate to slit your wrists."

"Jesus, Neil. Glad to hear you think so highly of my old man." I chuckled at the visual.

"He and my dad are cut from the same cloth. I don't have a use for either one."

Neil had never recovered from the shit his parents had pulled our senior year in high school. Their relationship was never the same—in fact, it basically didn't exist. And Natalie had deserted him when she hadn't been able to dictate his path. He even now had a niece he'd never met because she refused to see him. He only found out about the little girl from Facebook. However, his situation had been slightly different than mine. My parents hadn't screwed me over or cut me off—they'd just been absent the way most parents in Geneva Key were. Au pairs, nannies, and house staff raised children, not mothers and fathers.

Neil had stopped by my apartment on his way home to get signatures on documents he needed while I was gone. He hadn't been here since I'd moved in, and he seemed uncomfortable, although it could have been the topic at hand or my home itself.

"You get lonely living here?" Well, that answered that question.

I thought about lying to him, giving him the PC answer that would allow him to sleep without worry. Then I realized I had no reason to be dishonest. "Why do you think I'm never here?" I pointed to the closet in my room. "Hell, I haven't even unpacked all my stuff."

He sat in the chair in the corner, the one Cora had loved in the apartment we'd shared with Neil and Hannah. "What do you do when you're not at work? Surely you don't spend all your time at the bar in Midtown."

"Most of it. They've got decent food, great draft, and fairly good company." I shrugged as I continued to pack.

"You headed there tonight?"

"Nah, I'm going to try to get to sleep early. It's a long drive home."

"Remind me again why you aren't flying?"

I didn't have a real reason other than I hadn't wanted to. I didn't have a fear of flying, although I just didn't have any desire to get to my parents' house any sooner than necessary. "This way I get credit for coming a day earlier than I actually do and staying a day longer."

"You think they're keeping score?"

"Seriously? They're always keeping tabs. Not just for me but everyone they're acquainted with. They're never in debt to anyone and people always owe them favors. It's how my dad has so much leverage on everyone he comes in contact with. I remember when I was little, one of the maids had a fire in her apartment. My dad gave her money to help her get back on her feet, which she paid back with interest. Then anytime he needed her to stay late or work a weekend she wasn't scheduled, he'd remind her of just how generous he'd been."

I hated thinking about that kind of thing. I'd seen it my whole life, and it always felt wrong, although I didn't have a way to express that then. As an adult, I simply avoided owing him anything.

He crossed his legs at the ankles and put his hands behind his head. "Have you told them about Cora?"

"What about her?" I discussed as little as possible about my personal life with my parents. They were on a need-to-know basis—and there was nothing they needed to know about Cora.

"That you're not still together."

"They're aware she's in Paris and think our decision to pursue our careers was mature." I mocked my mother's tone when she'd made the proclamation herself.

"Susan Carpenter. Always finding the bright side to every dull piece of tin."

I just rolled my eyes and zipped my suitcase. "Especially when that tin is a Chase. They don't care if we're in love as long as we're well connected."

"You think that's what this weekend is about? Them furthering your connections?"

"There's an agenda…I'm just not privy to what it is yet. But rest assured, I'll know within an hour of my arrival. And hopefully, I won't be getting back in the car to return to New York without a decent night's sleep and breakfast in the morning. I pray to God my dad can keep his mouth shut so we can make it through the party. Anything after that is icing on the cake."

"Good luck, man. I don't see you surviving past dinner tomorrow night. I'll be rooting for you and hope whatever he has up his sleeve benefits us. I'm not ashamed of taking handouts."

"Be careful…sometimes the hand that feeds you slaps you in the face."

***

"I'm about to blow my top, James." Cora had been ranting for thirty minutes, although I'd yet to figure out what she was pissed about. "Ugh, insufferable, I swear. Maybe it's just this place."

"So come home." I used any opening, anytime, to get her back stateside. I didn't care what the reason was or who sent her in my direction, as long as she came.

"Ten more months."

"You could be on a plane tomorrow if you wanted to," I spoke into the air as I drove down the interstate heading back to Geneva Key.

"Well, that wouldn't do me any good. Where would I go? Hang out in the terminals?"

"Have you ever wondered if people do that? Like just spend days wandering around the airport? It would be a safe place for homeless people to go. Why don't people do that?" I'd drifted off topic, only realizing it when Cora laughed on the other end. It was the first bit of humor I'd heard from her since she called.

"Squirrel much?" She referred to the rabbit trail I'd wandered off on with that diatribe.

"If you're coming home, I'll turn around now." And I would. No questions asked. My parents could kiss off. If it came to a choice between them and Cora, that was a no-brainer.

"I'm surprised you're going home."

"It's my dad's fiftieth birthday."

"So your mom insisted?" The giggle she let out, correct in her assumption, elated me.

"Basically. My father wants to discuss business as well, but that's not until after the party. Lucky me."

"Wait, you're not just going to the party and going home?"

"It's a weekend of festivities, Cora," I mimicked my mother's voice.

"How long are you staying?" she shrieked as though she'd be dragged along.

"Unless I cut the trip short, I'm leaving Wednesday morning."

"It's only Thursday, James. Are you insane? There's no way you'll survive five days in that house. Please tell me you're staying in a hotel."

"Where on Geneva Key would you suggest I find a hotel, Cora?" The laugh came unexpectedly, yet it felt good. I'd missed these kinds of conversations with her—the ones that went on endlessly about nothing where we'd both forgotten why we'd called to start with.

"Maybe they've built one by now."

"Yeah, right next to the Walmart and McDonald's."

"It could happen."

"There's no way in hell with the money floating around in that town the citizens will ever let the conglomerates take over."

"Do you want to go back?" Her tone was introspective, and had she not just been on some tirade about France, I'd wonder if she longed to return. Then again, as it stood in her mind, anything was better than where she was.

"For good?"

"Yeah. I always thought you'd find your way home. Geneva Key suited you."

"It suits old people who smell like wealth."

"At some point, the tides will turn. Our grandparents' generation will pass away, and a new one will take over."

"Yeah, our parents who will replace them and reminisce about a time when things were different, and youngsters were more respectful. It's a cycle, Cora. There will always be an older generation spearheading that island until *we* are that generation." The miles kept passing as I cruised toward the destination in question.

"Maybe not, time could weed them out. And just like every other beach-front community, younger people seek refuge until they overtake it."

"Except there's nothing there to appeal to anyone who still has color in their hair."

"All it takes is one. One person to bring something in that appeals to others. You should think about that."

"Think about what?"

"Being that one person."

"This conversation has gone so far off course, I don't even

remember where we started." I knew exactly where it began—her hating France and my desperate attempt to convince her to come home...ten months early.

"That's okay. It served its purpose. You cheered me up and got my mind off how much I miss the US and wish I were home...well, until I just thought about it. Now I want to be back in the States again."

I didn't need to tell her "I told you so," because she already knew she'd made a mistake. This wasn't something I could fix or even ease her frustration of—she'd chosen a path away from me, and until she returned, there wasn't anything I could do other than lend her an ear. Although, if she asked me to come see her, to spend time with her, I doubted I could say no. Since that request hadn't come in the fourteen months she'd been there, I didn't expect it to come in the next ten.

"Any idea what your mom has planned?"

I'd zoned out and had no idea if she'd said anything in the past couple minutes other than the last sentence she'd just uttered.

"Not a clue. Torturing me might be the main event...you never know."

"You're so melodramatic. Besides, they'd never do that in public—it might tarnish their image. Do you think my grandmother will be there?"

The laugh that escaped my mouth broke through the words I spoke. "How would I know? She's your family; has she mentioned it?"

"The monthly newsletter hasn't come out yet, but it wasn't in the Fourth of July edition." The levity in her tone tugged at my heart.

God, I missed her.

"I'll tell you if she signs the guest book."

"Oh, oh, better yet. FaceTime me and then walk up to her with your phone in your hand. That will freak my grandmother out, and she'll spend the next hour talking about how inconsiderate technology users are. It'll be fantastic, and you can keep me live so I can witness it—it'll be just like I'm there."

This was the lightest I'd heard her since we'd started chatting again. The gaiety in her voice and the playfulness of her suggestion had a grin plastered to my face.

"I might take you up on that."

"Don't you dare!" Her gasp rang through the phone as though the air had just breezed right by my ear. I could almost feel the warmth of her words meeting my skin while I waited for her lips to follow. "Gwendolyn would disown me. It'd be a disgrace to the Chase name."

I couldn't quite tell if she'd gone serious or was continuing this charade of giving a shit what her grandmother thought. My best guess was she couldn't even recall the last time she'd talked to her. There was a tiny piece of me that felt sorry for Gwendolyn Chase. She'd tried over the years to make amends with Cora, yet the little spitfire had refused her advances and kept her at arm's length.

When the giggles subsided, and the line quieted, the weight of her tone rested firmly on my heart. "Are you really going to be all right there, James? I hate that you're going alone."

"I'll be fine. It's just my parents...and like a hundred of their closest friends." I tried to keep the situation from turning deep. She didn't need to worry about me, at least not this.

"Call me if you need me, promise?"

"Sure. But I'm a big boy, Cora. I can hold my own with my parents and the other socialites of Geneva Key."

"I miss you."

I longed for her to replace that middle word with one she'd used a thousand times. One day, I'd hear her tell me she loved me again. Until then, I clung to this as if the sentiment were the same. "I miss you, too, Cora."

8

CHELSEA

I HADN'T BEEN IN THIS TOWN LONG ENOUGH TO BE FAMILIAR WITH it. Even though the island was small, there were times details escaped me. It was easier to have Dottie drop me off than to risk getting lost. When I stepped inside, the flurry of activity startled me. Before I could get caught up in the anxiety that lingered in unfamiliar places, Jared—the guy who hired me yesterday—stepped out of his office.

"Hey, Chelsea. You're right on time. Everyone is loading up so go grab a seat in the van."

I'd bartended back home while I was in college, and it was an easy gig to fall back on. The tips were good without an abundance of hours, and while this job wasn't in a club, the owner of the catering company assured me their high-end clientele tipped well and made the obscure hours worth the effort. Yet money wasn't really a driving force. It gave me something to do and people to interact with, and there weren't many career choices available in Geneva Key.

I didn't speak to anyone during the ride. Instead, I took note of how we all looked similar in our tuxedo shirts and black slacks. The others had met before, but no one made conversation with me, so I watched the beach pass until we pulled up to a palatial home that made my own feel like a shoebox. Once we entered through the back door and were assigned to stations, I realized the vast opulence in this place left me cold. Dottie's house was nothing in comparison —it felt lived in, not preserved. Her little three-bedroom bungalow breathed life into anyone who walked through the door and quickly became a place I never wanted to leave.

The bar had been set up and stocked before I arrived, leaving me with nothing to do other than wait for a customer. Then before any of the guests arrived, the host paid me a visit. I plastered a smile on my face and willed my hands not to shake in her presence. She looked familiar, although wealth had a way of making things obscure. The woman looked like every other millionaire I'd seen here since I arrived.

She didn't wait for me to greet her before she informed me of her expectations. "My guests will be arriving shortly, so let me get you familiar quickly. We only serve top shelf, you're not to accept tips, and if anyone has the audacity to request a beer, it needs to be served in a chilled glass. Under no circumstances do I care to find empty bottles littering my home. Understood?"

A tremor shook my right hand, and I stuffed it in my pocket, hoping she hadn't seen it. "Yes, ma'am."

Jared made sure I knew that all hosts and their guests should be addressed with respect. The woman who'd never bothered to intro-duce herself gave me a quick nod and moved to the next employee, likely giving him a similar welcome. It shouldn't have bothered me. I was being paid to do a job, though I didn't think it would hurt if she smiled or even said hello.

I noticed with the arrival of the first party goer, the hostess had a different face—and likely personality—for those in her circle. Her plastic expression never dropped, and I watched her with interest until someone under the age of fifty came into view. He was attrac-tive and definitely tall, but it wasn't his good looks that held my interest. The way he carried himself told me he was no stranger to this type of gathering. He had a part to play, and he did it well; however, his eyes gave away his unhappiness.

The blue-eyed boy with mussed hair was clearly the adult son of the host I'd met earlier. And since no introductions had been made, I just sat back and watched his social torture unfold while I filled drinks for his parents' privileged friends. That was until I lost track of him when a wave of thirsty old men created a line in front of me.

By the time he'd made another appearance, the night was nearly over. My legs had grown stiff, and I desperately needed to move. Without anyone to relieve my post, I distracted myself by eaves-dropping on the conversation a few feet away.

When his father clapped his shoulder, I expected him to smile. Instead, he appeared bored and maybe even irritated.

Then his father spoke to the other man standing with them. "He's making the old man proud, Doug."

There was no recognition that crossed his son's face.

"Following in his father's footsteps in the Financial District in New York." His father laid it on thick.

So he lived in New York. It didn't surprise me. He had the air of a city dweller—Chicago had been full of them. Wealthy yuppies who had escaped their parents' world only to start one of their own in another town thinking they were different than the privilege they'd grown up in. While he didn't give off the arrogant vibe, there was no denying he wasn't here on his own accord.

"That's a fine career choice. I'm sure your father has been a plethora of help and a wealth of added opportunities." *Doug* gave his acquaintance a smug look that made me want to smack the taste out of his mouth.

There was something off, like the young guy wanted to challenge Doug's statement, or maybe even his father's. Instead, he bit his tongue. With a nod of indifference, he politely excused himself, an obligatory smile straining his lips—it was the same plastic grin his mother had repeatedly shown throughout the evening.

I straightened my spine when he made a beeline for the bar I tended, not wanting him to see my discomfort. I didn't have much longer on the clock, and I needed to make it to the end of the shift. Dottie had put in a good word with Jared to get me the job, and I couldn't let her down. She'd lived in this town for longer than I'd been alive—I'd make her proud if it killed me.

He glanced over his shoulder at the group of men his father still talked to when he stepped up. When I asked him what I could get him, he was either distracted or didn't hear me. I didn't think my voice had trembled, so I tried again.

"Sir?"

When he turned his focus to me, he was clearly taken aback. His crystal-blue eyes stared at my hair for an especially long time without meeting my gaze. I hoped he was admiring my unusual strawberry-blond hair and not something inappropriate clinging to it. His attention made me uncomfortable, so I cleared my throat, hoping he'd respond.

"Can I get you something, sir?"

"Do you have any beer back there?"

"Unlikely anything you'd drink." I winked at him, amused by the request. I'd been standing here for hours, and not one person had ordered a beer.

He looked like he needed to loosen his tie, prop his feet up, and kick back on the couch to unwind. I couldn't stop the mischievous grin that lifted the corners of my lips.

"Let me guess, Amstel Light? Or maybe Miller?"

"Both. Bottle. No draft."

He shook his head. "Miller, please. My mother thinks Amstel is a beer women enjoy because it has fewer calories, although she doesn't know a single female who consumes anything other than expensive wine. And Miller is her generation's form of a microbrew, I guess. Somehow, it's perfectly acceptable for a man to drink barley and hops, yet a woman should only partake of grapes."

"Glasses are chilled. Bottles don't leave the bar."

"Of course." He wasn't the slightest bit surprised.

I chanced to offer an introduction over the top of the bar. "I'm Chelsea. You must be a relative of the couple throwing the party." I'd already figured out the lineage, but I wanted to keep him talking. I hadn't met anyone here, and even though he lived in New York, it made me feel normal even if it were fleeting.

"Carpenter. My friends call me Carp. And yes, the only child of said hosts."

"Sorry for your luck." My tone was playful, and he clearly noted my comment was in jest. "I take it Carpenter is your last name?"

He nodded as I handed him the glass. I couldn't say with any certainty what he was thinking, though the taste of crappy beer didn't appear to sit well on his palette. And the urge I'd seen to toss one back hadn't driven him to down the one he had in hand. He needed something far stronger to escape whatever he ran from.

"It is."

"Do you have a first name?"

His hesitation to share his first name was odd, but he finally acquiesced. "James."

"Well, Carp, you've been the highlight of my evening. I get off in an hour if you don't have anything to do." I'd never been so forward and had no idea where my confidence had come from. I didn't have a car here and had no way to get back to Dottie's—although, I knew she'd understand and rescue me when I called.

"Sure. There's not much to do here. I guess we could go down to the beach. The moon's full so there's plenty of light."

"Sounds good. I'll just meet you at the back door they had us come in. Work for you?"

An hour later, I released the tension in my legs when I found a bathroom and changed clothes. Then I met Carp at the designated spot. Carp. It was odd, but James didn't fit him—it was too... formal. I'd just try not to imagine an ugly fish when I addressed him.

He appraised me the same way he'd done at the bar an hour earlier. Except this time, he didn't stop at my hair; his eyes roamed from head to toe without bothering to hide the fact he was checking me out. Yet where he'd been fascinated by my hair then, he now stared at my leather flip-flops, or maybe it was the ink covering my feet.

"Do you live around here?" I asked, hoping to get a narrower indication of where I'd find him on a map. We'd been playing the get-to-know-you version of twenty questions since our toes had hit the sand.

"No. New York City." The lack of details he gave wasn't lost on me. Either he was a private person or a guarded one. "You?"

"On the other side of the island about two blocks from the water. It's my friend Dottie's house. It's nothing like your parents', but I love stepping out on the back porch and hearing the waves in the distance." There was no indication of how much information he had an interested in learning, and since I hadn't had anyone my age to talk to since I'd moved here, I chattered away, believing he was fascinated. "I moved down here a few weeks ago from Chicago."

"Do you bartend full time?"

As much as I enjoyed the company, it was obvious by the looks and the lack of meaningful conversation that Carp was more interested in losing himself in my body than getting acquainted with me. I didn't want to cheapen myself, but relationships weren't a possibility, and I had the same carnal desire anyone else did.

"No. I just do it to earn extra money." I didn't offer him anything further regarding my employment. Nothing I said would compare to whatever he did in New York, and I wasn't interested in tasting regret. Not everyone lived to be a millionaire.

The moonlight reflected off the water, and my mind wandered

momentarily to the endlessness of the ocean: the crashing waves, rolling tide, and the way it married the horizon, even in darkness. The surf lapped at our now bare feet, and the warm sand between my toes reminded me that I now called this island paradise home. The simple things in life could be monumental if we allowed ourselves to appreciate what nature gave us for free.

"What do you do for a living?" I hated that question—moreover I hated that Americans defined their identities with careers. However, he'd just done the same to me, and he seemed bored strolling along the shore in silence.

"Wealth management."

"Ah, so the apple didn't fall far from the tree." My brow rose, not in judgment rather humor. There was no denying he and his father weren't close just in the little time I'd seen them together, yet he'd followed in the old man's footsteps. I kept my gaze in front of me.

I expected him to present a firm argument against my assumption. Instead, he dismissed the comment the same way he'd done his father's friends at the party—with dignified grace.

"Other than bartending, what else do you like to do?" There was nothing in his tone to indicate he had any real interest in my hobbies or preferences. He hadn't been rude; in fact, he'd been rather pleasant, even though both of us were well aware this wasn't going anywhere long term.

I quit walking, and he stopped a couple steps ahead of me when he realized I wasn't next to him. "Can we just be honest here?" I didn't say the words with accusation, yet the question was pointed.

He turned back, closed the gap between us, and met my eyes. "Yeah, sure."

"You don't live here. I'm not going to New York. Obviously, the two of us are attracted to each other, and neither plan on any kind of relationship. Am I right so far?"

His shoulders raised with an involuntary shrug he seemed embarrassed by. "I guess so."

I glanced around the deserted beach and then pulled a condom out of my pocket. "I'm not interested in romance, Carp, and I don't do relationships. There are miles of desolate beach and nothing other than moonlight to disturb us." My forwardness caught him by surprise.

His brow furrowed in contemplation. Carp mulled something over, and the silence hung between us while I waited. "Have you ever *had* sex in the sand?"

I shrugged and cocked my head to the side without answering.

"It's like rubbing sandpaper on your ass while you try to get off."

"Okay, I'll take the bottom." My coy grin lit a fire in his eyes. The cool blue warmed in front of me. "Or you could sit, and I could ride. Whichever suits you." I'd never been brazen. The girl speaking to Carp was as much a stranger to me as she was to the man before me.

But sometimes, when you have nothing left to lose, you have to take the bull by the horns. I refused to live by anyone else's rules anymore. Life didn't hand you what you wanted—you had to take it without regret. And just like that, I stripped off the tank top that covered my thin frame and glanced at my flat stomach when I shimmied out of my shorts. I dropped each piece onto the sand in a pile that I stepped over to close the gap between us. Hunger marked his face and lust traced his eyes. The second the moon reflected off the foil between my fingers he sprang into action.

Something happens to a single man in front of a naked woman —he loses all rational thought. Where there had been a hint of hesitation before, the pull of bare skin basking in the light of the moon was too much to resist. He looked like a sailor lost at sea, lending his ear to a siren.

I wasn't part of mythology, and he wouldn't get entranced by my spell. I was just a twenty-two-year-old girl who wasn't captivated by the unfamiliar or afraid of risk.

Even though the experience wasn't beautiful, I couldn't say it was tragic. Sadly, we hadn't bonded over the intimate act on the beach, although somehow, Carp's warning coming true had sent us both into gales of laughter and left sand in crevices I didn't know existed. I'd be picking grains out of my skin for weeks to come. I could mark this off my bucket list—sex on the beach was only appealing in Hollywood. The levity of the situation elevated his mood and dropped his guard.

We talked for hours after an epic failure to get rid of the grit on each other's clothes and scalp. If only he'd been willing to open up before he'd gotten undressed. I could have saved him from making a mistake he'd regret in the morning. And it had nothing to do with me, and everything to do with the girl he'd loved—and lost. The guilt he would wear when what he did sank in would cling to him like a wet shirt he couldn't get off.

We'd both known the encounter would be fleeting, even if for different reasons. He escorted me to the pier, and I'd texted Dottie while we walked. I assumed we'd say goodbye and that would be the end. Yet we exchanged numbers, and I saw her headlights coming down the street.

"Hey, Chelsea?" He stopped me from leaving to meet my ride.

"Yeah?" When I turned back, his features had softened, and whatever wall he'd had up disappeared.

"I have business to deal with in town for a couple days. Maybe we could get coffee or breakfast one day before I leave." Suddenly shy, he shrugged. "As friends." His brows rose, and his hand landed in his hair. It looked painful to see him pulling on it with nervous apprehension.

I giggled at the vulnerability of a man who stood head and shoulders above most, had a physique many males would kill for, and who'd exuded confidence from the instant I'd laid eyes on him until this very instant. "I'd like that."

He had no idea the olive branch he'd offered me. It was unexpected, yet certainly welcome. I looked forward to calling James Carpenter a friend.

***

"How are you holding up, honey?" Dottie handed me a cup of coffee and took a seat next to me on the deck.

Staring out at the horizon, I watched the sky color itself in a rainbow of oranges and pinks. Life in Geneva Key was different than Chicago, not better or worse. "Some days are better than others." My gaze shifted from the artwork on the horizon to the woman I'd known and loved my entire life. "It scares me to think I'm going to lose her, and that if I don't remember her, there won't be anyone around to share with the world how amazing she was."

Dottie patted my leg just like my mother would have done, and I wondered if she'd picked up the habit watching her over the years, or if she'd always been nurturing. "I think she'll always be in your heart. And as long as she's there, her memory will survive. Your mother has touched the lives of more people than you could ever imagine."

"My entire life, I knew this day would come. She never hid from me what the disease would eventually do to her body and her mind. I just thought I had more time. And the older I got, the younger she seemed, so it didn't dawn on me that she was losing the fight."

"Chelsea, you're young. Mortality shouldn't be on the mind of a girl your age. Don't regret living—Janie would never want that."

Dottie was right, my mother never questioned the things she did when I was growing up. It had always been the two of us, and she made every second count. Had I realized then how she tried to ensure she got joy out of every day, I might have paid closer attention and focused on what mattered. In the end, money wouldn't save her, neither would the best doctors in the world—and she'd known that since she was diagnosed.

"I miss her. The woman I grew up with. Sometimes I still see glimpses, although they're getting farther apart. It won't be long until they disappear completely. I miss the sound of her voice and the way she hugged me. Even the elegance of her handwriting. The little things are the biggest reminders of what all I stand to lose."

There had been a time in the not so distant past that acknowledging my mother was dying brought an onslaught of tears that would leave me in a blubbering mess. I was well versed in how this all worked from diagnosis to the onset of symptoms and through the stages before death. I'd seen it all my life at charity events, and it was my mother's life's passion to raise awareness and find a cure. I'd been to countless funerals, hundreds of events, and studied every bit of information I'd been able to find—I should be prepared.

However, as the Huntingtons progressed, I tried to let go of that emotion to focus on making her comfortable and providing the best finale I could to celebrate her journey. It was important to me to bring a smile to her face for as long as I was able, and even now that I neared the point where my mom would lose what little motor function she had remaining and her memory would fail her completely, I wanted her to have joy as long as possible.

Dottie wasn't a stranger to the thief who stole the woman I loved. She'd faced that same devil in the losses of countless people she and my mom loved and worked with over the years. And I think those experiences brought the wisdom and patience she'd shown me in the last couple of years. She always seemed to know when to talk, when to listen, and when to just offer support with her presence.

My head rolled toward my mom's best friend who turned to me. Soulful, blue eyes searched my face, and the corners of her mouth turned up in a gentle offering of love. Dottie was a beautiful woman in her mid-seventies, but she'd been exotic and stunning in her youth. I'd seen pictures of her with her late husband and vaguely remembered her arriving at our house when I was a child looking the way she had in the framed memories that scattered the living room we now shared. Dressed to the nines with her makeup flawlessly done, hair tightly wound into a French twist, and heels I'd never be able to walk in—she was the essence of dignity and grace. And even though her hair had lost the rich, chocolate color of her youth, and her skin wasn't as taut as it had once been—her beauty still radiated class.

"Do you think she's in pain?" The mere inability to communicate made my mom's impending death that much harder. I couldn't remember the last time she'd told me she loved me because I hadn't known I'd never hear it again. And because I hadn't paid attention, I'd missed it, and it was one more memory I wouldn't have.

"Medically speaking? Or just my personal opinion?"

"Your opinion."

"I think pain comes at the end of someone's life when they realize all they regret and have run out of time to make amends, to tell someone how special they are, have a picnic in the park. All the things we never have room for in our lives because we're so busy are the very things we wish we'd taken the time to do."

I hadn't known Pappy all that well, and had only met him a handful of times, but Dottie had changed when she lost her husband. He was wealthy and powerful, the kind of guy who valued his public image—and he'd had a big one to maintain—yet she was the apple of his eye. And I assumed, because I didn't want to ask, that she missed doing those things with him and had ended up burying a mountain of regret. The stories she told of the places they'd been sounded like a fairy tale—however, as I got older, I realized jet-setting left little time for walks on the beach. And every choice brought a sacrifice.

"Your mother never lived with regret. She made sure to do everything that interested her, she apologized freely, loved passionately, and never held a grudge, and in the end, not taking a single day for granted left her with no remorse, and certainly no guilt. So to answer your question, no—I don't think Janie is in any pain. And now that you're settled here, I believe she's ready to let go."

My phone vibrated on the table next to me with a text from Carp. I sensed Dottie watching me as I read his message, inviting me to lunch.

"A smile looks good on your lips."

"Do you know where Galen's is?" I hoped she didn't ask a lot of questions. I didn't have any answers, and nothing other than friendship would ever come of this.

Her brows arched, though she didn't pry. "It's just a few blocks from here. I can drop you off."

I stood and took my untouched coffee cup with me. "No, thanks. I'm going to shower and get dressed. Can you give me directions before I leave?"

She stared up at me from the Adirondack chair she lounged in. "Of course."

"Thanks, Dottie." I kissed the top of her soft-gray hair, and then went inside.

***

Carp looked different in the warmth of the mid-day sun than he had at night, and even more so without the stress that had marred his features at his parents' house. The tension that pinched his brow was gone, and the cargo shorts and Tar Heels shirt suited him better than the slacks and tie.

"Hey." He met me at the door with a smile.

"Hey, yourself." I doubted I'd ever even talk to this man again, yet for the next hour, I got to pretend like things were normal and enjoy a meal and conversation. If that meant hiding from the weight of reality, then so be it.

"Have you ever eaten here?" Carp's enthusiasm was endearing. His attention shifted briefly to the hostess. "Hey, Nina. Two please."

"No, but it seems you have."

"They have the best shepherd's pie in the country, and I think I've tried them all. Well, maybe not *all* but enough to confirm that this is top notch."

We followed Nina to a booth in the back. The tiny restaurant felt more like a pub, except where the lights are dimmed in a bar, the restaurant bathed in sunshine from the front windows. It was a good thing I didn't come for the ambiance, because the wooden booths with green pleather upholstery reminded me of leprechauns and seemed kind of cliché.

After sliding in, Carp turned to Nina and asked her to give us a few minutes. The menu consisted of a single page of comfort food no one should eat on a humid summer's day in Florida. I kept it simple and went with Carp's selection accompanied by a glass of ice water.

He handed the menus back to Nina before returning his attention to me. "It won't disappoint."

"So how long are you in town?" I really hoped we were able to find a groove like we had post sex on the beach. Sitting here staring at each other in uncomfortable silence for sixty-plus minutes didn't appeal to me.

"Probably leaving Wednesday—although, that depends on what my dad springs on me in his office tomorrow morning."

"Do you guys work together?" They lived in different states, but with the money in this town, there could be multiple locations in a family business.

"Nah. We don't really even speak to each other." He rolled the edge of a paper napkin between his fingers. "I left Geneva Key after high school, went to college and have only been back a handful of times since."

"Is it that bad here?" There was a hint of laughter at the end of my question. Thus far, I hadn't encountered anything that would make someone leave the state without looking back.

Carp's pale-blue eyes peered through his dark lashes before he actually raised his head and stopped fidgeting. "No, probably not. But I grew up here, and while I have great memories with friends, none of those people live here anymore. And visiting my childhood home doesn't remind me of joyous family Christmases past or playing in my fort in the backyard as a kid."

"What memories does it bring back?" I couldn't fathom not loving where I'd grown up, the physical place. That was the single hardest thing about leaving Chicago—my home, the one I'd lived in since the day I was born, would belong to someone else.

"Homework in the afternoons with nannies, meals alone at an enormous dining room table, and running in to show my mom something I'd done at school, only to find she'd left the country with my dad for another business trip."

"That's really sad. I can't imagine. I'd kill to be able to go home."

"Did you live in Chicago all your life?"

"Yep. Our house wasn't anything special and certainly nothing like the mansions in Geneva Key, but my mom worked hard to provide for me. She always made sure I had what I needed, and the rest she made up for with attention."

"How'd you end up here?"

"My mom is in a treatment facility in Tampa. And Dottie—that's her best friend—convinced us both we needed to be closer so she could help me."

"It's a shame so many people fall prey to addictions. I'm sorry you have to deal with that."

I sensed the shock that took over my face. "Oh no. Not that type of treatment. She has Huntingtons."

"Is there a cure?"

I shook my head and inhaled deeply. "She's lost the ability to speak and swallow, and the tremors are bad. I try to pretend there aren't signs of dementia and memory loss, but they're there. And most days, I still see the recognition in her eyes when she looks at me." I tried to put on a brave face. This disease had been at the forefront of my life because of my mom and her ties to charities and research, although most people didn't live that way.

"I'm sorry. I didn't have any idea."

With the flick of the wrist, I waved him off. "It's okay. This didn't sneak up on us. Even after she developed symptoms, it took years to get to this stage."

"Do you have any other family?" Genuine concerned laced his voice.

"Just Dottie, but she's not related by blood—just love. I don't know my dad, and my grandparents passed away when I was in high school. I'm the only child of an only child." I shrugged. Others saw that as sad, I didn't know any different.

The waitress saved us from the conversation going deeper. It was a welcomed reprieve—not for me, I could talk about my mom all day, but strangers didn't know how to handle death being prominent in my life.

One bite of the shepherd's pie had made me a believer. "Oh my God." I moaned after swallowing the calorie-laden entrée.

"Right? What'd I tell you? Amazing, huh? There's nowhere in New York that even comes close—and I've looked."

"How'd you end up in New York?"

"My best friend, Neil, and I bought a wealth management company after college. Cora, the girl I told you about last night, moved with me to attend grad school. Neil's girlfriend, Hannah, followed us, too. The four of us lived together until Cora went to Paris."

"How long has she been gone?" I'd learned some of the details from what he'd told me walking on the beach.

"Fourteen months." The longing in his eyes broke my heart.

"Do you think you two will be able to fix things when she comes home?"

"Guess that depends on whether she actually comes back. She's career-minded and in a prime position to go far. I'm not sure she's willing to leave the company she works for. Cora's boss is pretty influential in the world of engineering."

"Maybe she'll surprise you."

"Anything's possible, I guess." He didn't believe it.

"Do you want it? The relationship, I mean."

He studied me from across the booth, probably wondering how I could ask such a silly question. Carp had confided in me how much he loved her. He'd even gone so far as to tell me last night shouldn't have happened. I wasn't insulted. His remorse had nothing to do with me or the fact we'd gotten busy in the sand. It had to do with his own guilt for not waiting for a woman who hadn't given him any hope when she'd left, and thinking if he loved her, he should have held out.

"Of course."

"I don't know squat about relationships, Carp. I won't pretend like I do, because I've never really had one. Don't get me wrong…I've dated, although nothing ever lasted longer than a year or so. But my mom has known for years she might not make it to my wedding, and that she may never meet a grandchild. And because of that, she lived every day like it was her last. So if you love this girl, if you believe she's *it,* then you have to fight for her."

Carp paid the bill after a bit of a hesitation from me. It wasn't a date, and I didn't care for it to feel like one. I liked the guy, yet with the things going on with my mom, I wasn't in the headspace to bother with any type of commitment.

Standing on the sidewalk outside of Galen's, I wished Carp luck with Cora and thanked him for lunch. "It was really nice to have someone to hang out with. I love Dottie, but spending time with a woman old enough to be my mom's mom just isn't the same."

"You're welcome. Look, I'm not sure if I'll have any more free time while I'm here. But if I do, let's try to get together before I leave."

"I'd like that."

"And, Chelsea? Even if we don't, you have my number. Don't hesitate to use it. If you need someone to talk to or just a distraction —I can always lend an ear."

I nudged his shoulder with mine and tried to hide the goofy grin that had taken over my face. "You, too."

9

JAMES

CORA CALLED SUNDAY NIGHT TO SEE HOW THINGS HAD GONE AT MY dad's party. It was nice to hear her voice, even if the conversations were surface level and came at two in the morning—time zones were a killer, but I didn't give a shit. I'd make it work to hear her sing in my ear every time she said "hello." We never discussed anything of importance, yet somehow, the familiarity seemed to spark what both of us had missed in our relationship the last year before she'd left.

I'd set aside my hope for salvaging the *us* part of the equation—temporarily—in favor of rebuilding the friendship. Neither of us had said those three magic words, or even mentioned the possibility of getting back together. However, every time we hung up the phone, we told the other we missed them. It had taken the place of the intimacy while confirming the tie.

"I'm sorry I haven't checked on you before now." Her apology seemed forced or maybe uncertain, or it could be the fog of sleep still hovering in my mind.

"It's not a big deal. I assumed you were busy." I had. We weren't together. She wasn't obligated to answer every time I called. Part of me felt like we'd taken several steps back, although the truth was we couldn't take very many forward while we were thousands of miles apart.

"Drake was in town, so I had a lot going on."

I hated even hearing the man's name.

Moreover, I hated how much control he had with Cora, yet I couldn't say anything. I had no right to question what she did or why. Drake Halifax made me want to vomit. I could have dealt with her being with Henry or Arthur—two guys she hung out with from work—or even some random bloke she met out on the town. It was knowing Drake was the reason the two of us weren't together that made me resent the hell out of him.

I had no clue what to say that wouldn't give my heart away, so I kept it superficial. "I'm sure having the big boss in town is stressful." I hoped she got my innuendo. I hoped for a confession—an admission of what had really happened. Maybe if I knew for certain that she'd carried a flame for him, then I could let her go so she could be happy. And if she vehemently denied any wrongdoing, then I could let my heart find its way back to her. As it stood, I felt like a moron who'd been played until she'd boarded the plane for Paris.

"He just expects perfection, and it's hard to deliver. I'm good at what I do, James, but that man has me questioning every decision I make. I feel inferior when he's around—so does every other member of his staff."

Whether it was fear, anxiety, or trepidation, something hung heavy in her voice, and I doubted she would share it with me. It was much easier to save face if one never admitted the truth.

"You wanted to play with the big dogs. Drake's experience comes at a price. Like you said, being mentored by one of the best in the business will put you in a position to make some serious waves in the industry once you've served your time."

"Yeah, if I ever escape." She let out a long sigh that held the weight of more to follow. "I feel like I sold my soul to the devil.

The more I learn from women around here, the more I feel like I made a mistake."

Rolling over in bed, I lay on my back and watched the fan spin into a dizzying frenzy in the dark room. I had to play the game. I couldn't just come out and ask how she couldn't know fucking her boss would end up screwing her career over in the long run. "How so?"

"He gets you with these huge salaries and promotions. Reels people in with big customers and high-profile projects—the high is like an addiction. Each one tops the last, and I'm constantly searching for one that's bigger and better. The little ones get you through to the next fix, but he expects the next fix to be brewing while you're still reveling in the one that got you high in the first place. I've reached the point where I can't enjoy the success because I'm afraid of the fall that might follow."

Not the answer I'd assumed she'd give. "So you're not the only one under Drake's wing, huh?"

"God no, I'm one of many. And he thinks women have an eye for detail men don't, so he leans toward females when he's scouting for talent. It's cutthroat—women are catty as hell and don't have any problem stepping on each other to get ahead. Nothing like a spiked heel to the eye to wake you up."

"I hope you mean that figuratively and not literally."

I couldn't help but think of them stepping over each other naked in Drake Halifax's hotel room while he played each one a different tune of romance. My hands started to shake as I imagined his skin touching Cora's. It made me sick to think of the way he manipulated women—although mostly, just one.

She laughed yet didn't respond to my comment about the shoe.

"Are you not going to leave at the end of your contract?"

"I don't know. I'm trying to save as much money as I can so my salary won't be a driving force if I return to the States to find a job."

I couldn't stifle the chuckle that escaped my lips or the sarcasm that followed. "It's not like you need the money, Cora. You could live off your inheritance and trust fund for the rest of your life. So could your kids and multiple generations after them. If you decide to leave, you can leave." It pissed me off to listen to her act like she didn't have options. We all had options, and we all made choices. Cora chose to stay in Paris under Drake's thumb.

"That's not fair."

"What's not fair about it, Cora? If you don't want to work for Halifax when your term is up, then don't."

"It's not black and white."

"You'll have to help me understand that. I might see how that would be true for someone who didn't have Chase money, but not for you."

I heard someone in the background speak to her just before she covered the phone to muffle what was said.

"Hey, James. I need to go. I'll call you later, okay?"

"Sure."

I didn't wait for her to tell me she missed me or say it myself. I just hung up. And realized after I'd done it just how shitty it was. She'd opened up to me about an insecurity, had really started talking to me, and I'd gotten pissy about it just because it was Drake.

I hadn't stopped fucking around with Letty and didn't even want to think about how Chelsea fit into that equation—my expectations of her were a bit hypocritical. However, Drake Halifax had everything to do with the shifts that had happened between us. I couldn't blame him completely; had our bond been as tight as it should have, there wouldn't have been room for him to force his way in— although he certainly played a part.

As much as I loved Cora and missed her, she was in France for another ten months, and even then, there was no guarantee she'd come home, much less to me. After staring at the wall for however long, the remorse wormed its way in until I finally caved and sent her a text. I couldn't bear to be the reason her day got worse. And even in the darkness of my childhood bedroom, I could see the hurt on her face and didn't want to be the cause for it staying there.

Me: I miss you.

Her unexpected reply came immediately, rubbing a little salve into the open wound of my tattered heart.

Cora: I miss you too, James.

Even text messages, I could hear her voice, and to this day, I loved the way my name rolled off her tongue like a whisper through trees—peaceful and serene. Yet what I loved even more was that she was the only person who used it. At work it was Mr. Carpenter, my friends called me Carp, my parents—when I talked to them—called me son, and Cora called me James. Somehow, from her, it was sacred—a prayer.

***

My father slid a stack of folders across his ornate desk two days later. The birthday festivities had kept him occupied until the last guest left on Sunday. And then the following morning, he was business as usual.

"What's this?" I'd never worked with my dad or participated in any of his financial endeavors. I was well aware of what he did for a living and could have used his contacts to build our business, but I had refused to ask, and he'd never offered. Until now.

"I'm letting go of most of our smaller clients to focus on larger accounts. As I move toward retirement, the board decided to shift gears for the company as a whole. These are all people I've done business with for years that I don't want to give over to anyone I don't trust."

"You're referring business to me?" I couldn't hide the doubt in my voice. My father didn't *give* anyone anything. It all came with a price tag that I couldn't afford.

"I've followed your firm from the sidelines since you bought the business, son. You and Neil have worked hard, made good choices, and weathered the storm. This will only strengthen your portfolio, and in time, draw more investors in your direction."

I eyed him suspiciously before speaking. "What's the catch?"

"Not everything in life comes with stipulations, James." He'd used my name—which definitely meant there were stipulations.

"And you don't give handouts without expecting something in return." I hadn't meant it to come across as disrespectfully as it had, although once the words were out, I couldn't take them back.

"I'm sorry you feel that way, son." Now we were back to terms of endearment.

"Dad, I'm not trying to be an ass—"

"Then don't."

"You've never given me anything without the expectation of something in return. We aren't close; you haven't even been to my place in New York, you don't even know about Cora—"

"I'm aware of more than you give me credit for." His interruption threw me off track, and I stared at him, waiting for him to continue. "Just because I've given you the freedom to start life on your own without being with you every step doesn't mean I don't love you or that I haven't paid attention. I know Cora is in Paris working for Drake."

Of course, he did. I should have expected my dad to be on a first-name basis with Drake Halifax. Which in turn meant my dad realized my girlfriend had left me for another man.

"I'm also cognizant of the fact that she's not happy there and would prefer to come home."

My jaw hung open, and no matter how hard I tried to formulate words or simply close it, it refused to cooperate.

"Drake and I have known each other for a lot of years. Cora being the granddaughter of the Chase family, who happened to live down the street from us, was a topic of conversation. Maybe I shouldn't have done it, but that's neither here nor there—you loved the girl, and I wanted to know her intentions."

Thoughts raced through my head, my brain unable to complete any of them before diverting to another. "W-what intentions?"

He let out a heavy sigh, stood from his chair, and rounded the desk to sit on the edge. For the first time in my life, my dad stared at me like a concerned friend instead of an overbearing, absent parent. "There's no doubt you've heard the stories of Drake's escapades with younger women, several of which worked for him."

I barely managed to move my head in a semblance of a nod, unsure I could bear to hear what he wanted to share.

"She wasn't one of those women, James."

My jaw finally clamped, and my mind shut down. *She wasn't one of those women.* It was the only thing that replayed like an echo bouncing off the walls of my skull.

"And Drake tried. She's a beautiful girl." He paused and stared at me as though he waited for me to catch up mentally in the conversation. "Her heart belonged to you."

I should have been elated, seeing fireworks behind my eyelids, rejoicing that Cora hadn't involved herself with Drake Halifax, but instead, my heart squeezed painfully just as my lungs constricted, preventing air from flowing freely. I hadn't believed in her. I hadn't trusted her enough to believe she was mine. Even if I'd never questioned it verbally, I'd thought it all in my head—and then I'd played out my retribution, using two other women's bodies as my targets. She hadn't failed me; I'd given up on her.

"James?"

My hand clutched my shirt, and the other pulled at the tie around my neck, desperate to loosen the hold it had on my airway. "How do you know?" It was all I managed to utter, but I needed confirmation before I found the nearest Catholic church to start confessing my sins and reciting Hail Marys.

"He told me. He didn't have a clue what he was admitting to when he brought her up. Or that the beau she fancied was my son."

"Did you tell him?" The sentence came out raspy and desperate, although I wasn't sure why.

"Not until I was certain she was loyal."

I wanted to hate him for the sentiment, but the truth was, if it were my child we were talking about, I probably would have done the same.

"Women like that are hard to find when you come from the life you do."

"What?" That was the dumbest thing I'd heard since Chelsea telling me my mom made the staff use the back door.

"Whether you believe it or not, you're privileged, and people will use you to raise their station—"

"She's a Chase, Dad. If anything, she'd be elevating my social status, not the other way around."

"Don't fool yourself, son. Lots of women prefer to marry into the life they were raised in with little respect for the sanctity of the union. And I didn't know Cora from Eve."

"That's because you were never around." I'd mumbled it, yet it had been loud enough for him to hear.

He unfolded his arms from his chest and rested his palms on either side of him, just before his shoulders and face fell slightly. "I deserve that."

Jesus, I didn't have a clue who this man was or what he'd done with my dad. I was starting to wonder if he'd been diagnosed with some terminal disease and was trying to right the wrongs of his past.

"I hope you make better choices if you have children. It's easy to point a finger after the fact, but I did the best I knew how. I mirrored what I'd seen my father do. Those were different times, back when mothers, even those who had nannies, stayed home while fathers worked to provide for their family. It's what my grandfather did and my father after. I wanted you to have the best of everything. I just never considered—until it was too late—that I'd sacrificed the only thing you cared about having the best of…a father."

I'd entered the Twilight Zone. Soon, my mother would come through the door in a prim dress with a belt cinched at the waist, pearls around her neck, and a plate of freshly baked cookies in her hand.

"I can't change our past. I can only hope you have a better future. And I hoped to make sure this Cora girl was it."

"That's it?"

He let out a hearty chuckle before clapping my shoulder and helping me up from the seat I sat in.

"If you don't want to end up just like me, stop taking life so seriously…and maybe find time to make your way to Paris."

I felt my brow draw down, and my lip curl up; I could only imagine what my confusion looked like from the outside. I was lost with this whimsical man who stood before me and wondered if someone had slipped a hallucinogen into my morning coffee.

***

"James, I swear, dating men in Paris is like dating hell in the United States. For a city that's filled with love, these guys have no idea how to treat a lady."

I abhorred hearing her talk about other men, although I secretly smiled each time she told me about a date gone wrong. None of them had been horrible; they just weren't *me*. Cora had yet to figure that part out; she assumed it was the men, when in fact, most women would have swooned at the accent alone.

"They dress like pop stars, James. A guy shouldn't look better in skinny jeans than his date. And they pair them with fitted shirts. It's like boy band gone wrong."

I couldn't help but laugh. "Cora, not every guy in France dresses like Justin Bieber."

"The ones I've met do."

"Maybe it's the industry you're meeting them in. Aren't they all rather artistic in some form or fashion?"

"No." The humor danced in her voice. "What gave you that idea?"

"I just figured engineers were artsy." I shrugged as if she could see me through the phone.

"No, silly—they aren't artsy, they're mathematical. The fashion here is just different."

"So are you going to come back looking like the cover of *Vogue*?"

"I wish. Unfortunately, long hours have done nothing for my complexion or my figure."

"Are you starting to resemble the Toad of Babylon?" I chuckled at the reference. Cora could never be ugly, much less an abomination.

"Oh my God, did you just refer to me as a whore?" Her laughter rumbled through the line.

"I said *toad*! Okay, poor choice of words. Now that I think about it, it didn't make any sense anyhow."

"Thanks, I'll call you the next time I'm feeling particularly heinous, and you can talk me off the ledge."

"I'll sing for you." Third Eye Blind instantly came to mind, and I grinned at the high school memories and times I'd listen to that album on basketball trips. "I wish you would step back from that ledge my friend." I was tone deaf and had massacred that one line.

"That would certainly bring some levity to my day, even if it didn't make me feel any better about my horrendous appearance. Don't quit your day job—the stage is not the place for you."

"I'm sure you're just as beautiful as you've always been." The words were sincere. She'd always been the most stunning woman I'd ever seen.

"It doesn't feel like it in the fashion capital. Everyone here is exotic and thin and just…I don't know…intimidating."

"You've never been intimidated a day in your life, Cora. And if that's how you truly feel, I have to wonder how the benefits of this job outweigh the damage it's doing to your psyche."

Her tone changed, and she giggled playfully. "It's not quite *that* bad. But it would be nice to have one decent date. I don't need anything remarkable or off the charts—just a romantic evening in a spectacular city." I could hear the fairy tale in her voice. She'd had that once, and somehow, we'd both let it slip away. "What about you? Anyone new on the dating scene?"

I hated the direction of this conversation. I'd purposely avoided this topic for fear of where it would lead and our inability to come back from it. Cora may have thought she wanted details, just like I itched for them about her life, yet neither of us really needed to imagine the other with someone else.

"Nah. Just doing the casual thing." *And waiting on you.* I didn't say that last part, although it hung in my thoughts like straight dialogue.

The silence lingered on the line. It was comfortable, the way we'd always been with each other.

"Hopefully we'll both find what we're looking for," she whispered.

I didn't have to find it. I knew exactly where it was—I just couldn't reach it right now. But that would change in ten months if I had anything to do with it. For now, I had to bide my time and remind Cora of why she needed to be here instead of there. "I'm sure we will."

"I need to get going."

I glanced at the clock realizing it was almost one in the morning in France. "Sweet dreams, Cora. I miss you."

"I miss you, too."

***

I tried calling Chelsea on my way home from Florida, but it had gone straight to voicemail. I hadn't heard from her since we had lunch, and while we both agreed there was no possibility of a relationship, she seemed like she needed a friend. The last two days I was in town had been filled with my dad and conference calls with the clients he turned over to our firm. I'd crashed after dinner both nights and left early Wednesday morning to make the trip back to New York. I didn't want her to think I'd used her. I enjoyed talking to her and felt like we could both benefit from having the other to confide in.

Cora was at work, but I sent her a text telling her I was in the car if she got a chance to talk. The silence that came with the open road never bothered me, although now, for whatever reason, it ate at me with each minute that ticked by. I'd stopped several times for gas and snacks, then again to piss—anything to break up the monotony.

By the time Cora's name finally lit up the screen on my cell, I was near the point of insanity.

"Hey." Even though I'd been sitting in the driver's seat doing nothing other than holding the wheel for over an hour, my greeting came out breathy, as if I'd had to run to catch the phone before it quit ringing.

"Hi. How's the drive?"

"I'm ready to leave my car at an airport and fly home."

She snickered. "That bad?"

"I'm just restless. Geneva Key does that to me."

"How'd things go with your dad?"

"It was the strangest experience of my life. He gave me hundreds of thousands of dollars' worth of portfolios for the business, we had lunch like friends, and he told me to go see you in Paris." I hadn't meant to admit that last part. She didn't need to know I'd spoken to my dad about her, much less that he'd suggested an impromptu vacation.

"Yes, yes, yes. That would be perfect."

I'd expected her to brush over it, not extend an invitation.

"Oh, James, could you? I'd love to see a friendly face."

"We could do that over FaceTime." I could have slapped myself for that insensitive remark. It was like I was determined to be an ass to the one woman I'd ever loved as some form of pseudo punishment that only hurt me.

She giggled, thankfully. "Why don't we ever do that? The thought hasn't occurred to me because I don't use it. But that way, we could see each other…I mean, if you won't come to France."

I could envision the way she'd be staring up at me from beneath her long lashes, pushing out her bottom lip just a hair, and waiting for me to give in to her whim. And if I could have driven across the ocean, I would have detoured in that very moment. The drive back to New York didn't exactly tickle my fancy—at least a ride to Paris would have resulted in a pot of gold at the end of the rainbow.

"I wasn't trying to invite myself to a foreign country, Cora." I needed her to confirm she wanted me to come, not that she'd been polite.

Her tone suddenly changed, and her voice dropped. "You didn't. I asked." The hurt in those four little words fractured another piece of my soul.

"I'd love to see you." It was a dangerous admission, yet I needed to confirm where she stood. When I told her I missed her, I meant I missed loving her. *She* could just need a friend.

"Promise me you'll look at your calendar as soon as you get home. It's a long flight, but even if you could come for a couple of days, I'd love having you."

"Can you take time off work?"

"Of course. I've been with the company for over two years, James. I'm not a slave…well, mostly."

I hated knowing she felt that way—she'd worked like a Trojan. And since she was still homesick, she hadn't made a lot of friends— which also meant that other than the handful of bad dates she'd told me about, she didn't socialize much. I couldn't stand the thought of all the socializing I'd done when she left—or with Chelsea on the beach just days ago. My stomach churned again. I had to remind myself no less than twenty times a day since that Cora and I weren't together. Technically, I hadn't done anything wrong—it was just soul-crushing guilt that plagued my conscience.

The two of us talked until she was yawning through every sentence out of her mouth. The time difference had been a killer since we'd started these calls, and as much as I didn't like hanging up, the possibility of planning a trip to spend time with her made it easier to let her go.

"Promise you'll have some dates for me tomorrow?" She was cute like this. It was easy to picture her curled up next to me in bed the way it had been for so many years.

"Promise." Nothing would stop me from giving her what she asked for.

"I miss you, James."

"Miss you, too, Cora."

When the screen went dark after the line had disconnected, I said, "But I love you more," to no one.

Since I couldn't sit and ponder my agenda while barreling ninety miles per hour down the interstate, I did the next best thing. I called Neil.

"Hey, man."

"Hey, Carp. How was the trip?"

"I'm still making it, but if you're referring to the time with my parents, it was interesting."

"Yeah? What'd your dad want?" He didn't try to hide the skepticism from his voice.

"To give us twenty-three clients."

"I hope you told him to shove them up his ass." He snorted like he'd said something funny.

A week ago, I would have scoffed alongside him. However, something had changed on this trip. I wasn't sure if my dad suddenly realized his mortality and this was his attempt at atoning for his own transgressions, or he'd recognized that I had become an adult. Either way, it didn't matter—for the first time in my life, I'd had lunch with my dad and not my father.

"Nope. We spent two days going over each account, and together, we reached out to every single one of them. Which means...we're going to need to hire another investor to manage the additional workload."

"Why the hell would you take your dad's handouts? I was kidding when I said I wasn't ashamed to take charity."

"Because there were no strings attached."

"There are always strings." His agitation started to tick me off.

"Trust me on this, Neil."

"What has you in Daddy's pocket?"

I wasn't in his pocket, but if my best friend cared to know what had changed, I'd gladly tell him. "He looked out for Cora." Technically, he'd been looking out for me, although when you loved someone, you could twist things any way you chose. I loved her, and I believed my dad loved her for me.

There was a moment of silence on the other end of the call while I assumed he collected his thoughts. It abruptly ended when he shrieked, "He did what?"

"I was shocked myself. Apparently, when he found out she was in the crosshairs of Drake Halifax, he made sure to find out his intentions."

"Please tell me that dirty old man never touched Cora."

"No, but it wasn't for a lack of trying. She didn't want him."

"Well, no shit, Sherlock. Everyone other than you saw that."

I chose to ignore that. "She asked me to come see her."

"In Paris?" He screamed so loudly I had to pull the phone away from my ear. His voice was distorted to the point I couldn't tell if he was shocked or pissed that I might be out again.

"Yeah."

"When?"

"That's why I called—"

"Dude, you cannot be gone for a week, bring back twenty-three new clients I know nothing about, and jet off to another fucking country. I'm pretty fucking impressive, but I'm not Batman."

"Thank God for small favors. No one needs to see your ass in tights. And I sure as hell could never be your Robin."

"Not to worry…Hannah definitely has Harley Quinn covered."

Gross.

"I realize I can't go in the next week or two. I was going to ask you to look at my calendar to see when I might be free in a few weeks. That would give us time to get someone hired and familiar with the portfolios, so you wouldn't be drowning."

"Surely you don't think I'm your secretary?"

"Not at all. If you'd like me to ask *her*, I certainly can have her tell me the moment my calendar is free and get her to book a flight." I let the weight of that settle…which didn't take long.

"Fuck that. She'd have you out of here within hours of you pulling back into the city. She's too efficient for her own damn good."

I didn't try to stifle the laugh.

We spent the next hour talking about the clients I was bringing back, the type of person we needed to join our team, and going over our schedules. As great as the added business was, it meant there was no way I'd get back out of the office for a week—or even a few days—before November…and that was pushing it. And unfortunately, until we hired at least one more person, maybe two, there was no way I'd be airborne, much less practicing my high school French.

10

CHELSEA

I KISSED HER CHEEK AND TOLD HER HOW MUCH I LOVED HER BEFORE I left. Each visit became progressively harder; she'd lost weight living on a liquid diet, and her eyes were tired—not sleepy, but weary. I felt like I should offer her permission to let go; however, selfishly, I wasn't there yet. I wanted to hold on for another day, another week, another year. There would never come a point where I could open the gate to eternity for her. I'd always need her, and not even Dottie could take her place.

Dottie waited for me to say goodbye just outside the room. It had become our routine. She always gave me time alone with my mom. She did it in case it was the last time I got to see her. And while I refused to believe the door closing behind me could take my mother with it, I appreciated her consideration all the same.

I hadn't let my mom see me cry—she couldn't console me, so the tears seemed selfish. But as I left today, Dottie took me in her arms and kissed my temple. I didn't have to tell her I was scared— she could see it written all over my face—and I couldn't hide the way my body shook before the sobs began. There in the hall, with people passing us without a glance, my heart finally acknowledged what my brain had known my entire life.

My mother was going to die.

Soon.

With her arm wrapped around my waist, Dottie led me back outside. "How about a walk before we drive home?" It was about an hour drive from here back to Geneva Key, and sitting in a car for that length of time in the shape I was in would make for a difficult night.

"If you don't mind. Curling up on mom's bed for hours makes me stiff, and the sunshine will do me good."

"Sweetheart, there is nothing I'd rather do than spend time with you."

She dropped her hold on my waist to take my hand. Somehow, it didn't seem strange to walk around the path down to the pond just outside the facility with our fingers laced. Maybe it was our age difference or that my heart was so heavy I needed to feel tied to something that wouldn't allow me to sink into an abyss. Either way, the warmth of her touch lightened my mood and tipped my lips into a meager smile.

"Do you remember when the three of us went to New York? You couldn't have been more than four or five years old." We did a lot of reminiscing these days; Dottie was either determined to ensure I recalled things from my childhood or she tried to keep them fresh in her own mind.

"I remember going to Central Park and my mom begging me to ride in the horse-drawn carriage."

"And you were scared of the horses running off if someone scared them. When she gave up and realized you weren't going to budge, she decided to stroll through the park on foot."

"There were people everywhere. It wasn't anything like the parks I'd been to. There wasn't a playground or a sandbox—everything was green for as far as I could see."

"We must have walked a hundred miles that day. Your mom and I kept thinking you'd get tired. But you were relentless. We didn't leave until the sun started to set, because the fear of the dark was scarier than the appeal of the adventure."

I hadn't thought about that trip in years and had forgotten Dottie was the one who'd taken us there. She always came up with the best things to do. I wasn't aware of it at the time, but her adventures were more extravagant because money had never been an issue. My mom's were always fun, regardless of the fact we were on a tighter budget. And even though we didn't have financial freedom, I never wanted for anything.

She stopped walking and faced me to take my other hand. "Your mom's adventure is ending. This time, you can't be afraid of the dark."

I stared into her baby-blue eyes. Dottie hurt as much as I did, yet she was determined to get me through this. I couldn't speak. Everything she said was true. So I gave her a weak nod, and we walked back to the car. The ride home was quiet—neither of us even turned on the radio. Trees and billboards and cars passed by; however, nothing drew my attention away from my confused thoughts. I should've been able to prepare for this, but nothing readied a child to lose their only parent.

When we arrived home, she followed me into the house. I didn't stop in the kitchen for coffee like I normally did. I needed some time alone, time to think. The best place for me to do that was behind the closed door of my bedroom where I was free to release emotion.

"Chelsea?"

I turned suddenly, lost in my thoughts, to acknowledge Dottie. Before I caught a glimpse of her, the sound of glass breaking drew my attention to the clatter. In my haste to steady myself before falling, I reached out to grab the end table and sent the vase flying. My ass hit the floor with a hollow thud, and shooting pain resonated up my arm. With tears welling in my eyes, I jerked my hand to my face to pick out the little shards that had lodged themselves in my skin upon impact. My cheeks were wet as the droplets fell to my palm, mixing into little crimson pools.

"Oh, sweetheart, are you all right?" Dottie asked as she squatted next to me. She took my hand in hers to look at my wounds.

I was fine. My ego was bruised, but the little nicks were superficial. I nodded and looked around at the damage I'd done. The vase broke into several large chunks, and I'd shattered a picture frame that contained the only image of her and her teenage son that I'd ever seen. The edges of the glass created gouges in the photo paper, covering the image of his face in scratches that hadn't been there before. Carefully brushing the debris away, I held it up.

"I'm so sorry. I didn't mean—"

"Shh, it's fine. I can get another frame." But she couldn't get another picture. There weren't many of him around, and she kept this one close enough to see regularly. This one was special.

I'd never known her son. All the pictures she had were of him as a child through maybe sixteen or seventeen. I'd asked my mom once what had happened to him, and she told me that was Dottie's story to tell, and then encouraged me not to ask. It was the only time I remembered seeing my mother sad, as though she grieved the loss, too.

"But the picture's ruined," I blubbered, desperate for a tissue to blow my nose.

"Chelsea, yes…I love the photo. However, my memories aren't contained on that piece of paper. And now there's another layer of value on it, anyway. Every time I see it, I'll think of you being here…with fondness."

I looked into her eyes and chanced the question I'd never dared to ask. "How did you go on after you lost him?"

Dottie let out a long sigh and sat on the ground next to me. She picked up a large piece of broken ceramic and used it as a cup to collect the others. "It was a slow progression. By the time he passed away, he was already gone. I struggled with regret for a lot of years, but I couldn't change any of it. I made mistakes, and I wasn't the best mother I could've been. I loved him, although looking back, probably not in the right way. Finally, I realized I had to let go in order to keep living."

The same look I'd seen on my mother's face the day I asked her about the boy in the pictures showed on Dottie's face today. Her grief was just below the surface, and I could tell it was a wound that never healed. "I shouldn't have asked. I'm sorry."

"Nonsense." She patted me on the knee and stood. "Let me help you up. You need to get some tweezers and make sure you don't leave any glass behind."

I took her offered hand, though I didn't let her exert any force and pushed myself off the floor. Dottie cupped my face and wiped the tears away with her thumbs.

"You're going to be okay."

I let her words sink in like a promise—even though it was one she couldn't keep.

***

I'd seen the missed call and listened to the voicemail from Carp the night I came back from seeing my mom. However, after the vase and picture frame incident, Dottie had spent an hour picking glass out of my palm because I was unable to keep the tweezers steady. My nerves were shot, and I was exhausted. I wanted nothing more than to close my eyes and chase the day away with sleep.

Then I'd worked three days in a row for the catering company doing different gigs and hadn't gotten around to it. We'd texted a few times, but Carp had been busy with work since he'd gotten back to New York and a phone call just hadn't happened. Still, I'd thought of him and wondered how things fared with his plight to win Cora back.

The phone rang three times, and just when I expected the voicemail to pick up, he answered, clearly winded. "Hello?"

"Hey, Carp." I tried to keep my voice sounding optimistic. It took effort not to let the circumstances with my mom take over.

"Hey, Chelsea. I wondered if we'd ever actually connect."

"Did I catch you at a bad time?"

"No, I was down the hall in Neil's office and had to race to get my phone."

"You're at work at eight o'clock?"

"The work days keep getting longer. My dad's clients are far more time-consuming than those we had in-house…just because we're learning them. We've had a couple interviews, but so far, we haven't hired anyone to help with the additional load."

"Yikes. That makes for some long days."

"It keeps me out of trouble." If he'd been in front of me, I swear a wink would have followed that statement. "What have you been up to?"

"I've worked the last few days doing parties around town. And Dottie and I went to see my mom."

"Yeah? How's she doing?"

"Not great. But thanks for asking. Did you call Cora?" I needed to change the subject quickly before I succumbed to the emotions.

"I can't believe you remembered her name."

"Yeah, well, having a guy cry on the shore about another girl after having sex with you is kind of memorable. It'd be hard to forget her name." I giggled, hoping he could tell I was just giving him a hard time. "My ego took quite the hit that night. It could be years before I recover."

"Wow." He laughed through the word, and the sound barreled through the receiver. It was hearty and playful, and there was no doubt he'd gotten my intention. "Way to make a guy feel like a schmuck."

"You can make it up to me by living out an amazing second-chance romance. One that authors and producers fight over owning the rights to. So spill it, have you guys talked?"

I didn't know this girl and likely never would, but he'd been so enamored with her when we talked on the beach in Geneva Key, that I found myself rooting for them. When things in my life were so uncertain, it made me happy to listen to a hopeless romantic talk about the woman he loved. And Carp was *in love* with Cora.

"We have. A couple times, actually. Right now, I think we're rebuilding the friendship. Plus, hearing her voice again gives me hope."

"Has she said any more about coming back when her contract is up?"

"She's unhappy there, but she won't commit to anything. I haven't pushed it. *Yet*." The determination in his voice was clear, and I grinned believing he'd get the girl. Carp just seemed like that type of guy. "Oh, she asked me to come to Paris."

Why he hadn't led with that baffled me. It was far more interesting than hearing about a budding friendship for people who'd been lovers for years. "Really?" I was almost as excited as I would have been if it were me crossing the pond. "When are you going?"

"I'm not sure. The timing is horrible. With the increase in business, I can't leave right now. Neil and I have to get someone trained before I can consider taking off for any length of time."

"Don't wait, Carp." I thought about my mom and what I'd give to have more time with her. "There's nothing in your office that won't be there when you get back. Make people your priority, not money." It was easy for me to spout off crap about life lessons. I wasn't a business owner—hell, I could barely even say I had a job. And I certainly didn't have anyone other than my mom and Dottie to worry about.

"I'm going to go as soon as I can. I just don't have anything set in stone. I'll keep you posted, promise." He probably thought I was an idiot for insisting he chase down another woman after our one night. "What about you?"

I was confused. Either I'd missed something Carp had said, or I was lost. "What about me?"

"Picked up any more lonely guys at dinner parties and seduced them on the beach?"

"Har, har, har. I hope you don't think that's something I do regularly." I rolled my eyes.

Carp's opinion shouldn't matter. He lived in another state. And if he was passing judgment, it was rather hypocritical since he'd been the one naked in the sand with me.

"More power to you if you do…just play it safe. Women should have just as much freedom sexually as men do. Although, be careful about who in Geneva Key knows—the old people there can be kind of critical."

"Does anyone under the age of fifty live in this town?" I didn't go out much. Other than the grocery store and to work, I stayed close to home. Even though the island was small, I didn't chance getting lost; not to mention, everything I needed was already here, and those that weren't could be ordered on Amazon.

His laughter wasn't encouraging. "Yeah, but they aren't legal. There's a black hole from eighteen to forty-nine. Even though I can't say for certain, I think the portal is down on Beaches Boulevard, close to the grocery store. I left before it could suck me in at nineteen."

"That's encouraging. There has to be *someone* here my age."

"Sorry, sweetheart. Unless you want to become the trophy wife to a blue hair, you're out of luck. Give it twenty-seven or so years, and you'll be one of them."

"A blue hair?" I had a hard time talking. The voice he'd used sounded like William Shatner, and all I could see were people getting sucked into this imaginary hole in the ground, and then being spit back out when they were old enough to return to the Geneva Key society. I was dying with laughter.

"Yeah, you know…the smarmy old men with lots of money who die their hair black leaving it with a blue tinge?"

"Totally not my cup of tea."

"What about the people you work with?"

"Most of them are considerably older than I am and don't live on the island. They drive in for the jobs and leave. And even if they were, I never actually work with anyone. I'm always at a bar by myself. Not much of a chance to make friends."

"I wish I had great advice. It's been so long since I've lived there, I really don't know of anyone still around and haven't met anyone new who's moved in."

"It's not a big deal. I didn't come here to make social connections. My focus should be on my mom and Dottie, anyhow."

"Even so, everyone needs to have friends to hang out with. What about your friends in Chicago?"

I didn't want to admit I didn't have any. We'd all gone our separate ways after high school. Most of them went to college, and when I stayed home because my mom was sick, the relationships just kind of drifted. Nothing bad happened; we all just led separate lives. "I still talk to them some, but it's hard to keep up long-distance friendships. You know, with work and family."

"You should get involved with some of the women's groups in town. There are tons of volunteer things and charity crap always going on. They wouldn't be your age, although it might give you something to focus on and maybe make you feel good in the process."

"I'll have to see what I can find."

"My mom is pretty heavily involved. I can have her reach out to you."

He'd lost his mind if he thought I had any desire to talk to his mom. She terrified me. "I doubt she'd be interested in mingling with the help. But thanks. I'll be okay." I hoped I hadn't hurt his feelings, but based on what I'd seen of him with his parents, it was unlikely.

"I get it. Just don't sit around wasting away while taking care of everyone else, okay?" If only he knew how true that sentiment was.

"I won't."

"I need to get back to work so I'm not here until midnight. Don't be a stranger."

"Night, Carp."

He said goodbye, and we hung up. I knew I was where I was supposed to be—with Mom and Dottie—but sometimes, the loneliness closed in and made it hard to breathe. I wanted to be like my mom had been my whole life—to live every day as if it were my last—however, knowing any day could be my mom's last kept me from my own adventures. I felt selfish thinking that way; she'd give me everything and had always been my best friend. I owed it to her to give her some of me, and hope when it was over, there was still time left to have my own life.

***

My hands trembled as I handed the money to the cashier at the drug store. When I grabbed the plastic bag and my receipt, the rustling sound echoed in my ears like thunder. My arm jerked in response, and I felt like a spaz when the guy behind the counter stared at me with wide eyes.

"Thank you." I tried to smile, although the awkward grin did nothing other than earn a confused stare in return.

I hadn't asked Dottie to bring me because I refused to admit what I needed. Yet now that I was carrying a bag from the pharmacy, I wasn't sure how I would explain what I'd picked up on my walk. My legs got stiff a lot, and she never questioned how long I was gone, though I never wanted to give her a reason not to trust me, either. Lost in my thoughts, I took the wrong turn, and it ended up taking me another fifteen minutes to find my way back to the cottage. Thankfully, when I walked in, Dottie wasn't home. She'd left a note on the counter informing me she'd gone to the grocery store. I wasn't sure how I hadn't seen her pass me but was grateful for the reprieve.

I considered praying before I sat down on the toilet, except prayers hadn't changed anything up to this point in my life, and I doubted they would change the outcome of this test. Whatever was meant to be would be. I only hoped I was late due to stress. The last few weeks had been nothing but turmoil and sadness going back and forth to Tampa, and it had taken a toll on my health. Hopefully, this was just another side effect.

When I set the stick down on the granite and washed my hands, something told me I wouldn't like what I saw. I was right—two pink lines stared at me, blazing like neon lights. With the test in my hand, I sat down on the floor and cried.

James and I had developed a strong friendship. Even though we talked all the time, I wasn't interested in sharing a baby with him, and there wasn't a doubt in my mind he felt the same. He was in love with Cora, and this would destroy any chance he had of getting back together with her. No woman in their right mind would want to be with a man who had gotten another woman pregnant. It wouldn't matter that they hadn't been together when it happened or what he'd done since.

"Chelsea, sweetheart, why are you crying?" Dottie's concern came from the open bathroom door.

I didn't know how long I'd been sitting there, but I hadn't heard her come in, and I couldn't hide the evidence still in my hand.

"Did something happen to your mom? No one called me."

I just shook my head, unable to respond. As much as I wanted to hide my dirty secret, there was no way I could face this on my own. And without being able to go to James, I had no other choice than to tell Dottie. I dreaded seeing the disappointment on her face, though it was less daunting than destroying James's life.

I didn't dare make eye contact when I gestured with my outstretched hand, offering her the explanation for my tears.

"Oh." That was the only thing she said. She didn't yell or blow her top. It was one word, one syllable—that was all Dottie gave me.

Until she sat on the bathroom floor and leaned against the cabinets that held me up. She patted my knee and gave it a gentle squeeze. "Children are blessings regardless of the circumstances under which they enter the world."

I rolled my eyes up to her, wondering what kind of drugs she'd done while she was out of the house. "You can't be serious. My life is a total mess. How could I possibly bring a child into this chaos?"

She pulled tissue off the roll of toilet paper and handed it to me to blow my snotty nose. When I finally cleaned up my face, she said, "What about the father? Won't he want to help?"

I proceeded to tell Dottie all about Carp without giving his name or Cora's. They had both grown up in this town, and I couldn't risk it getting back to them—not before I figured out what I planned to do. There was so much more to consider than just being a single parent, and I wasn't sure I could handle it all at this point in my life.

"I can't tell you what to do, Chelsea. And I wouldn't force you to do it even if you told me the boy's name. However, I think any man who fathers a child has a right to know. You weren't the only one who conceived that baby, and you certainly shouldn't be the only one responsible for raising it."

I never knew my dad—not even his name. I'd never seen a picture, heard my mom talk about him, nothing. Not a Christmas card, a birthday present, or even a "hello" along the way. But I never missed him because I'd never known anything different. I'd had an amazing childhood, and other than my mom, Dottie was the only family I'd had.

"I think it would do more harm than good. Plus, I didn't have a dad, and I turned out okay."

"You're incredible…but, Chelsea, your mom didn't always have it easy. She worked really hard when you were little, and she struggled at times. Just because you never saw that doesn't mean it wasn't there. And she knew throughout your entire childhood that she would get sick at some point, leaving you alone. She took a huge risk by not involving the father."

"Then why'd she do it?" Despite my asking this question more times than I could count, my mother had never given me anything to go on.

Dottie's head dipped and her eyes closed. I could tell she was on the verge of revealing a piece of truth that had the potential to change how I'd viewed everything in my life. I held my breath, waiting for her to speak.

"All of this happened before I met her, so I can only tell you what little I know."

My chest rose and fell dramatically, and my heart raced.

"She dated a man at work, but he traveled a lot. They had a casual relationship as far as my understanding goes. Your mother cared for him, even if she didn't love him. They saw each other frequently and talked regularly. When she told him she was pregnant, he finally admitted to her that he was married."

I gasped, unable to believe anyone could carry on an affair, even a casual one, and the wife not be aware it was happening.

"You have to remember this was a different time, Chelsea. Social media didn't exist, cell phones were relatively new and not widely used. She had no reason to believe he was anything different than what he told her he was."

I was speechless. I'd never imagined my mother in some sort of sordid affair. That was the opposite of the person I grew up with. Although, it also made Dottie's story believable. My mother wouldn't have slept with another woman's husband had she known she existed.

"So what happened? Did his wife find out?"

"I think he realized what he stood to lose by his wife finding

157

out, and I believe he loved his wife, he just got caught up in something he shouldn't have. So he offered your mother a lot of money to go away, which your mother refused. To the best of my understanding, he never told his wife, and your mother never spoke to him again. You were never an option for her—she loved you from the second she knew you existed. It wasn't in her to be part of a scandal either, and she never would have destroyed a marriage that could have been salvaged. I don't believe she ever spoke of him again. She was determined to do things on her own, and for you to have the best life possible."

"If she knew she had Huntingtons then, why wouldn't she take the money?"

"She wasn't sick and hadn't shown any symptoms at that point. And I think she wanted to keep you pure. In her eyes, accepting money for her silence meant she was ashamed. So she adamantly refused."

It didn't change anything for me, even if it blew me away. My mother was still my rock, and I loved her. I hated that she struggled because she'd refused help, but in the end, it made our relationship what it was.

"So the guy never asked about me? He never called her to check on me or anything?"

"Not that I'm aware of. I think it might have been the wakeup call he'd needed, although that's just my assumption. Your mother believed his image in the community played a part, and an affair would have destroyed him and his family. It wasn't something she wanted on her shoulders, so she let it go and never looked back."

I considered asking if she knew my father's name, then I realized that at this point in my life, it wouldn't do any good. Nothing positive could come of me finding him. If his wife still wasn't aware I existed, all I'd do by locating him was create exactly what my mom had spent my entire life avoiding.

"Your circumstances are very different than your mother's, Chelsea. Don't carry this burden alone. There's too much at stake."

I couldn't begin to consider destroying Carp with this information right now. I was swimming in the similarities between me and my own mother's history, and it was frightening how alike they were. But right now, I couldn't think about James or Cora. I had to figure out what *I* wanted to do before I ruined anyone else's life.

11

JAMES

I'D HAVE A MIGRAINE SOON IF I DIDN'T STOP BEATING MY HEAD against the desk.

"You promised me, James." Her tears broke me.

I'd been trying to get to France since I left my parents' house in August. However, the stars hadn't aligned, and I'd done everything in my power to send the moon into retrograde. We'd been bombarded with new clients. The two investors we'd hired turned into four, and somehow, we still couldn't keep up. I hadn't been to Sideways Shots since I'd gotten home because I'd worked every waking moment in order to clear a few days in my schedule. Oddly, I hadn't heard from any of the people at the bar either, but I guessed that was how the whole "casual" thing worked.

"You keep getting my hopes up only to tell me you can't come. It's not fair. Why can't Neil make do without you for a few days?" Wails had turned to whimpers, and I couldn't take it.

Every fiber of my being yearned to comfort her, hold her, kiss her forehead, and protect her. I couldn't do shit from thirty-five hundred miles away, and she'd chosen that. That wasn't a decision we'd made together or one I'd even been consulted on—even still, a little piece of me died every time she shed a tear of unhappiness.

"Baby..." I didn't even care that it had slipped out. I was exhausted, there was most definitely a bruise forming on my forehead, and I still had another five hours of work at minimum before I could walk out the door. Glancing at the clock, I realized it was already four thirty and dropped my head again.

"I miss you, James. I want to see you. You promised you'd come."

"Cora, sweetheart, I'm trying my best. I swear, I am. Did something happen today that has you so upset?"

"Yes."

"Can you tell me what it was?"

"You delayed another trip."

I couldn't help the chuckle that formed in my chest and rose through my throat and out of my mouth. She was so fucking cute, and I was miserable without her. It had been over seventeen months since I'd seen her other than the picture that flashed on my screen when she called. She refused to FaceTime, declaring it heightened the anticipation of seeing each other in person. I bet she regretted that shit now.

"Why are you laughing?"

If I hadn't known better, I would have sworn a five-year-old held the phone on the other end of the line. "I'm—hell, I don't know."

She sniffled, and I stifled the urge to laugh again when Neil popped his head in my office. I covered the phone when he didn't leave. "Give me five."

He nodded and walked off.

"Cora, you know I miss you, too. I promise, before I go home tonight, I will book a flight."

"Non-refundable?"

I chuckled, "Yeah. Non-refundable."

"Okay."

"I have to go deal with Neil. I promise when we talk in the morning, I'll have dates for you."

With that pledge, I hung up and dealt with Neil and a hundred other fires that needed to be put out. By the time I pulled up flights, it was after ten, and I hadn't eaten since noon. The last thing I wanted to do was think about traveling, but at the end of that grueling flight stood Cora—so I'd endure.

I'd told Neil what my plans were, and he agreed; I just had to go. There wasn't going to be a break in the schedule, and there was no such thing as a good time. He knew how desperately I missed her, and I loved him for encouraging me.

Chelsea called in the midst of my travel planning, but I sent her to voicemail. My brain was too fried to do more than one thing at a time, and I had promised Cora I'd have an answer for her tomorrow. Chelsea would understand. Hell, she'd probably book it and set the itinerary for me if I told her what I was up against. She'd been bugging me for weeks about when I was going, but I'd put her off the same way I had Cora. She wanted me to be happy, and she chastised me regularly for not realigning my priorities. It was one of the things I appreciated most about her—she was selfless and wanted the best for those she knew.

I'd wondered if a friendship with another woman would ever work. I wasn't sure anything platonic could really exist between two people, especially two people who'd had sex—albeit, very bad sex that we laughed about afterward—but sex nonetheless. However, she'd proven there was nothing else there, no ulterior motive, no desire to try to keep something going between us other than friendship. Even Cora's skepticism over Chelsea waned the more she learned, until she'd started asking about Chelsea's mom, Janie, and even Dottie. Then again, that was who Cora was, too—loving and nurturing.

I barely remembered driving home, much less getting into bed, but I couldn't wait to call Cora. We'd made tentative plans more times than she'd let me forget, and until now, I'd yet to book a flight—this was set in stone. And I'd already started counting down.

"Hello?"

"Hey, babe." I shouldn't let the pet names flow so freely; however, they'd felt right last night, and she hadn't stopped me or corrected it, so I was going with it.

"You're awfully chipper this morning."

"I made you a promise."

"Do you have dates?" Her voice went from casual to animated in seconds.

"How about Christmas in Paris?"

"Seriously?"

"I bought the ticket last night, so I hope that works for you."

"Non-refundable?"

I laughed heartily while I answered. "Yeah. So if you don't want to see me, I either just wasted two grand, or I'm going to hang out with the pigeons in the park."

"They like bread crumbs."

"Are you feeding me to the birds?"

"Nah, but it does get cold here in December."

"Like New York cold?"

"No, it's not that brutal. Oh my God, James. I can't believe I get to see you in—wait, what date are you actually arriving?"

"December twenty-second."

"Eeep. How long do I get to keep you?"

I never thought those words would be so appealing or that I'd hear Cora squeal like a child.

"Forever if you'll have me, but I fly back out on January second."

"Ten days?" She totally skipped over forever. "Really? How will Neil breathe without you around to force air into his lungs?"

"I haven't told him how long I'll be gone."

She erupted in laughter, and it was the greatest gift she'd ever given me—next to her love. "He's going to Hulk out on you."

"I doubt he'll turn green and have muscles popping out everywhere. Plus, he encouraged me to go. He thinks it will be good for us."

"How is having you gone good for Neil?" The way her voice dropped half an octave when she was confused brought a grin to my face. The nuances that were Cora were endless, and I missed every single one of them.

"Not good for him...good for us—me and you." My laughter died, and I held my breath while waiting for her response.

"James..." My name was nothing more than a whisper on her lips.

I didn't push it. I'd hinted at where my thoughts were—it was no secret I'd never wanted her to leave—and if flying to France didn't prove to her I still loved her, then maybe my presence there would.

"So, promise me you'll take some time off, and when I get there, you'll show me around like a tourist. There's only one place I'd like to go on New Year's Eve, so leave that day open. Although, feel free to fill in the rest with whatever you want to do or see."

Luckily, Cora didn't ask what I had in mind, and instead, just prattled on about the places she'd meant to explore since she arrived but hadn't been able to because of her work schedule. It wouldn't matter if every one of them sucked; hearing her excitement made them appealing. Never in my wildest dreams would I have thought I could rekindle my love affair with Cora Chase in Paris, yet now that the opportunity had arisen, I couldn't fathom a better place.

***

It wasn't uncommon for Chelsea and me to play phone tag for a week at a time, still, she hadn't read or responded to my texts in a couple of days. When I called today, I half expected to get her voicemail, but she picked up on the last ring. And immediately, I knew something wasn't right.

"Chelsea, what's wrong?"

There was a long pause, and her deep inhale wasn't a sign of good things to come. Even though I didn't want to pry, if something had happened to her mother, I should be there for her the way she always was for me. I couldn't replace her mom—I could, however, keep her from feeling alone.

"My mom has pneumonia. I'm sorry I haven't answered your calls. I've been in Tampa. I'm still here—well, at the hotel. Dottie stayed with her."

"Pneumonia's treatable, though, right?"

"For lots of people, yes. For someone with late-stage Huntingtons, it's more likely a death sentence."

Hearing her cry was almost as bad as listening to Cora. And in both cases, I wasn't anywhere near able to help them or comfort them. Chelsea might as well be in Paris with Cora in terms of distance. I didn't know anyone who'd lost a parent. The closest thing I'd ever experienced was Cora's grandfather passing away, but they weren't close, and she hadn't even gone to the funeral because of school. I was in unchartered territory.

"I'm so sorry. Is there anything I can do?" There wasn't; it just seemed right to offer.

"Tell me something good. I don't want to think about this right now."

I was hesitant to tell her I'd finally booked a flight to Paris. I hated to come across as insensitive—like I was gaining someone I loved while she lost the same. "Umm, I had an Egg McMuffin for breakfast, and they accidentally put two eggs on it."

She giggled on the other end. "Not really what I had in mind, although I'm glad to hear you were able to complete the egg heist of the year from the golden arches."

"It may not seem like much, but that extra protein put a pep in my step. They even upsized my coffee for the extended wait in the drive-thru."

"What are you going to do with all that good fortune, Carp? You should go out and buy a lottery ticket right away. Luck like this doesn't come along often."

"I'll get one for you while I'm at it."

There was a slight lull, though nothing uncomfortable. I wondered if she was thinking about winning the lottery like I was and what she'd do with that kind of money. However, before I could ask, she shot out her own question.

"I wanted to talk to you about something." We both said the words, almost verbatim, at the same time.

"You first," she insisted.

I couldn't imagine what she had to talk to me about, but her tone had been serious, and I wondered why she didn't go first. Maybe it had to do with her mom and putting it off as long as possible was preferable.

"I finally booked a trip to Paris." The words raced out as though I'd be burned with their touch if they lingered on my lips too long.

"Oh."

That wasn't the reaction I'd expected. Before I could say anything else, she spoke again.

"Carp, that's wonderful. When are you going?" Her excitement didn't seem genuine, but I couldn't say for sure. She could have just been expecting something else.

"Not until the end of December. I'm going to spend New Year's there."

"That's great. How long are you staying?"

"Ten days. You don't sound interested; we can talk about this another time." I tried to give her an out. I'm sure it was hard to be ecstatic for me with what she was dealing with in Florida.

"No, no. I'm sorry. I'm really excited for you. Are you going to make a list of things to do with Cora? You have to go to the Eiffel

Tower at night." Her tone changed instantly when I'd pointed out her indifference.

"Have you ever been?"

"Uh-uh, but it's on my bucket list, and the pictures at night are stunning. So just in case I never get to go, you have to visit and tell me all about it."

"I'm sure you'll get to go. You're young. Maybe you'll honeymoon in Paris." The moment the words slipped out, I regretted them. She didn't even have any friends, much less dates that might evolve into a marriage. And I couldn't imagine it was even something she was considering. "I'm sorry, Chelsea. That was insensitive."

"It's fine. I promise. I won't always be waiting for my mom to die." Something else hovered in her voice, but whatever it was, she didn't say it.

The conversation stalled, and I felt awkward sitting with the phone to my ear when I remembered she'd had something to say.

"What was it you wanted to talk about?"

The moment she responded, I knew she was blowing me off. "Oh, nothing. It's not important. Your news is way more interesting."

I hadn't mapped out the trip because Cora had places she picked to go, but I was excited to have someone to share my only plan with. I hadn't even told Neil. However, Chelsea had been such an advocate of my relationship with Cora that I wanted her to be the first person to know that I intended to propose. And figured she might even be able to help me figure out what to do about the setting I'd never purchased and the best place to pop the question.

If she'd been shocked, she didn't say it, or even hint at it. Her enthusiasm spurred my decision on. Chelsea was as much of a hopeless romantic as I was, and part of me thought her ideas were what she'd fanaticized her own proposal being. I couldn't make that happen for her, although I could certainly work it into what I did for Cora. I hadn't heard Chelsea this happy in all the times we'd talked.

She was genuinely excited for me and promised to keep her fingers crossed that Cora would say yes and finally come home. God, I hoped for the same thing.

***

"Are you sure you're making the right decision?" Neil questioned everything I did in regard to Cora, likely because *Hannah* questioned everything I did in regard to Cora. However, he'd been sworn to secrecy about this, and if Cora found out, there was only one place it would have come from.

"Maybe not, but at least I won't have any regrets. And Chelsea thinks it's romantic, so I'm sure Cora will, too."

"I'm not sure taking another woman's advice on proposing is the best thing to do. Not to mention, spending thousands of dollars you can't get back to ensure you don't regret anything is asinine. You can propose after she comes home."

"I had planned to propose before she ever left."

"Yeah, but you haven't been together in a year and a half. You aren't dating. What if she turns you down?"

"I'm not thinking that way." I couldn't. Chelsea was convinced she'd say yes, and I was too. I had to believe Cora loved me and had only needed time to grow into who she was destined to become before she came back. She'd turned down Drake Halifax even after we'd broken up; that had to mean something—other than she wasn't into rich old men.

"Dude, I get that Paris is like the City of Love or whatever, but this is reality, not some fairy-tale fantasy. Chelsea isn't thinking about real life; she's thinking about some twisted version of a romance novel. Cora doesn't have a script she's reading from; she'll be reacting to your whim based on a life she's lived for eighteen months without you."

"Why can't it be both?"

"Maybe it can, although I don't think that's realistic. I just don't want to see you go through the breakup phase again. I wasn't sure your liver or your dick were going to survive that the first time."

"First of all, my dick was always securely wrapped, and secondly, just because I hung out at a bar didn't mean I was mainlining tequila."

He held his hands up in surrender. "Don't say I didn't warn you."

I had refused to consider rejection, unwilling to believe Cora was meant to be with anyone other than me. And Chelsea's confidence meant more than Neil's disbelief.

"Are you going to tell her what you've been up to while she's been away?" The way his eyebrows rose irritated me—like I'd somehow maligned her because I'd gone out with other women.

"If she asks, I won't lie. But am I going to volunteer information? No. That would be relationship suicide."

"Hate to break it to you, man, but you're not in a relationship with her. Just because you quit dicking around with other people doesn't mean you're committed."

"I'm sure she's been with other people while she's been gone." At least that's what I told myself to keep my own guilt at bay.

"Yeah? Has she told you that?"

"Not in so many words. Why? Has she told Hannah something I should be aware of?"

"I'm not getting in the middle of this."

"You're absolutely smack dab in the center of it all because you tell your girlfriend everything I do."

My assistant came and shut my office door when my voice rose enough for the rest of the staff to hear me.

"You never kept secrets from Cora. Why would you think things would be any different with Hannah?"

"I never told Cora *your* secrets." And I hadn't. Not that Neil had many, but I didn't tell her about the financial problems he'd had when we first bought the business. I'd helped him cover them so he wouldn't have to admit any of that to anyone.

"And I haven't told Hannah yours. I may have talked to Hannah about my concerns with where your social life was headed when you were making stupid decisions because I was concerned for my best friend—not because I was a gossip train pulling into the station."

Both of us had gotten far too worked up over something that should have been a happy occasion, one I needed his support in. Hell, even my dad had been ecstatic when I'd told him my plans—cautious, yet happy. Oddly, he had truly acted like a father since I left Geneva Key, one I wished I could spend more time with.

I lowered my voice to continue talking to him. "Neil, I've never loved anyone other than Cora Chase, regardless of what I did after she left. I haven't been in another relationship or even considered one. I had a friend with benefits—who wasn't really a friend, considering the day I stopped coming around, she disappeared—and Chelsea. Cora knows about Chelsea, even if she doesn't know I had sex with her...*once*." I emphasized the word to make sure Neil remembered it hadn't been anything more than a bad decision. "But if Cora's in a relationship, or you think there's a reason besides separation that I need to be concerned about, then as my friend, I need you to tell me—even if you don't give me the details."

As he let out an exaggerated sigh, he ran his palm over his fore-head, down his nose, and then dragged it through his hair. The pained expression on his face indicated a desire to unload, as well as confusion over whether or not he should.

"I don't know a lot, Carp. I do know that she's dated and none of them have worked out beyond one or two dinners."

"But there's something else you're not telling me." I let that hang in the air and waited. I wouldn't push it. I never would have violated a trust Cora had put in me, and I didn't expect him to do that to Hannah.

"She misses you. And she doesn't believe she'll ever be happy in France until she's sure things with you are over."

Over. While that one word replayed in my mind, Neil gave me the time to process it without speaking. I refused to believe things with Cora and me would ever be *over*.

"Are you saying I'm making this trip for Cora to determine she doesn't love me anymore so she can move on?"

With his elbows on his knees, he cradled his head in his hands. I watched silently as he once again ran both sets of fingers through his hair to the back of his neck where he massaged the tension that had suddenly made him uncomfortable. When he finally made eye contact with me, he sat up. "Hannah thinks she's trying to convince herself it's over because you haven't made any attempt to come after her. She also believes Cora will never love anyone else, the same way you won't, and that once the two of you see each other again, the doubt will wash away. And *that's* when Cora will come home."

"This is all Hannah's assumption, right? I mean, Cora hasn't actually told her she doesn't still love me?"

He shook his head. "No, she hasn't. And I can tell you, if Hannah knew what your plans were, she'd be on board. She thinks like a chick—emotionally. She'd be on the crazy train with Chelsea. You need to be thinking rationally. And there is a fifty percent chance she will say no."

The side of my mouth turned up in a cocky grin. "There's a fifty percent chance she'll say yes. And unless the odds tip out of my favor, I'm going forward with my plan. Why else would she have asked me to come to Paris? She could have asked Hannah if all she needed was a friend."

"If you're going to propose, I think you need to be upfront about what happened while she was gone. And she needs to offer you the same thing. The two of you have never had secrets, and it will eat at you until you give her the truth. Having it come to light after a wedding could be catastrophic."

I couldn't deny his point and hated that Neil had become a voice of reason. Yet I couldn't imagine telling Cora I'd slept with anyone else, much less *two* other people. She wouldn't care that it had been meaningless sex. Unless she'd had sex since moving to Paris, she would see it as betrayal—regardless of the fact she'd been the one who had left.

"And exactly how honest would you be?" As long as I had Neil looking out for my best interest, I might as well get the whole picture.

"Don't give details. Cora won't be able to forget them, even if she doesn't hold it over your head. I would tell her you made some poor decisions after she left, and open the door to let her ask what she needs to know. Then protect her from shit that won't benefit her in the long run. Transferring guilt from your shoulders to hers just to make yourself feel better won't help her down the road."

Luckily—or unluckily, I wasn't sure which yet—there were lots of details I couldn't give, even if she asked, because I'd been too intoxicated to remember them. The thought of divulging any of it to Cora made me sick to my stomach, but Neil was right. I'd never be able to live with the weight of remorse in the long run. I couldn't risk that happening after marriage, which meant I'd have to risk it happening before.

He stood while I was still in thought, drawing me back to the present and out of my head.

"Just my advice—that shit needs to be done face-to-face, not over the phone. You'll have more control over the situation if she can't hang up. And don't be surprised when it stings the hell out of her."

I bobbed my head to acknowledge him while considering what he'd said. I'd have to tell her before New Year's Eve. Neil opened the door yet stopped with his hand on the edge.

"Whatever happens, Carp, at least you'll know when you come home whether it's time to move on and let her go completely."

"I just hope it doesn't come to that."

"Me too, bro. Me too." He grimaced and then hesitantly turned around. After finally walking out, he pulled the handle with him and closed me off to the rest of the office.

12

CHELSEA

"When are you going to tell him, Chelsea?" Dottie's voice was elevated, although it wasn't in anger. She simply didn't want me to face raising a child on my own.

"I already told you." I struggled to remain calm. I'd repeated this same thing so many times I was tired of hearing myself talk, all because Dottie refused to listen to reason. "I'm not going to put that on him before he goes to Paris."

"Why is his relationship with another woman more important than his responsibility to his child?" She wouldn't let this go. I couldn't tell if it had more to do with my own mother having walked away from my father, or her desire to resurrect her relationship with her child, or a million other things. All I knew was that her constant pushing me to do what she thought was right suffocated me.

"It's not, but they'll never get together if she's aware he has a baby on the way. He's leaving in a couple weeks to go see her. It's not like I'm waiting until after the baby's born." My voice cracked under the strain of remaining respectful.

"So you're going to wait until they're engaged? I don't follow your logic."

"If they get engaged, I'm not telling him. End of story." I'd intentionally left Carp's name out of all discussions with Dottie, thankfully. I wouldn't be surprised in the least to find out she was friends with his family, and that would only spell disaster if she felt like going around me to them. At this point, she believed it was a guy I worked with. Clearly, she hadn't noticed there wasn't anyone under the age of forty in that crowd.

"Chelsea, you have a lot going on. You need his help, even if it's only financial."

"I'm about to lose the only thing I have going on, Dottie. So unless you're going to kick me out if I don't tell him, I don't need his help. I'll be okay."

She stood from her seat at my side and turned to face me. With her hands on her hips, she huffed. "You and I both know that's not true. At some point, you're going to have to face your future…I just don't want it to be too late." Her words were like a hard slap across the face, one that knocked the taste right out of my mouth.

Dottie had never talked to me that way. She'd never been so cruel. It didn't matter if there were any validity to anything she'd said, it stung.

I'd struggled with this decision since I found out I was pregnant. I didn't arrive at this conclusion on a whim—I'd agonized over it. The weight of either choice held dire consequences, but if Cora said yes, then she and Carp had a fighting chance at the love of a lifetime. I'd never have that and refused to rob him of it, or her. And no matter what scenario ran through my head, I always wanted Carp to get the best life he could have. I didn't care to saddle him with my problems or a child. And if he ever found out, it'd be too late to change anything.

Lying back on my pillows, I propped my feet up on the end of the bed. My tummy had started to pooch just a bit with the hint of a baby underneath. I hadn't told my mom, although at this point, I wasn't sure it would matter. She'd been virtually unresponsive for days, and the end was near. I rubbed a shaky hand over my belly and talked to the bump as if the baby inside could hear me.

Maybe I was selfish, and it had likely shaped my decision, but I was okay with this baby being mine. My mother had been the center of my universe all my life, and I hated to admit that being on the cusp of that ending made me want to complete the cycle with my own little version of me. I strived to be the mother Janie Airy had been. She'd fulfilled all her dreams—even knowing she would get sick—with me in tow. It was probably naïve to think she'd preferred it that way, but I'd always believed she did.

Either way, I still had time to change my mind. Carp wouldn't be back from Paris until the beginning of January. And one way or another, he'd have an answer either way when he returned. I'd only be a little over five months along, so if they weren't engaged, that was more than enough time to pull the trigger and allow him to be involved. And if he didn't, I would be prepared for that as well. However, if they *did* get engaged, I hadn't gotten my hopes up to begin with.

I had no desire to be with James Carpenter. I wasn't in love with him, and I had zero romantic interest—taking the love of his life away just seemed like a cruel punishment. My phone rang on the nightstand next to me, breaking me out of the vicious circle of thoughts I couldn't escape on my own.

Speak of the devil. "Hey, Carp." I had to make a concerted effort these days to keep my voice light. He knew I was dealing with something that kept me from being super cheerful, although he thought it revolved solely around my mom.

"Hey, Chelsea. I'm glad to see you haven't fallen into the portal."

"What?" I didn't have a clue what he was talking about.

"I haven't heard from you in a couple days and was afraid Geneva Key had swallowed you up with the rest of the youngsters."

"Nope, I just avoid that part of town." I giggled. It was nice to hear his voice and have him joke around. Dottie was so serious about everything these days that, sometimes, I felt guilty for smiling. "Are you getting excited about going to Paris? You're only a couple weeks away."

"Nervous. I can count on one hand the number of life-defining moments I've had, and this is definitely at the top of those. I don't know what—"

The phone beeped, interrupting what he was saying. "Hang on just a second, Carp. Someone's on the other line." Before I could answer it, the call had gone to voicemail, but it wasn't a number I recognized. "I guess I missed it. What were you saying?"

"Um, I don't remember. Sorry, I'm kind of scatterbrained these days."

Dottie burst through the door, her face streaked with tears. "Chelsea?" The moment she said my name, I sat up, and she saw I was on the phone.

"Carp, let me call you back. Something's wrong."

"Yeah, sure."

I didn't say goodbye or wait for him to, either. I terminated the call and stared at the woman falling apart in my doorway.

Standing quickly, I tossed my phone onto the bed. "What is it? Is it Mom?"

Her hands cupped her face, and when she nodded, long strands of gray hair surrounded her thin, delicate fingers.

I didn't move.

I didn't say a word.

I remained still, committing this moment to memory.

This was the time I'd learned my mother had died.

***

I'd never attended a funeral, much less been forced to plan one. It didn't seem fair; she was too young to lose her life to such a cruel disease. I hated that there was no cure and that it was such a painful, degrading way to go. By the time she'd left us, she couldn't talk, couldn't control her motor functions, couldn't swallow, and essentially, lived trapped in a body that refused to work.

I'd never be able to say with any certainty just how cognizant she'd been of anything going on around her or if she'd understood when I told her I was pregnant. I knew she'd kept my secret until her dying breath. I'd told her everything I could about James Carpenter: how we'd met, our laughable sexcapade on the beach, all the way to his undying love for Cora. She'd blinked rapidly when I told her about their fairy-tale romance. It may have been a reflex, but I believed she wanted their love story to work out as much as I did. I also believed she understood why I hadn't told him about the baby. She'd made the same choice, even if my circumstances were a little different. She hadn't wanted my father to lose his marriage.

Sitting in the pew of the mostly empty church, I tuned out the minister giving the service in favor of remembering the last conversation I'd had with my mom. I had told her Dottie confessed about my dad, and that I loved her for thinking I was special enough to endure the hard times alone. I also made sure she knew I held no ill will for her decision to keep it a secret. I refused to let her think she would carry that to the grave. It might not have given her any peace because she might not have even been aware of what I said, although I felt lighter with her secret out in the open.

"Chuck Plahniuk once said, 'The unreal is more power than real, because nothing is as perfect as you can imagine it, because it's only intangible concepts, beliefs, fantasies that last. Stone crumbles, wood rots. People, well they die. But things as fragile as thought, a dream, a legend, they can go on and on.' Janie Airy will go on forever as a legend in the legacy she left. I've never met a woman more dedicated to a cause than Janie was to finding a cure for Huntingtons, and in the fight, she touched so many people that her memory will live in the hearts of others for generations to come."

I recognized the man from the Huntington Foundation. My mom had done fundraising for them most of my life. He was as old as

Methuselah, yet he'd known her well. It was nice to think he believed my mother was a legend that would stand the test of time, one as powerful as a dream and as fragile as a thought. I had missed his taking the podium and the preacher stepping down, but I was glad I'd heard that if nothing else.

The music played, and the twenty or so people who'd attended the funeral in Tampa made their way to her graveside. There were more flowers than I could think of what to do with from out-of-state mourners who were unable to attend. However, their sentiment wasn't lost. The volume of beautiful blooms surrounding her casket and her grave were reminders that my mom had been well-loved. Dottie and I had received countless cards where hundreds of thousands of dollars had been donated to the Huntington Foundation in her memory. She would have been elated that not only had her life brought meaning to those who suffered, but in her death, she'd made one final contribution.

I was numb to it all. I'd shed so many tears over the last year that I almost felt relief it was over, that she wasn't in pain anymore, and she no longer had to endure in a body that gave out long ago. My face was the only one that was dry next to the gravesite, though no one commented on my lack of a breakdown. It would come, I was sure of it—most likely when I felt safe knowing that no one would witness my final goodbye.

After everyone departed, Dottie waited in the car while I watched them lower her casket into the ground. There was no music playing, no words spoken, just a silent exodus from the earth. When the first shovelful of dirt hit the wood, I couldn't bear the sound, the hollow thud, knowing my mother was underneath. And I turned and fled.

Once back in the car, I took the passenger seat. I was in no shape to drive. My hands hadn't stopped shaking since Dottie came into my room, and I felt like I was in a continuous state of confusion. Although, Dottie assured me it was natural to feel so disorientated after losing a loved one. My attempt to steady my fingers by placing them over my belly worked for the time being, but probably only because I fell asleep.

"Sweetheart." Dottie's hand patted my leg and gave it a gentle squeeze. "We're home. Let's go inside."

My eyes fluttered open only to realize it hadn't been a dream. And every day from now on, I'd wake up as an orphan.

I just sat there and stared through the windshield at the sky changing colors as the sun set, wondering if it would get any easier. My mind struggled to process that she was really gone and not still lying in a hospital bed in Tampa. It had been ages since she'd had an active part in my daily life, but I struggled to let go of the notion that I could go see her tomorrow.

Stretching my legs in front of me, I reached for the handle to open the door. Yet when I went to get out, the tingles in my limbs left my legs more like Jell-O than something sturdy enough to walk on. And before I could sit back down or steady myself on the door, I stumbled to the ground, landing on my side.

"Chelsea? Are you all right?" Instantly, Dottie was by my side to help me up.

"Yeah, my legs were asleep. I'll be okay." I pushed myself off the ground, thankful I hadn't landed on my stomach, and dusted myself off. My bruised ego was nothing compared to my broken heart.

"Come on, I'll make us some coffee." She linked her arm with mine to escort me inside without making me feel like she was coddling me.

"I'm really beat, Dottie. I think I'm going to lie down." I didn't mention that I was going to call Carp. She still didn't know his name, and I had no interest in revisiting that argument. It had been a long day, and I wanted nothing more than to say hello and then sink into the comfort of my mattress and bury myself in covers.

***

"Tomorrow's the big day, huh?" I hadn't made the phone call to Carp the night of my mom's funeral. I couldn't bring myself to dial because I couldn't bear for him to ask how things had gone.

"Yeah, I leave in less than eight hours. I've got to be at JFK at oh-dark-thirty."

"I should let you go so you can get some sleep."

"I can talk for a bit. I doubt I'll sleep anyhow."

I went through the checklist of things he needed to remember… like I was his mother instead of some strange cell phone pen pal he'd picked up at his father's birthday party. "The ring. If you don't remember anything other than the ring and your passport, you'll be fine."

"Got them both."

"Don't put the ring in your suitcase. I've heard the airlines search them, and you could lose it to someone who gets grabby in security."

"Jesus, that would send me into a tailspin. Can you imagine?"

I couldn't, which was why I told him not to do it. "Nope, it would be horrible. Have you finalized your plan for how you're going to propose?"

Knowing it had to be perfect, he'd debated on this for weeks. I tried to listen as he shared his final ideas with me on how he'd ask Cora to be his wife, except my mind drifted when the little life inside me fluttered. And I wondered for the umpteenth time if I was making the right decision.

"What do you think my chances are?"

I jolted back to the topic at hand. "Of Cora saying yes?"

"Yeah. I mean, you don't know her, but what would you say if you were in her position?"

"I'm a romantic at heart, so I wouldn't be able to resist. If she loves you the way you do her, she'd be a fool to say no. Have some confidence. This is what you want, right?"

"Definitely."

"Then the only way to get it is to ask for it. You can't control what happens from there." *And if she says no, you'll have another surprise waiting for you when you return.* Although, I didn't say any of that, or even hint at it.

He yawned, and I needed to let him go. He didn't need to miss his flight because he'd been on the phone all night.

"You sound tired, so I'm going to let you get off here. Promise me you'll let me know what she says."

"Of course. You'll be the first person I tell."

"Have a safe trip."

"Hey, Chelsea?"

"Yeah?"

"I'm sorry about your mom. I know you haven't wanted to talk about it, but I've been really worried about you."

I took a deep breath and fought back the tears. "Thank you. I'm doing as well as can be expected. I just miss her."

"I'm here anytime you need to talk. I really mean that."

"I'm sure you do, but it won't bring her back—it'll only bring you down. I'll find a way to move on. I'm sure I'll have something else to take my mind off it in a couple months." He had no idea how true those words were. "Promise, I'll be okay."

"Maybe when Cora comes home, the three of us could get together. I'd love for the two of you to meet." He meant well, but he didn't have a clue what he was suggesting. "She could tell you all about Paris, and you could regale her with stories of the socialites you work with in Geneva Key." The humor in his voice made me smile. In another time and another place, his wish might have come true.

What he didn't know was that by the time Cora came home, her fiancé would have a baby that was almost two months old, a baby neither of them was aware of. I doubted she'd welcome me and an infant carrier to New York with open arms. Only time would tell.

"That would be great." And it would be, if there were a chance in hell it'd happen. but However, if Cora said yes, my time with James Carpenter would come to a close. I wouldn't lie to him, but I couldn't tell him the truth, and the only way to avoid that was to disappear the same way my dad had done.

"Get some rest. I'll let you know how things go."

I didn't expect to hear from him until after he proposed, and likely not before he returned from Paris. It would be a long ten-day wait. I'd put destiny in the hands of fate, and now I just had to wait to see which way she leaned.

13

JAMES

SEVEN AND A HALF HOURS ON A PLANE SEEMED LIKE AN EXORBITANT amount of time until I was on said aircraft waiting to reunite with my future at the other end. It had flown by in nervous anticipation, and when the wheels hit the ground, my stomach threatened a revolt. My anxiety hit the roof, and I was afraid I wouldn't be able to get out of my seat and down the aisle unassisted. I didn't even want to talk about the form I had to fill out for customs—it wasn't even legible my hands shook so badly.

I fumbled with my luggage and got in the endless line to trudge through customs. They were going to think I was a heroin mule due to the volume of sweat pouring off my face—and fuck, my heart raced like I'd just swam across the ocean instead of flown. I looked guilty, and no one would believe it was just jitters from seeing the love of my life.

Thankfully, by the time I got to the front of the line, I'd chilled out. I answered the man's questions regarding why I was entering the country and where I was going. He scanned my passport and waved me through without ever cracking a smile.

Cora was like a beacon of light standing on the outskirts of the crowd of people coming and going. I would have seen her a mile away, even if she hadn't spotted me and waved frantically. A smile stretched across my face at her enthusiasm. Never in my wildest dreams had I imagined she could be more beautiful than the last time I'd seen her, but somehow, she was. I couldn't pinpoint what had changed, yet whatever it was looked good on her.

The instant I broke free from the massive hordes, she took off in my direction, and I dropped my bags to catch her in my arms. The force she hit me with caused me to step back a bit to brace us from falling, but the moment she hugged my neck and her legs wrapped around my waist, I knew she'd come home. The scent of her lavender shampoo filled my nostrils when I inhaled deeply, and she buried her face in the crook of my neck. Nothing ever felt so right. Had we not been standing in an airport, I would have held her as long as she'd let me. But we were, and there were people everywhere, so I reluctantly set her on her feet and kept her close.

With no regard for consequences, I captured her face in my hands and tilted it up. Her eyes were filled with tears, and the smile told me they were of joy. My lids closed, and I bent down, meeting her lips with mine. There was no hesitation, no retreat—she joined me, parting to allow my tongue entrance. Each pass sent a tingle straight to my dick, and if I weren't careful, he'd be standing at attention. Every cell in my body responded to her touch, her scent, her taste—I could feast a lifetime on Cora Chase.

The catcall from out in the distance broke the kiss, and she blushed a warm pink before she blotted at her mouth with her delicate fingers.

I picked up my bag, slung the strap over one shoulder, and rolled the other behind me.

She took my free hand. "We should get out of here."

"Lead the way." I'd follow her anywhere she wanted to go.

The two of us jabbered on like we hadn't spent a day apart in eighteen months. Cora pointed out everything she could as we drove, yet I couldn't take it all in fast enough. Once something caught my attention, she pointed in the other direction. And while nothing was off, it dawned on me that Cora lived in another world —one I knew nothing about.

Her flat was small, even in comparison to apartments in New York, although she'd made it her own. I'd never seen a single thing in the place, but I could have identified it all as hers. Girly and classy, with a hint of edge. Industrial feminine—I should coin that term. The kitchen was the size of my bathroom, the living room the size of my kitchen, and a queen bed took up the majority of the space in her one bedroom.

"It's small compared to spaces in the States. In order to live close to work, I gave up certain luxuries. I'm comfortable here, though." The graceful grin that hugged her cheeks made me swoon in a way only Cora could.

"It's you. I like it."

She took my bags and set them in the corner of her room before turning her head, suddenly appearing nervous. "So, should we go out? Stay in? Take a nap?"

I'd flown through the night, but even if I hadn't, I'd be too wired to sleep. I only had ten days to remind Cora of why she belonged in the United States—I wasn't wasting time napping... unless she was naked next to me.

"Can we go for a walk, talk? Keep it low-key today?" I'd struggled with whether or not to bring all this up on my first day; although, I also couldn't wait until the last, either. There needed to be as much distance as possible between my confession and proposal.

"Absolutely. I can make dinner when we get back, and we can have wine and catch up. Just let me put on some tennis shoes." She kissed my cheek before going to dig through her closet.

The two of us strolled hand in hand down the sidewalks of Paris. The streets were narrow and the architecture stunning, though nothing rivalled the company. She led me to a park, and our pace became much more casual. The wind whipped around us, yet the cold was nothing compared to the wet chill of New York in December.

"I've told you this a million times since we started talking again, but I've missed you, James." Even though her attention was set off in the distance, her words were inviting.

"I've missed you, too. I feel like this is a dream I'll wake up from and wonder how I'll recover."

"Doesn't have to be." The hope in her voice launched butterflies in my stomach.

I felt like a nervous teen out on our first date again. Except instead of the beach, we were in a park—and this time, I was at her mercy instead of her at mine.

"Do you miss *us*? As a couple." With her last word, her eyes met mine.

"Every day."

"I have a confession to make." The sheepish look on her face made my stomach flop, and not in a good way. "I thought when I saw you again that I wouldn't love you anymore."

I hadn't expected that. Neil had been right, or Hannah —whoever.

"I knew my heart would know. This may sound dumb, but I argued with my head and my heart for weeks before I left. My heart longed to stay with you; my head insisted I go. In the end, I convinced myself this would be best for both of us."

"How could leaving someone you love be best for either of us?" There was no hiding the confusion or irritation from my voice.

She stopped and dropped my hand in favor of my cheek. The weak smile she offered did nothing to calm my ragged breath. "I needed to be certain I had lived for me. We'd been together since we were seventeen. I'd never even dated anyone else. You were my world."

"And you were mine, so I don't see why that was a bad thing."

187

"It wasn't." Her brows rose, and her eyes glistened with unshed tears. "I just never wanted to resent or regret following you around the country. I never wanted to look back and wonder *what if.* I needed to know that at the end of the day, we both experienced what life had to offer and chose to come back together, not because we'd never tried anything else, but because we never *wanted* anything else."

"I just wish you'd talked to me about it."

"Would you have let me go willingly?"

The wind rustled through the trees, creating a static around us that offered me a moment to contemplate my answer. "Truthfully, no."

"Please believe, I never wanted to leave. I always thought we'd find our way back together. But I couldn't tell you that, or you wouldn't have lived while I was gone…just existed."

"I never thought I'd hear from you again, Cora. The months after you left were not my finest hour."

Her thumb stroked my cheekbone and then grazed my jawline before she spoke. "I worried about you. Hannah tried to keep me informed, but she said you cut her and Neil out not long after you moved out."

My fingers wrapped around her wrist and moved her hand from my face. I held it loosely between us. The opportunity presented itself, and I had to take it. "I made a lot of mistakes."

"Me too."

I doubted very seriously we were talking about the same things. "No, babe. I made mistakes that might change the way you feel about me."

She huffed a bit of a laugh. "That makes two of us."

"How much did Hannah tell you?" This might help me figure out how to delve into my admission.

Her teeth tugged her bottom lip into her mouth where she chewed on it for several long seconds like she was trying to find the best way to tell me what she already knew I'd done. "I heard you gave your liver a run for your money."

"Why does everyone think I was a raging alcoholic?"

"I don't think anyone believes you were an alcoholic. Neil and Hannah were only concerned about your sudden lifestyle switch. And when you shut them out, that increased tenfold."

"Right."

"I also know you became friendly with the owner of a bar, and of course, there's Chelsea." She held my stare, yet instead of anger, I saw sorrow.

"I'm sorry. I never would have touched another woman if you'd told me our separation was temporary. I would have waited had I had any inclination."

"Don't apologize. I don't like it, but I did nothing to stop it. I knew about it when it was going on, which was why you didn't hear from me. And trust me, it took everything I had not to reach out and beg you to wait. The only reason I didn't was because that wouldn't have been fair to either of us."

"I would have killed to hear your voice." My mind drifted back to the place of darkness after she'd left, the one where I didn't give a shit what or who I did, I just searched for pleasure to kill the pain.

"I wasn't perfect, either. I dated. I played. It just wasn't ever right. And the hours I was keeping at work kept me from falling too far down the rabbit hole."

Even though I didn't want any details from her, I had to give her the chance to ask me questions before we shut this topic down permanently. "I don't want to know. I can't stand the thought of another man touching you, and I'd prefer to pretend like they never did. If there's anything you need to ask, I think you should do it now. Let's clear the air completely, and then decide if we can move on. Because if we can, I never want to bring it up again. We weren't together, and it's not fair for either of us to hold that time against the other." That was easy for me to say since I'd been the one to act like a slut.

"Was there anyone other than the woman who owns the bar? What's her name—Letty?"

We'd talked about Letty and Chelsea. She also heard about Eric and Cason. I'd mentioned them on numerous phone calls, and while I had assumed she knew something had taken place with Letty, I had never admitted to it.

"Colette, but yes, Letty." I wasn't sure she really needed a name, though I gave her one.

"So one?"

"And Chelsea."

"Wow. I didn't realize you and Chelsea had done anything. I thought it was platonic. You really enjoyed your time away, huh?" She swatted playfully at my chest, but I caught her hand.

"Cora…"

"Were you safe?"

I looked her dead in the eye and made sure she saw the truth in my next sentence. "I've never been with another woman unprotected. Not once. And Chelsea is nothing more than a friend, I promise."

Her pupils dilated just slightly, and her chest swelled with something akin to pride, although I wasn't sure why.

"Anything else?"

She shook her head. "You?"

"Did you, uh…um—fool around?"

She held my stare and squared her shoulders. "Yes. With Henry from work. Huge mistake, and it caused a lot of problems."

"Is that what spurred your desire to come home?" I had to have confirmation that she chose me and not that she simply had to get away from the guy in her office.

"No, James. I want to come home because that's where I belong."

There was no further discussion of our past when I took her mouth to seal our future.

***

Never in my wildest dreams did I imagine Cora would let go of our time apart as easily as she did. I assumed it would come back up, that she'd have more questions, try to delve into the depths of my misdeeds, even insist I stop communicating with Chelsea, but not once did she broach the subject the entire time I was in Paris.

She dragged me all over the city doing the tourist bit, and I loved every minute of it. It was as if time ceased to exist, and the world ushered us into a cocoon of isolation where the two of us reunited. Every minute we spent together—whether it was at the Eiffel Tower or the Arc de Triomphe—was perfection. I'd laughed when she told me we were going to Disneyland Paris, but we had the time of our lives with Mickey and the gang. The Louvre and Notre Dame were just as magnificent as I'd expected them to be, yet it was magical getting to experience them with Cora by my side.

She convinced me to try foods I'd never considered in cafes that only existed in novels. We shopped, walked what seemed like a thousand miles, and talked endlessly. The city made for lovers reconnected us emotionally and healed a part of me I thought would remain forever broken. And at the end of each day, exhausted but full of life, we crawled into bed next to each other and made out like teenagers before she'd crash in my arms.

Tilting my head to see her nestled into my side leaned against my chest filled my soul with hope. Whereas her soft breathing would have lulled me to sleep any other night, tomorrow was New Year's Eve, and the day belonged to me. She didn't make any plans as I'd asked her to let me take care of it. However, lying here in the shadows created by the glow of the moon through the open curtains, nervous anticipation prevented sleep. My mind raced through a thousand scenarios about how tomorrow would play out, although I refused to let myself consider that she might turn me down.

Looking for reinforcement, I tried to text Chelsea. Except she didn't respond, and reaching out to Neil seemed to violate the bro-code in more than one way. Plus, he'd tell Hannah, and I'd never hear the end of it when I got back to New York.

So instead, I focused on her saying yes, and how each day that passed after would be one more day closer to her coming home. We hadn't talked about our future or our past; we'd simply enjoyed our present. It only served to confirm what I'd known for years—Cora Chase had claimed my heart in the cafeteria our junior year, and no other woman would ever satisfy my soul.

I had drifted in and out of fitful sleep all night, and when the sun finally erased the night to welcome the morning, I couldn't lie in the bed any longer. Cora stirred as I eased out from under her, yet instead of waking, she rolled onto her side. The way the sunlight hit her dark hair that flowed over on the pillow stopped me in my tracks. I'd never seen anything more stunning and peaceful—her bare shoulder peeked out from the sheets, adding just a hint of arousal to the picture. It took everything in me not to crawl back in bed and have my way with her naked body, but I'd promised myself I wouldn't take that step unless she said yes.

After pulling on some basketball shorts, I made my way to the kitchen to make her breakfast. I wanted everything about today to be perfect. I'd even gone so far as to have Hannah teach me how to cook Belgian waffles to make sure I had something special each step of the way. Of course, she'd only agreed to cooking lessons after I'd confessed my plans with a promise of secrecy on her part. Thinking about Hannah bouncing up and down, clapping with excitement, only fueled my fire and brought a smile to my face. She believed in Cora and me, and that had meant the world. I needed to channel hers and Chelsea's positive energy and faith.

"Good morning." Those two words came off in a raspy, sleep-filled haze from behind me. "Something smells delicious. When did you learn to cook?"

Cora wrapped her arms around my midsection and kissed my shoulder blade. When she pressed her cheek to my skin, I leaned back into her embrace, wondering how I'd survived eighteen months without her.

"I might have coerced Hannah into teaching me some basics." I grinned over my shoulder while finishing breakfast. "Are you hungry?"

"Starved. Should I make coffee?" The heat of her breath made it hard to focus on the task at hand.

"Already brewed. And these are done." I turned in her arms to kiss her sweet lips before carrying the plates to her tiny, two-seater table by the window.

I watched in anticipation as she poured the warm syrup over her waffle and then placed a piece on her tongue. I didn't have a clue if it was even edible, although it looked fantastic.

Her eyes closed as her lips released the fork. "Mmm."

There was no denying she either loved the waffle or had given a performance that rivaled that of Meg Ryan in *When Harry Met Sally.* But when I took a taste of my own, I confirmed it was the former. Hannah had done me proud.

"These are fantastic, James. Please tell me Hannah taught you more than just breakfast."

She hadn't, but that didn't mean I couldn't learn between now and the time Cora actually came back to New York. "I'm learning."

Cora leaned back in her bistro chair and crossed her legs. With a cup of coffee in hand, she eyed me with curiosity and sipped from her mug. "Tell me, what other surprises do you have in store for me today?"

In the time we'd been apart, something had changed in the girl I loved. However, it wasn't until that moment that I recognized what it was. When she'd left New York, she'd still been a young adult, youthful and spirited. She was still that same person, yet a year and a half of international living had matured her, not aged her appearance, just softened her already smooth edges. The woman before me was the picture of class and sophistication in a casual, lovable way.

"Hopefully, a romantic excursion and day we'll remember for the rest of our lives."

"This isn't like the road trip to New York and the world's largest ball of twine, is it?" Her eyes danced with humor at the memory.

"I thought we'd go explore the history of the bidet." I cleared my expression, waiting to hear her response.

"Do you think we'll get to try them out?" She challenged my bluff.

"I didn't ask. I assumed you washed your bum on the regular now that you were a Parisite."

"Parisian."

"Huh?"

"You called me a parasite…like a fungus. The term is *Parisian*." The giggle she let escape turned into a full-blown laugh that caused her cheeks to warm and her eyes to water.

"I'm an idiot. I knew that."

"For real, what are we doing? We aren't going to have fountains sprayed up our butts. And the list of questions I have about bidets couldn't possibly be answered in twenty-four hours. We should save that for another trip."

"When you're done eating, we'll get dressed and go find out."

Eager to see what I had planned, she finished her coffee and waffle in record time. She popped a kiss on my mouth after she stood from the table, and I wrapped my arm around her waist to bring her to me. "I'm right behind you."

The week had been perfect, and today would make or break us. I needed to either move forward or move on—her answer this afternoon would determine which direction I went at the crossroad before me. I could only pray our paths were the same.

"Are we on a timetable?"

"Not really, we have reservations at eight thirty tonight. Nothing's set in stone prior. Why?"

I stood and gathered the plates from the table, but before I could get more than a couple steps away, she latched onto the waistband of my shorts and pulled me back to her. "I want to take our time getting cleaned up." Her expression hinted at mischief, yet when she pulled her bottom lip between her teeth, it turned erotic.

The dishes could wait.

"Lead the way." I didn't care where she took me or what she had in mind—I'd follow…even if I hadn't expected it to be a sensual shower together. My willpower was waning. Every touch of her skin against mine left me weak, and my resolve not to fuse our bodies into one neared failure.

Cora was wanton, and I was the last guy in the world who should try to refuse her. I managed to escape the shower without penetration or making her feel rejected. She'd played along with my unwillingness to consume her, even though it was evident she was growing leery.

It took monumental effort not to strip off the tight skinny jeans she'd just slathered over her legs and have my way with her. Instead, I forced myself to face a wall while the two of us finished dressing.

"You ready?" Eager to get this show on the road, my excitement came out like a prepubescent boy.

She giggled and eased up on her tiptoes to kiss my lips with a smile. "Been ready."

Hannah wouldn't spill the beans, but that one comment and the way she'd said those two words made me wonder if she had some premonition of what today would hold. I hoped to keep it a surprise. Although, if her radiant joy came from knowing what I had planned, I had to admit that put a huge puff of wind in my sail. I wasn't ready to beat my chest, but God, I prayed I was in full-on caveman mode by eight thirty tonight.

With the ring uncomfortably in my pocket, I took Cora's hand and led her out the door and into the last December day of the year. The sun shined so brightly it created a halo around everything in the distance, and the warmth it offered was unseasonable yet welcomed. There was no breeze or bite to the Paris air, and the birds sang happily as traffic eased by at what seemed an unusually slow pace. I chose to believe Mother Nature had orchestrated a perfect day and the world was in cahoots with her, but instead of thinking beyond the sounds of silence, I opted to enjoy the company of the woman at my side.

"You going to tell me where we're going?"

"Down the road a piece."

We walked in relative silence other than the few things Cora pointed out along the way or the architecture she couldn't resist. I knew long ago that my ability to enjoy Cora's company without words or something to occupy us was a connection I'd never shared with anyone else. Simply being next to her was enough.

As we approached the Pont des Arts, Cora squeezed my hand. I wished we'd made this trip before the city quit allowing lovers to add locks, but she'd understand the meaning and why I'd chosen this particular location to drop to one knee. It wouldn't matter that we couldn't put our own lock on the ironwork, the sentiment would remain.

"Up until a couple years ago, we could have had a padlock on the bridge." The comment managed to come out as smoothly as I'd hoped...by the grace of God.

"I've read a little about it. The weight threatened the integrity of the bridge." She turned to look up at me, still holding my hand. "Somehow, it's like we have one here anyhow. All I feel is love and romance. Silly, huh?"

We weren't where I'd intended to be on the bridge, and the water wasn't as visible from this location as I'd hoped, but Cora had stopped *here*, and I took that as my cue. I said a quick prayer while I stared into her emerald eyes, and without dropping her hand, dug the black box from my pocket and took a knee.

If she was aware I was going to propose, I couldn't tell. Her free hand touched her lips in shock, and her eyes glistened with unshed tears. Cora didn't pull away or tell me no. She didn't look around to see who might bear witness to my request. She honed in on my eyes and refused to let go.

"I had planned to ask you this two years ago, but think maybe you were right. Maybe we both needed to explore who we were to establish who we're meant to be. There has never been a question in my mind of whether or not you were meant to be in my life; I've known since that day in the cafeteria when we were seventeen that there would never be anyone else."

She blinked, sending the tears that pooled in her eyes cascading down her pink cheeks. They clung to her jaw with the same anticipation that lingered in her eyes. Her emerald irises were smiling, even if her expression was that of shock.

"I don't want to go another day without knowing you're mine. Eighteen months has been a year and a half too long. Will you marry me? I promise to love you endlessly, care for you faithfully, and protect you at all costs."

She nodded, although her head barely moved. "Yes," she croaked, and it was the most glorious sound I'd ever heard. "Yes. Yes. Yes. A thousand times, yes." The smile that hung in her eyes took over her face, and the tears that had held on let go at the last possible second.

I dropped her hand to remove the ring from the velvet and then slid it onto her slim finger. Before it was even fully on, I stood to take her mouth in an uninhibited kiss that would embarrass old ladies. But I didn't care. Cora Chase had agreed to be my wife despite my downfalls, stupid mistakes, and transgressions during our time apart. I'd shout it from the mountaintops as soon as I reached a peak.

When I finally allowed Cora to breathe her own air, I glanced around and noticed the area was primarily deserted. No one appeared to have witnessed our monumental moment. And somehow, that seemed perfect. I watched as Cora stared at her hand in awe, her gaze shifting to me then back repeatedly, and I tried to commit every moment to memory.

The details of the remainder of the day paled in comparison, but the cruise down the Seine and the sights we took in only added to the experience. We were both on cloud nine throughout our time on the river and our four-course meal that followed. The sights of Paris at night were nothing short of breathtaking and completely different than they'd been during the day. Chelsea had been right; the Eiffel Tower alone was worth the trip. We kicked off the new year together, engaged, and all was right in the world as the fireworks exploded over the city in what I'd forever remember as a celebration of us.

As promised, I sent Chelsea a text as soon as I could with a picture of the Eiffel Tower lit up as though it owned the sky, and a caption that read, "She said yes." She didn't immediately respond, and I hadn't wanted to spend time away from Cora waiting for my phone to chime. I'd talk to her when I got home; I just let her know she'd been right.

Staring out over the edge of the boat with Cora in front of me, wrapped in my arms, nothing could have been any better.

Until she said, "Promise me we'll get married as soon as I get back to the US."

And we did just that. Six months and two weeks later, Cora Chase became Cora Carpenter in a small ceremony in Geneva Key with Neil, Hannah, and my parents in attendance.

14

PART THREE—PRESENT

CORA

FIVE O'CLOCK TRAFFIC WAS UNUSUALLY LIGHT, OR MAYBE I'D hoped I'd get caught behind a six-car pileup that would take me well into the night. When that hadn't happened, I pulled in behind James. The drive hadn't prepared me to have this conversation with my husband—nothing could.

While I sat in my car taking deep, cleansing breaths to keep the anxiety attack at bay, James had gotten out of his and walked toward me. He tapped on the glass with his knuckles. With a silent prayer and a quick deal with God, I grabbed my purse from the passenger seat and got out to greet him.

"Hey, babe." James kissed me the way he did every night when he came home, except normally it was in welcome. Tonight something was off.

"Why are you home so early? Does your head still hurt?" I peered up at my husband, aware my brow was knitted and concern creased my forehead. He wasn't prone to migraines, but he'd had one last night that put him in bed before the sun went down.

He snaked an arm around my waist and squeezed me to his side. Everything always felt so perfect next to him. The two years we'd been apart had been a self-imposed hell I never cared to revisit. I thanked God every day when he walked in the door that, somehow, we'd found our way back to each other. Now I worried with the news I had to share, this might drive another wedge between us the same way it had seven years ago.

"No, my head's okay. How was your day?" His voice shook just a hint, like maybe he needed to clear his throat. Or maybe I was hearing things because of what lay in front of us.

Leaving the cocoon of his embrace, I reluctantly opened the door to walk inside, dreading what was coming. "It wasn't great."

He still hadn't answered my question about why he was home so early, but before I could ask again, he probed me. "Anything in particular?"

The weight of my purse hitting the counter when I set it down made a hollow thud. From the corner of my eye, I saw James set his bag on the floor and wondered when I'd begun to find metrosexual attractive. He watched me move around the kitchen—I was clearly on a mission—and then his eyes widened in surprise when I pulled out a bottle of wine and two glasses. And I wasn't shy with the servings. I could only hope alcohol softened the blow and lessened the yelling.

He took the glass I offered, hesitating to drink when I didn't propose a toast, although we probably should have just drunk straight from the bottle and saved ourselves the hassle of cleanup. It could have been Mad Dog 20/20 in that glass, and it wouldn't have mattered. James tried not to guzzle it, but I had thrown caution to the wind, taking large gulps before finally meeting his eyes when I swallowed the last drop.

"Drake offered me another international position." The sting of trying to hold my emotions at bay burned until my eyes brimmed with tears.

I couldn't read his thoughts from his blank expression. I watched in slow motion as he lowered his glass from his lips and set it on the counter. The corner of his eye twitched, and his pupils dilated slightly before returning to normal. Then his hands went to his hair and pulled at the roots. This did not bode well for me.

"W-what?" he stammered as though he'd consumed a bottle of wine on his own.

"Yeah, Italy." Once the waterworks started, they'd continue for most of the night. "James, I did my time. I don't want to go overseas. That's great for people who are single, but how can he expect employees with spouses at home to just take off for two years?" The trickle started down my cheek, and I swiped furiously at the never-ending stream.

"Tell him you can't take the job."

His answers were always so simple. James wasn't taking into account this was my career. I'd been with the company for close to a decade counting my internship. The hiccup that escaped my mouth exaggerated the shake of my head. "If I don't take it, then there won't be a job at Halifax for me. I've been with them for nine years—*nine.*"

"I don't think you'd lose your job if you turned down a position in Italy." His words were harsh and insensitive, and by the scowl he tried to hide, he was aware of it. He'd hated Drake Halifax for the better part of my career. And even worse, he hated the control Drake had over the staff. James thought Drake was the master of manipulation, and this was a prime example.

"He was pretty clear that it wasn't optional. So the question becomes, what are we going to do if I lose my job?"

I'd worked hard to get where I was. The education alone took years to obtain, and I'd put in more than my fair share of hours to impress the man behind the company name. It had paid off; he'd noticed me—it had also nearly cost me James. I refused to let that happen again.

"We don't need the income if that's what you're worried about. Even without taking money out of savings or drawing off either of our trust funds, I make enough to cover our expenses. The question really isn't what are we going to do; the question is, what do you want to do? The last time he made you an offer like this, you jumped at the chance to leave the country." Hurt still lingered in his eyes; I'd nearly destroyed him then.

"James…"

"Just be honest with me, Cora. You have to tell me what you *want* to do so we can figure out what *we* are going to do." He emphasized my desires and our plans, and I loved him for that.

"I have no interest in moving to Italy." I didn't, but even if I had, I loved my husband more than any job, and if he wasn't on board, then we weren't leaving.

"Have you really thought about it? Or is this you saying what you think I need to hear?" He rubbed his temples. There was something weighing on him other than Drake Halifax and us relocating.

I cocked my head to the side and stared at him, taking him in. There were bags under his eyes that normally weren't there, the sides of his mouth turned down unnaturally, and a permanent crease stretched across his forehead that I'd never noticed before. "What's going on with you?"

He inhaled deeply and slowly released the breath he'd just taken. Twice. "I think we need more wine."

Jesus, this couldn't be good. My eyes tracked him through the kitchen as he grabbed another bottle and the corkscrew. He motioned with his head for me to grab our glasses, and then I followed him out to the back porch. The sun still hung in the sky, providing a warm evening in New York. I loved this time of year. The nights weren't too hot, yet not so cold I needed a sweater—and the sunsets were unbelievably colorful.

He turned his chair to face mine and took a long swallow of wine, or three, before finishing the glass. I stared at each movement as though I might find an answer in it. However, when he put his elbows on his knees and took my hands, I had to fight against more tears. All I saw on my husband's face was total devastation.

"What's wrong? Please talk to me." My voice cracked and my throat closed. The lump hurt to swallow past.

"There's no easy way to tell you this."

I wanted to holler at him to just spit it out, but my mouth refused to open.

"Do you remember Chelsea?"

Of course I did. Even though it had been years since her name had come up, at one point, they were pretty good friends. While I never admitted to the jealousy I harbored for her, it existed. My feelings hadn't been hurt when I came back from France and found out she'd flittered off into the unknown. But if she had resurfaced, that couldn't be good. At some point, I must have nodded.

"She passed away."

"Oh, I'm so sorry. How did you find out?" I *was* sorry. She was close to us in age if I recalled correctly, and he had cared for her. I had feigned interest when he spoke of her during those years I was gone, so I was sure he thought it would matter to me.

"I got a letter from her attorney in the mail yesterday." He looked up from our hands to meet my eyes.

"Why would her attorney contact you?" My head pulled back in confusion, waiting for his answer.

Instead of responding, he handed me the envelope he'd received in the mail. I glanced at the sender—Clary, White, & Boyd—not recognizing any of the names from Geneva Key. Unfolding the piece of paper, my eyes bounced back and forth between James and the sheet in front of me. When my gaze finally met the words on the page, I didn't have to read it; the entire contents stood out in just a few short words: *paternity test (DNA) for minor child Airy.*

"You said you used a condom!" I wasn't sure what that proved at this point. "Her kid can't be yours. You promised me."

"I *did* use a condom. I'd never lie to you about that."

"Then how can she claim you're the father of her child?" I rarely raised my voice. However, as we sat on our back porch, it dawned on me that I was screaming at my husband over something that happened six years ago…when we weren't together.

He handed me another piece of paper—this one already unfolded. "I have no idea, Cora. All I can tell you is she had a condom, and we used it. It didn't break. I know she didn't go back to get it off the beach. I have no clue how she got pregnant."

Ninety-nine point nine percent. James had fathered a child he'd never met and knew nothing about. And now the mother of this child was gone.

My mind went blank, my heart hurt, and my chest constricted. I grabbed my wine and raced into the house with James on my heels.

"Please don't walk away." The anguish in his voice ripped at my heart. "I'm scared, Cora. Please help me."

Never, in all the years I'd known and loved James, had I ever heard him admit he was afraid. And when I turned around, he stood in front of the sliding glass doors, shoulders slumped, tears streaming down his cheeks, completely broken.

"Please." It was nothing more than a whisper, almost a prayer.

And I couldn't bear for him to endure this alone. I couldn't even be angry that we now faced an issue no one should ever deal with. I couldn't imagine why Chelsea had kept the baby a secret, but we'd never have an answer to that question. We wouldn't get the answers to lots of questions. All that mattered was my husband was destroyed, hanging on by a thread…and somehow, we'd figure out a way to get through this. Together.

***

At that moment, I needed to connect to my husband, the man I loved, the one I'd committed my life to, because the world didn't make sense without him. I needed a reminder of the bond we shared and that the world fell away when his skin was flush with mine.

James didn't question me when I pulled him to our bedroom, or when I undressed him before removing my own clothes, or when I pushed him down on the mattress. And when I straddled his waist and he sunk into me, his eyes remained focused on mine without a word uttered between us. He let me be the aggressor, expending the negative energy his news had brought, casting aside my disdain for Drake Halifax, and when the tears began to fall, he rolled me over, reminded me of how desperately he loved me, and brought me back home...to the place where nothing could hurt us, as long as we were together.

Lying next to each other—my chest pressed to his, our sticky skin cooling off—he ran his fingers through my hair and traced my cheek with his thumb. The light through the window had started to wane, and shadows fell around us, yet I could still see his crystal-blue eyes focused on me and searching my features. Everything in our life was suddenly uncertain, but I knew for sure that I'd walk through a burning house to save this man, and I wouldn't leave his side.

When James finally spoke, it was obvious he thought I was saying goodbye, when in reality, I'd been taking his hand. "I'm sorry. I'm lost over what to do. You never wanted children, and this one isn't even ours."

With more conviction than I actually felt, I tried to reassure him. "I can't say I'm happy. The only thing I can tell you is that we'll get through it together. Somehow, we'll figure it out."

"How do you figure out a kid? It's not like you're pregnant and we have nine months to formulate a plan. This child is already here and just lost its mother."

"Do you have any information about it? Is it a boy or a girl? Who has the child now? Is it in foster care?" That was only the tip of the iceberg of the questions we needed answered.

He closed his eyes and shook his head. "I didn't ask anything. What kind of father does that make me? I don't know the first thing about my own child."

It was hard to comfort him when I needed so much myself—we both had the same uncertainty and neither of us had any answers.

The truth was, we were just going to have to wade through it and hope we didn't drown in the process. "Don't be too hard on yourself. It's hard to be informed when things were intentionally kept from you."

"I can't imagine why she never told me. It wasn't like the two of us never talked again." Something had just crossed his mind, a realization, though he hadn't shared it. "She would have been several months pregnant when I left for Paris."

"So you think she didn't tell you because of me?" I highly doubted that.

"I never spoke to her again after I came back from France. I texted her the night we got engaged to tell her you'd accepted. She never responded, and I didn't think much about it. Once I got home, I tried a couple times to reach her. We were so busy at the office that I didn't pursue it."

"Maybe she started dating someone." It was as plausible as his explanation.

"In Geneva Key? I don't think she had an affinity for older men in golf attire."

"Unfortunately, James, if she didn't give you any answers, I don't think you're going to find them now. Maybe she has a family member taking care of the child while all this plays out. That person might be your only hope for resolution."

He rolled onto his back, leaving my front cold and bare. His forearm crossed over his face, shielding most of his expression from view, but I knew he was upset by that action alone. "I have to go to Geneva Key."

"Yeah, you do."

"You don't have to go with me. I have no idea how long any of this is going to take. I could walk in, sign some papers, and they shove the kid my way. Or they make me take parenting classes and do visitation before they turn over custody. What if this isn't about custody at all and just about child support?"

"I think you need to figure out what role you want to play in the child's life. The torment that kid is feeling losing its mother has to be horrible. Chelsea's family may try to keep custody—you need to be certain before you get there if you're choosing to fight."

"She doesn't have any family. Her mother died right before I came to see you in Paris. The only other person in her life was her mother's best friend, Dottie."

"Then you're prepared to take custody of a son or daughter you've never met?"

He lifted his arm from his face and looked at me like I was an idiot. "No. I'm not prepared to take care of a kid. But I can't walk away, either."

"Then there's your answer. So when are we leaving?"

He kissed my lips so tenderly that I melted into his embrace. When he tipped his forehead to mine, if I hadn't already determined I'd be by his side, that would have sealed the deal. There hadn't been a single day since James Carpenter had walked into my life that I'd ever doubted how he felt about me—although seeing it never got old. And if he made a decision to love a child, it would be with the same abandon he loved me.

"I guess I need to go in to work tomorrow and talk to Neil. Then book a flight. What are you going to do about the job offer?"

Clearly, he still didn't get it. I wasn't going to Italy without him, and that wasn't an option since we were both going to Geneva Key. "My guess is he will let me go tomorrow when I inform him I'm not taking the promotion and that I need an undetermined amount of time off to go home." I offered James a gentle smile, the one my heart naturally forced upon my lips anytime my husband was around.

"I love you, Cora. More than anything in the world." And he did. I'd never questioned that.

"I love you, too."

He kissed the top of my head and wrapped me in his arms.

207

Thoughts ran wildly through my head, though my heart was content. The *what-ifs* and *whys* tried to take over, but the circles he traced on my spine relaxed me until I fell asleep in his embrace.

***

Sitting on a plane, waiting to taxi down the runway, I couldn't help but wonder if I'd made the right decision. I hadn't been surprised when Drake had let me go two days earlier—I couldn't say I was upset, either. I loved my job, on the other hand, the man who owned the company left a lot to be desired. He'd taken far too great an interest in me since the day I'd started. Flattery had quickly turned to irritation when he scrutinized every move I made. And James was right, we didn't need the money. Although, it still felt like failure.

James and I hadn't talked much since the night he told me about Chelsea. He was lost in his head, and I was content to let him stay there. It wasn't that I wasn't supportive, I just wondered how our lives were going to change and whether or not I could handle it. I'd never had a desire for children, however, I didn't have an aversion to them. I didn't want for my child exactly what I'd grown up to face and what this poor kid was facing at such an early age.

Yet I had to believe my fear was nothing more than uncertainty. Even though I wasn't typically a wishy-washy woman, my thoughts on this had waved like a flag in the breeze, bending whichever way the wind blew at that moment. Hopefully, once we found out what we had to deal with, the pieces would fall into place. They had to.

"You okay?" James squeezed my hand reassuringly.

"Just nervous."

"About flying?"

I scoffed. I didn't have a fear of planes. "No." And I rolled my eyes.

"Is there any part of you that's excited?"

"Cautiously, maybe. I guess not having any details makes this harder than it has to be. I think I'll feel better when we're in the attorney's office and things start moving."

He nodded in agreement but didn't respond. His eyes closed, and his head tilted back against the seat as we took off. I leaned against his shoulder and stared at the tray table in front of me. In a couple hours, this ball would start rolling, and I hoped it didn't go so fast that it spun out of control.

A few hours and a rental car later, James and I opened the door that would irrevocably change our lives.

"Clary, White, and Boyd. How may I direct your call?" The receptionist clearly hadn't been the recipient of one of the firm's letters, or she wouldn't be nearly as peppy answering their phone.

When she finished with the call, she greeted the two of us standing in front of her. The only sign of fear either of us showed was the trembling in our clasped hands.

"James and Cora Carpenter. We're here to see Karen Clary." My husband's voice was calm and cool.

She typed something on her computer, waited for a moment, then stood and escorted us back. The conference room sat empty except for the pitcher of water, a carafe of coffee, and cups in the center of the table.

"Mrs. Clary will be right with you. Please help yourself to coffee and water. There are some snacks on the table in the corner if you'd like anything to eat." When James nodded at her, she turned and closed the door behind her as she left.

I didn't have a chance to finish making a cup of coffee before a woman in her mid-fifties strolled in. She was full of confidence, primly dressed, and wearing the most fabulous heels. Any other time, I would have inquired about them, unfortunately that seemed a tad inappropriate given the circumstances.

"I'm Karen Clary. You must be James and Cora. It's nice to meet you." As she shook both of our hands, the two of us remained silent and let her lead.

"As you know, Chelsea Airy passed away two weeks ago, naming you the sole guardian of her five-year-old son, Legend."

It was totally inappropriate, but I couldn't stop the giggles that erupted. James glared at me, horrified by my outburst. Regardless, no matter how hard I tried, I couldn't stop running this kid's name through my head. Legend Airy—legend-ary. Who would do such a thing to their only child, their first born? It was horrendous—poor guy was going to be the laughing stock of the playground.

"What is wrong with you?" James hissed at me under his breath while giving the lawyer a sideways glance to show he didn't have a clue what was going on or approve of my behavior.

"I'm sorry." I tried to whisper, but my voice carried. "Legend Airy…that's your son's name." The weight of what had just come out of my mouth hit me. And then the tears did as well. My fingers met my lips, and in total wonder, my giggles morphed to awe. "You have a son." Those four words were barely heard.

The hand that had hidden my astonishment now cupped his jaw. I didn't bother to hide the overflow of emotions from my husband or the attorney. I kissed his lips and repeated myself. "You have a son." I smiled as if I'd just given birth and the doctor had presented us with our new addition.

Karen didn't interrupt our moment or rush us back to whatever information she needed to share. She gave us time to process what we'd just learned. When we finally turned back to her, she waited with a smile on her face.

"I have to admit, Mr. Carpenter…I worried about how this would all play out when we first spoke. I'm glad to see you and your wife are open and possibly even excited about your son."

"He doesn't have any other family who wants custody?" My eyebrows rose in question, and suddenly, it seemed hard to imagine that no one would fight us for this little boy. My emotions were all over the place. If I weren't careful, I'd give myself whiplash.

"Chelsea didn't have any family, but Legend has been staying with Chelsea's friend—"

"Dottie?" James interrupted her.

"Yes. Chelsea and Legend lived with her, so the court granted temporary custody to her until the paternity testing was completed and you were able to get back to Florida."

"So, he's okay?" The worry in James's eyes was something I'd never seen before—not on him. Although, I'd seen it cross my own father's expression countless times when I was a child.

"As well as can be expected. Chelsea did a good job of preparing him for her death."

"He's five...why would she have prepared him? Did she have cancer or something?" James wasn't quite as eloquent as I would have liked him to be. He responded based on emotion, and I'd just had an explosion of inappropriate laughter.

"Mr. Carpenter, Chelsea had juvenile Huntington disease."

"Her mom died of Huntingtons. I thought it took years, and the decline didn't start until her forties or later."

"I'm fairly ignorant about the disease; I just know that Chelsea was in late stage one when she was pregnant with Legend. Juvenile Huntingtons is very aggressive, and death usually occurs in less than ten years."

James sat there stunned, apparently unaware this girl had been affected by the disease at all. Although, now wasn't the time to ask him how he could have missed something so monumental.

"When will we meet him?" My question was soft and shy.

Somehow, I felt like it wasn't my place to ask. At the same time, this was my husband's son. Now *our* son. Nervousness and excitement rolled into an emotional ball of frenzy that whirled around inside my mind and did somersaults in my stomach. One minute the idea of James having a child was terrifying, and the next, almost natural. My heart and mind bounced over all the emotions in between, but never at the same time.

"Does he know about me?" James had been relatively quiet sitting next to me, so when he blurted out this question, it was as if the answer was the difference between life and death.

"He does. He's also been told that someone special is here to see him. Since you hadn't communicated what your intentions were, Dottie didn't think it was in his best interest to get his hopes up, and then you walk away."

"But he's mine. I get to keep him, right?"

"He's not a dog, James." I rolled my eyes at his insidious question, choosing to ignore that I could have done a five-minute comedy routine on the kid's name alone.

"Legally, yes. Chelsea named you his sole guardian and parent. However, if for some reason the two of you are averse to those roles, Dottie is prepared to have you sign over custody and all parental rights."

"She wants my kid?" My husband's face grew angry, and the crimson crept up his neck and into his cheeks.

"Not in a malicious, or even greedy way, Mr. Carpenter. She has been with Legend every day since he was born. She is the only family, other than Chelsea, he's ever had."

"But she has to be like a hundred years old," he screeched his disbelief.

"James." Now it was my turn to hiss at him.

The attorney chuckled at his outburst. I, on the other hand, was mortified. "I assure you, Mr. Carpenter, she only has Legend's best interest at heart. Dottie thought it would be best if you met Legend in a place less formal than this, one he'd be comfortable in."

"Like her house?"

I wanted to laugh at the expression on his face. Neither of us had a clue how to handle any of this. James was doing the best he could, even if he hadn't managed to hide his dismay.

"No, he likes to play at the park by the pier. She thought it would be a safe place for him to welcome you into his world."

My mind had retreated back to a place of uncertainty. This was about to happen, and I wasn't sure I could face it. If it hadn't meant leaving James, I would have been out that door without risk of it hitting me in the behind as it closed.

"When?" James's face was unreadable. His eyes danced with excitement, even though his knee bounced with anxiety, and his thumb stroked mine in soothing love. None of his body languages agreed with each other.

"Today at three if you're available." Karen's eyes were kind and understanding as if she'd dealt with this type of thing a hundred times before.

James glanced at me for approval, and I just nodded, wondering where the hell life would take us in two hours.

15

CORA

MOTHER NATURE HAD DELIVERED A PERFECT DAY TO MEET THE newest member of our family. I wanted to believe it was a sign that everything would work out. However, in the time since we'd left the offices of Clary, White, & Boyd, James had already pulled back. It had nothing to do with me and everything to do with the apprehension over meeting his son, who was not a newborn, but a child who knew little about him. I expected us to do this together, though now I felt like I was somehow intruding on their initial meeting.

"Do you not want me to go?"

We sat in the car at the end of the pier, staring out at a place the two of us had been hundreds of times before. It was as familiar to us as New York. I couldn't count the number of memories we shared on that very pier and along that shore.

"I do. I'm just afraid we'll overwhelm him. And I've never met Dottie. It's not you. I'm just a mess. I absolutely need you here, just bear with me. I'm flying by the seat of my pants, and I'm about to lose my shit." The only way past this was through it. He knew it; I knew it. Yet neither of us were comfortable with it.

With the windows down, it was easy to hear the waves in the distance and the seagulls crying. I didn't miss Geneva Key, but I missed the way the air smelled of salt and how the wind blew through my hair in even the slightest breeze.

From our vantage point, we could witness every person who approached the playground from the parking lot or the beach. It had remained vacant until a few minutes after three. I couldn't make out the features of either person who approached, other than it being an older woman and small boy.

"Do you think that's them?" James asked as if one of them was the boogeyman, and I'd somehow gained superhero powers to thwart him.

"I'd say it's a safe bet."

"Are you ready?"

I still wasn't convinced he wanted me to do this with him, but I'd regret staying behind. We were meeting our destiny—whatever that might be—and I was determined to be a part of it.

"As ready as I'm going to get." I put on a brave face and unbuckled my seatbelt.

James and I met at the front of the car, and hand in hand, the two of us made our way down the pier to our future.

The woman lingered on the opposite edge of the playground, while the little boy ran to the jungle gym and immediately started climbing like a monkey. His exuberance brought a genuine smile to my face, and when I glanced up at my husband, I saw the same exuberance shining brightly on his.

"Dottie, look at me!" the small child yelled to his friend as he hung upside down by his knees from the metal bar.

When he began to swing, she called back, "Be careful, Legend." Her silvery hair blew across her face when a gust of wind kicked up.

We stood at the edge of the pier and watched him play like any other kid. James squeezed my hand and met my eyes with wonder and love. I only hoped the two of us remained as optimistic while this all unfolded.

"Should we go introduce ourselves to Dottie first or Legend?" he asked as if I had the answers to this situation.

"I guess Dottie."

He took the first step, and I followed behind him. My feet slowed when we hit the sand, but James always accommodated my shorter steps. If we'd been any place else under any other circumstances, he would have had me get on his back—however, it would be inappropriate here.

The closer we got to the woman, the more familiar she looked; although, her gray hair that whipped with the wind and her relaxed beach attire threw me off. Her gaucho pants swayed with the air, and her feet were bare, but when she moved her hair from her face to tuck it behind her ear, my heart stopped and so did my feet.

"What's wrong?" James had continued to walk until my arm refused to follow. He turned to stare at me, wondering what was going on. He looked toward his target and back at me. "Cora?"

"That's my grandmother." When my heart started pumping again, it did so with a vengeance. The beat thumped loudly in my ears, drowning out the sounds of the waves and the giggles of the little boy on the playground. Not even the piercing cries of the seagulls could be heard.

"Baby, that's Dottie. You heard him call her name." His free hand took my jaw, and he kissed me sweetly on the lips "Come on. It's okay."

But it wasn't; none of this was. I knew my grandmother. He'd never met her. In all the time we'd been together, even in high school, not once had I ever introduced them. And while I needed answers, now wasn't the time to try to get them. I had no clue why my grandmother would have temporary custody of a five-year-old, nor why she would have been living with his mother—the woman who'd slept with James years ago.

The realization struck her the moment her attention pulled away from Legend to greet us.

Before she could speak, James stuck his hand out to introduce himself. "I'm James Carpenter, and this is my wife, Cora."

Her eyes were glued to mine when I identified her first. "Gwendolyn Chase," I spoke with malice and discontent. And refused to extend my hand as my husband had done.

"Cora." It was a whisper the waves could have carried in with the wind. Her eyes were filled with something akin to remorse, while mine remained hardened.

"Dottie, watch!" Legend drew our attention toward him as he did a flip off the bar and landed on his feet in the sand just before he bottomed out.

The little boy was captivating and charming and a temporary reprieve from the woman behind me. His fiery-red mop was overgrown and a tad shaggy, and the way the sun reflected off the slightly curled ends made him appear angelic. I couldn't help but notice his large, brown irises and the smattering of freckles that dotted his face and arms. And he was exceptionally tall. The only thing hinting at his younger age was the innocence in his sad eyes.

When he stood, he dusted the sand off the back of his shorts and then rubbed his hands together to remove the grit from them as well. It wasn't until then that he realized he had an audience greater than one. He stopped, didn't move an inch, and took his dad in from top to bottom before his eyes shifted to me. The grin that had fallen from his face when he first noticed us slowly appeared until the corners of his mouth tilted up in childlike innocence.

"Who's your friends?" He ran over to us as he spoke and then grabbed my grandmother's leg.

"This is your daddy and his wife, Cora."

"I'm Legend, it's very nice to make your acquaintance." His little hand jutted out like a confident man. First to me, which I eagerly took and shook, and then to James.

"He's been practicing that all afternoon." Dottie's eyes glimmered with pride, but I had a hard time not reaching up to gouge them out.

"It's nice to meet you, too, buddy." James had released my hand in order to squat and see his son at his level.

"You're really tall. Will I be as tall as you?" He rambled like most kids did, and I could already see adoration for James in his eyes.

"Maybe, it sure looks like you're well on your way."

"You wanna see the tricks I can do?"

"Of course. Show me what you've got." Legend took James by the hand, and with the first step they took, Gwendolyn was close on their heels.

I reached out, latching onto her forearm. Once the two of them got a few paces ahead, I whispered, "What are you doing here?" It was more like a hiss between clenched teeth, even though I tried to play nice.

She patted my fingers, and I jerked back, recoiling my arm. "Cora, sweetheart. Now isn't the time." And then she smiled at me in a way I'd never seen her do—as though she actually cared about someone other than herself. "Come on, don't let our past shape his future." She nodded toward Legend and James, but I wasn't sure which she referred to.

***

I managed to keep my cool at the playground, although only by the grace of God. We had stayed for about two hours and then wandered down the street to grab an early dinner. I was shocked by how easily James and Legend had fallen into a groove. He'd never indicated a desire for children, yet seeing him with the little redhead made it obvious he was a natural.

Luckily, Gwendolyn—or Dottie, whatever her name was—focused on James and Legend and left me to myself to stew over her reappearance in my life. Legend monopolized the conversation, telling James everything he'd ever done, all his favorite foods, favorite color—blue, favorite superhero—Green Lantern, and anything else that came to mind. I interjected where I could without disrupting the flow of the conversation, but mostly, I watched in disbelief. I witnessed a side of my husband I'd never seen and met a version of my grandmother I wasn't aware existed. And I wondered why she hadn't been that loving with me when my parents had passed away.

Here she sat with a child she wasn't even related to, playing the doting family friend, while she couldn't be bothered to stay home to help me acclimate to a new town and school when I was forced to leave New York. I couldn't decide whether to resent her more for it or be grateful she'd been here for Legend when he needed someone. Selfishly, I wanted to focus on the first, even if I knew it should be the last. It just didn't make any sense to me. The woman I'd just spent the last four hours with wasn't the one whose house I'd shared as a teenager or the one my father had painted a picture of. I liked Dottie, I loathed Gwendolyn, but I had a hard time differentiating between the two.

There was never a point during the afternoon or evening that provided an opening for me to pull my grandmother aside to find out what was going on, and we ended up leaving without Legend or an explanation.

Once we were back in the car, James put his hands on the steering wheel, and before he backed out of the parking space, he said, "That went really well. Don't you think?" He started to drive waiting for me to respond.

I was at a crossroad. Either I confirmed for him how well things went with Legend, or I brought up how unnerved I was by Gwendolyn's involvement. One would draw us closer while neglecting the other, and one would push us apart while accomplishing nothing.

"Yeah, it did. He's a great kid. I've never seen such an infectious smile. It was hard not to scoop him up in a hug and refuse to let go. Are you excited to spend some time alone with him tomorrow?"

Dottie thought it would be best to make a slower introduction and have Legend go home with her tonight and then us spend more time with him the following day. I agreed. Ripping him away from the only place he'd ever lived wasn't a good idea, although I hated thinking of him being so little in that enormous house. I'd felt lost there as a teenager, so I could only imagine how tough it would be for a small child.

"You ready to face the firing squad?" He acted as if seeing his parents would be worse than what I'd just endured. He hadn't had much of a relationship with them until the last few years, but they'd never been unkind to me, just indifferent.

"It won't be that bad. What did they say when you called them yesterday about us coming?"

"They were really excited we wanted to stay with them." The way his tone lingered told me that wasn't all. "But I didn't think this was news I should give them by phone."

"You haven't told them?" I screeched and jerked my head in his direction. "Are you insane? They're going to murder you in your sleep. I'm tired. I can't sleep with one eye open. We need to get a hotel."

He laughed like *any* of this was funny. "We'd have to leave the island. You know there's no hotel anywhere nearby. Plus, it's possible they might be excited."

His optimism wasn't humorous. His parents would not be the slightest bit amused by finding out they had a grandchild born out of wedlock five years after the fact. This was the stuff scandals were made of, and their appearance was of utmost importance in their circles. The Carpenters and the Chases ran in similar crowds—none of which approved of marrying outside of the pack, much less fathering children with people not of the same social standing.

I sat back hard against the seat and crossed my arms over my chest in protest. "Fine, it's your funeral."

"Don't be so melodramatic. I'm in my thirties; what are they going to do?"

"Disown you? Publicly humiliate you? Stone you? Burn you at the stake? Do you have a preference? If so, I'll try to get them to lean in that direction—possibly tar and feather? My powers of persuasion can be hard to resist."

He stopped and put the car into park. His hand slid up my thigh and rested between my legs, and then his lips were on mine. James could distract me from just about anything with his touch, but a make-out session at a stoplight wasn't going to get him anywhere with his parents. Or the car honking behind us. I fought him off with a laugh as the guy behind us came around the car, shaking his fist in irritation.

"Just drive. Might as well get this over with."

Geneva Key was a hop, skip, and a jump from one side of the island to the other, but we were only a hop away from the Carpenters' house. When we pulled up, the lights were on out front, and it was the same house I remembered visiting in high school. Not even the landscape seemed to have changed. But where there was always a butler or a maid who'd answered the door then, his mother welcomed us before we knocked.

Instantly, her arms were around her son, and she pecked him on the cheek. As quickly as she'd latched onto him, she let him go to embrace me. My arms were stuck at my sides, yet I did my best to return the greeting with an awkward pat on her back and a contorted grin she couldn't see. After she finally released me and blood returned to my limbs, I looked up to find Brock Carpenter standing behind her. His stern features had softened over the years, and the intimidating expression that had always lingered in his eyes had been replaced by warmth.

"Hey, son. It's good to see you and your beautiful bride." His baritone timbre made me blush.

Thankfully, he wasn't an affectionate man—at least, not with James or me. A man in a suit appeared flanking Brock's side before silently moving past us to grab our luggage.

Susan waved us along as she spoke. "Excuse my manners. Please, come inside. You must be tired from flying. There's fresh coffee and dessert in the kitchen."

"Actually, Mom, we got here this morning."

Oh crap, so *this* was how he planned to lay things out—just dump it all on the table and then sort out the pieces. It was the same way he put together a puzzle—zero logic or planning. James was not an outside-edge-first kind of guy, and he never looked at the picture on the box. No part of this scenario could go well. If I thought I could hold my breath during the entire revelation, I would, just so I didn't miss a single word. It was a sadistic kind of anticipation that my husband wouldn't fare well in.

"This morning? What on earth took you so long to get here?" she asked as she passed mugs and dessert plates around the island in the kitchen.

This was where his plan came to a grinding halt.

I loved my husband, but when it came to matters of the heart, he didn't take calculated risks—he went all in with everything he had. It was part of what made him such an amazing man and incredible lover—although, I didn't get the impression Brock and Susan Carpenter were going to be besotted with his admission.

"We had to stop by an attorney's office." When James paused, his father's brow drew in. However, he wasn't given long to interject before James continued. "And then we went to the playground at the pier. And we had dinner with my son." He took a sip of coffee as though he'd just told them we had enjoyed a sunset stroll along the shore.

I shouldn't have worried about missing anything over the sound of my breathing, because *nothing* was said. The silence was eerie and unnerving. More minutes ticked by with my attention flicking to each person huddled on barstools around the counter. The only one who met my gaze was Susan.

"Oh, Cora." Her eyes filled with tears, and those two words had me stumped.

"No." It instantly dawned on me what she'd assumed. "No, no. Susan, this didn't happen while we were married—or even together. It was while I was in France."

"That can't be right. That would make the little boy around four or five years old. Why are we just now finding out about this, James? Who else knows? Brock, did you hear that? We have a grandchild."

And *that* was exactly the reaction I expected from her.

"Just calm down, Mom." James's tone was far too harsh for his father's liking.

"Remember whose house you're in, son."

If I could have backed my stool away to avoid the line of fire without anyone noticing, I would have. I was close enough to get caught in the crosshairs from where I sat.

"Can everyone relax, please?" My husband pleaded with his parents, not so much with his voice, but his expression. His eyes said far more than his mouth, and thankfully, they both noticed it and stopped.

"Okay, son, we're listening." His mom's voice returned to the mellow tone she'd had when we arrived, before he'd dumped the weight of a tiny human on her unexpectedly.

He proceeded to tell them the events in the order in which they happened for us: the letter, the paternity test, the lawyer, telling me, the flight, meeting with the attorney, the playground, dinner, then here. They listened without so much as a peep, even though I could see the questions forming in his father's eyes.

"That's where we're at. *We* just met Legend a few hours ago, so it wasn't that I was keeping anything from you; I didn't have any information to give. I wasn't certain if I was even expected to take custody of him or if another family member was going to fight me. It's all a tad overwhelming."

"Legend? The boy's name is *Legend*?" Susan asked and James nodded in response. "Does he have our last name?"

I was about to lose my composure again. I could only imagine it was the stress of the situation that made a child's name so humorous —or unfortunate, however I looked at it.

"No, it's hers. Airy."

The glint of amusement tugged on her cheeks, which only served to feed my own issue. Both of us snickered, and neither man thought it was the slightest bit funny. Although, I doubted Brock had said the full name in his head.

"My grandson's name is Legend Airy?" She tried to cover her mouth as the laughter escaped, but she was as unsuccessful as I'd been at the attorney's office.

Just before James erupted in irritation, his father chuckled and tried to disguise it as a cough.

"Seriously? You guys are laughing at my son."

"No, baby…just his name," I choked out the words mid-chortle.

He threw his hands in the air. While I knew he was frustrated, it had completely diffused what was otherwise about to get out of hand quickly.

"When can we meet him?" His dad's question surprised me, and James, too.

"I'm not sure, Dad. I don't have a clue how all of this will work. He's lived here his entire life and just lost his mom. Are we supposed to tear him away and whisk him back to New York because that's what's convenient?"

I hadn't even thought about that. I assumed he would come home with us, but when James put it that way, my own history came rushing to mind. I had desperately wanted to stay with Faith in New

York after my parents passed away, and Gwendolyn and Owen had refused to even consider it. Now I wondered if we needed to contemplate staying here, at least for a while, for Legend to get to know us.

"We're spending the day with him tomorrow; maybe we could ask him if he'd like to meet your parents. If he's open to it, then I don't think it would hurt. Do you?"

His mom's face lifted in hope. She clapped her hands together and held her fingertips to her lips, waiting on James to respond.

"Would that work for you guys?" he asked them both.

Brock nodded to Susan, and she stepped around the island to throw her arms around her son. "Thank you, James." She never called him by his name—no one did. It was strange to hear.

As if someone had flicked a switch, the focus went from my husband to me by the least likely subject, Brock. "Cora, sweetheart, how are you handling all of this? I can't imagine it's easy finding out you're now the proud parent of another woman's child."

Other than Neil and Hannah, the Carpenters were the nearest thing I had to family—and we weren't close. Gwendolyn had sent me sporadic emails since the day I'd left Geneva Key, though I almost never read them and often just clicked delete. An email did not a relationship make. This might just be the very thing that changed the dynamic between the four of us, that opened a door that had been partially closed as long as I could remember. This could be the opportunity for us to create what we hoped for in a family.

"It's a struggle." I chose not to lie. In the end, it wouldn't do me any good. "But James and I weren't together when he met Chelsea, and she was a good friend to him when I was in France. I'm trying to be open to the situation while remembering there's an innocent child who was left in the middle between adults' mistakes." I offered Brock a meek smile.

"Cora never wanted children."

I was surprised James revealed that. Most people didn't understand and assumed I didn't like kids. Before his parents had a chance to respond, I offered my own explanation. "My parents died when I was a junior in high school. Children shouldn't go through that." I shrugged, acting as if it didn't matter, yet hoping it answered their questions without starting a discussion.

They continued talking around me, and my thoughts drifted back to a time before my parents had passed away. Unfortunately, I got stuck in a loop in the limo coming home from the concert, seeing Faith's face when she got the call, hearing myself cry out in disbelief. I hadn't talked to her in years and wondered how she had faired when we lost touch. I hadn't been able to maintain a relationship with her because it hurt so much, although every once in a while, she'd creep into my thoughts and I would once again regret pushing her away.

While they continued to talk—about what I no longer knew—I excused myself, needing some time alone.

***

I left my shoes at the house in favor of strolling on the beach barefoot. The sand was warm between my toes, and the waves licked it away as quickly as I took another step. I loved the dark blues of the sky just after the sun had gone down and the moon had taken its place. The ocean rippled with peaks of light, while the water appeared black. And the shades of indigo that turned onyx as they rose off the horizon reminded me of Van Gogh's *Starry Night*. It was picturesque in a way that belonged exclusively to Geneva Key and one of the few things I adored about this town.

James hadn't been given much longer to process this news than I had, but he had a couple days, and he seemed to be faring far better. I wanted to meet him at the place he was mentally, yet making that happen wasn't as easy as clicking my heels together. Since arriving in Geneva Key, my parents' death and what followed after had hung heavy in my mind and on my heart. I'd never been close to my grandparents, and the only truths I had were the things my father had told me growing up. He never made them out to be bad people, just indifferent—self-absorbed maybe. He'd always acted like Gwendolyn and Owen couldn't be bothered to spend holidays or special occasions with us because their life was on the road —business and charity. Yet I wondered—seeing Gwendolyn with Legend—if there hadn't been more to the story. Everything he'd said about them lined up perfectly with exactly what they'd done when I was forced to live on this little island a thousand miles away from the only life I'd known.

I couldn't remember the specifics of when Gwendolyn had actually tried to reach out; I just knew in high school how isolated I'd felt. And I believed then the only reason they'd taken custody was to keep up the image of who they were with their friends and business associates. But the woman I met today was nothing like the one whose house I'd lived in over a decade ago—not even her hair or her clothes resembled that person.

When I stopped long enough to take in my surroundings, I found myself on the beach behind my grandmother's house. I hadn't stepped foot in it since leaving Geneva Key at eighteen. The lights shined like beacons through the windows, and I could see people moving behind the curtains. It wasn't all that late, although, late enough that I imagined Legend would be in bed, and I might be able to talk to Gwendolyn alone. It wasn't a secret how she felt about visitors who arrived without invitations, but I hadn't cared what she thought before now, and I didn't let it stop me from ringing the bell at the front door.

I wasn't the least bit surprised when a woman I didn't recognize greeted me. Gwendolyn's staff had probably turned over ten times since I'd left for college.

"Hi, is Gwendolyn home?" I squared my shoulders and raised my chin with confidence.

"I'm sorry, you must have the wrong house."

I stepped back to inspect the front porch to confirm I hadn't somehow wandered up to the wrong place. "No, this is the right place. I'm looking for Gwendolyn Chase."

"This is the Morris residence, ma'am."

"That's not possible, my grandparents have lived here for years. Well, my grandfather passed away, but my grandmother lives here." I was rambling about stuff I was sure the woman didn't care about —she had to be mistaken.

"I'm sorry, ma'am. Mr. and Mrs. Morris have lived here for nearly a decade."

My stomach rose into what felt like my chest and bile lingered in the back of my throat. "I-I'm sorry to, um...to have bothered you. Thank you." I stammered most of the sentence and tried to ignore the look of pity in the woman's eyes. I felt like a fool.

Ten years. My grandmother hadn't lived in this house for ten years, and I wasn't aware of it. I couldn't fathom why she would have ever left; everyone knew where the Chase family lived—it was a statement just like their lives. Giving it up meant losing part of her identity. None of it made any sense. That mansion had been as important to them as their bank account. And she hadn't bothered to inform me she'd moved.

The tears only served to irritate me. I wasn't sad they'd left; that house meant nothing to me. And we weren't close so I couldn't figure out why I cared if she moved without sending me her new address. Yet some part of me felt violated and totally out of touch— a stranger to the only person remaining on this earth who shared my DNA. She'd moved on and left me behind.

I ran down the steps that led to the beach. The motion detectors illuminated a path as I navigated the stairs before my feet hit the warm sand, and the sounds of the crashing waves welcomed me back to the white space where time ceased to exist and noise was swallowed by the ocean. And there at the water's edge, I stood with my face tilted toward the moon and let the emotion fall from my eyes and the tides steal it away.

By the time I finally wandered back to the Carpenters' house, it was after ten, and most of the lights were out. James waited for me in the kitchen with a cup of freshly brewed coffee. He'd changed into jersey shorts without a shirt or socks, and his bare chest brought me home—back to the only comfort I'd had since my parents passed away. His skin was warm against mine, and his powerful arms tucked me into impenetrable security.

"Did you find what you were looking for?" he whispered into my ear.

I shook my head, sobbing into the crook of his neck. His hand stroked my hair, and he kissed my temple. James had been my rock since the day I'd laid eyes on him in Harbrook High, and I knew without a doubt, no matter what we had to go through, I'd never leave his side—because he'd never left mine.

16

CORA

"YOU READY TO GO, BUDDY?" JAMES APPEARED AS EXCITED AS Legend was when we got to Dottie's door.

I was too surprised by her new address to say much. She'd given it to James this morning when he called to arrange a time to get Legend. It was nothing like the home she and Owen had shared. We only stepped foot inside the foyer, but it was cozy and welcoming. There was no staff, she didn't have ten thousand feet of unused space, and there were pictures everywhere. I couldn't imagine what had happened to take her from the life of luxury that was prevalent when I was around to upper-middle-class suburbia now.

Just as we were about to leave, I met her stare and saw that same thing I'd witnessed yesterday, something similar to regret, although I still couldn't imagine why. And once again, it wasn't the time or the place to question what all had changed since I left Geneva Key, or why she hadn't been this attentive when I'd needed her most. So instead of poking the bear, I gave her a meager smile and a tiny wave over my shoulder before leaving with my husband and his son.

"You guys have fun. Just give me a call when you're ready to come home." Dottie cringed just slightly at the last word.

It had likely started to dawn on her that this wasn't going to be Legend's home much longer. And I had to wonder what role she planned to play in his life once we were gone and he was in New York. That too was a topic for another time, and certainly not one to be had in front of Legend. James and I had avoided it as eagerly as we had the presence of her in Legend's life to begin with. I assumed he feared lighting a flame inside me he couldn't extinguish along with the one he already fought figuring out he had a child.

The three of us hopped into the rental car and went back to the Carpenters' house to utilize their semi-private beach-front property. Legend didn't even notice the monstrosity of a house. His eyes were set on the sand and the water in front of us.

"Daddy, will you play in the waves with me?"

My heart skipped a beat hearing Legend call James "Daddy" for the first time. He hadn't hesitated, he wasn't unsure, he owned it as though James hadn't missed a single day of his life.

"Absolutely."

As soon as we were out of the car, I grabbed the bags from the back deck. James picked up Legend and swung him onto his shoulders. He jogged the rest of the way to the water's edge with Legend giggling and an enormous smile on his face. I was witnessing a side of James I'd never seen before, and it made me sad to think he'd desired children and never told me. He was a natural and exactly what Legend needed.

"Cora!" His little voice carried over the waves to where I laid out our towels and put up an umbrella. "Come in the water." He waved his hands to indicate just what water he meant.

I couldn't suppress the giggle or my desire to see him smile. Regardless of how my feelings had ricocheted back and forth about the situation, being in Legend's presence seemed to wash away the reality of what we were up against. Chelsea had given us a gift so precious, yet I hadn't even known I'd wanted it. I shimmied out of my shorts and removed my tank top. Just before I took off toward the man I loved and his little boy I'd grown undeniably smitten with, I kicked off my flip-flops and pulled up my hair. I'd never enjoyed the beach as much as I did that morning. The world around us ceased to exist, settling in together, splashing and having fun.

I never thought I'd be enamored with a child I barely knew and had just met, yet every time I picked up his little body, or he went chasing after a ball he'd dropped, or sent a Frisbee flying into the water, I couldn't stop the smile that spread across my face or the joy that filled my heart. Legend exuded personality and vibrancy—he was infectious in the best possible way. And each time that thought crossed my mind, a twinge of regret followed—I'd never get to meet the woman who'd raised such a gentle soul.

"Daddy, do you have floats at your mama's house?"

"I'm sure they do. Want me to go find out?"

His red head bobbed eagerly.

"You mind staying with him while I run up to the house?"

I waved him off as though his question was insipid, while inside, I was slightly terrified. The waves were huge, and the ocean could be a dangerous place. It would only take one wrong move for Legend to slip into the undertow and me not be able to get him back to safety. He was a strong swimmer for his age, but I held my breath until James returned. We laughed at him bouncing down the shore with two long rafts and a tube that beat against his legs with every step he took.

When he finally arrived back in the water, I released the panic I'd held inside and helped Legend into the tube. And as soon as I lay down on the raft James had given me, Legend reached out to me.

"Cora, hold my hand, so the waves don't take you away."

I was in awe of a child who had lost his mother being able to enjoy the world around him and worry about other people. At that moment, I realized just how great his capacity for love was, and how lucky we were to have him come into our lives when he had.

We'd only spent a handful of hours with him, yet somehow, I couldn't imagine never having met him.

Lying there, rolling with the motion of the water beneath me and the sun shining down, I let my mind go quiet and quit overthinking everything. And just as I'd settled under the warmth of the day with my eyes closed, certain James had one of Legend's hands and I had the other, I heard his little voice.

"My mama would think you're pretty."

I shielded my brow with my fingers to look his direction. His chocolate-brown eyes stared back at me with a hint of sadness he clearly fought. Before I could say anything, he kept speaking.

"She told me how much my daddy loved you, and when her turn with me was over, that you would be special. I'm glad she was right." His bottom lip trembled with his admission.

My heart firmly lodged itself in my throat, and I hopped off the float to find my feet planted on the ocean floor. I didn't ask Legend's permission or even look at James. My hands reached under the little boy's arms, pulled him from the tube, and held him against my chest. I knew firsthand the pain he was in, but his mom had promised him he would be loved even after she was gone, and he'd believed her. Chelsea had put so much trust in me that she encouraged her son to love me blindly—without ever having laid eyes on me or exchanged a single word. And for that, I was grateful. Even more, the faith of this child brought me to my knees.

"Oh, buddy, thank you," I whispered into his ear, hoping he could hear me although not caring to share our truth with anyone else. "I know how much it hurts. I hope you'll tell me all about her. Every day." I vowed to myself to ensure he remembered the way she loved him and the memories they collected in the short time they had together. I'd had seventeen years with my parents, and the memories weren't nearly as sharp as they were then. His would fade quickly if James and I didn't ensure he didn't forget.

"I promise."

I hadn't paid any attention to James getting off the raft when he lost hold of Legend's hand, and when I finally opened my eyes and still had Legend securely in my embrace, I looked over the little boy's shoulder to see his father biting back tears. Somehow, James knew Legend and I were bound by a loss he would never understand. He would never experience losing a parent as a child. That one exchange, just a handful of words, tied my heart to a child I wasn't aware I needed, yet now, I couldn't imagine never having.

When Susan and Brock appeared under the umbrella, it signaled lunchtime and the perfect way to escape the emotional overload. They were as excited to meet Legend as James had been. I'd never thought of them as the grandparent type, but here they were almost bouncing on their toes, waiting for us to come out of the water.

***

"James, your parents are here. And they brought lunch." I propped Legend on my hip like I'd done it a thousand times in the last five years and pointed at the huge picnic basket Brock held at his side. It had been the plan, but seeing the size of the basket, I wondered if they'd packed enough food to feed us for days instead of just one meal.

"Why don't you take Legend up there, and I'll get the floats."

I had forgotten all about the tube and raft that had drifted a bit when we hopped off them. James rounded them up while we climbed out of the waist-high waves and back onto stable ground.

When I put Legend down, he pulled on my hand and clutched it tightly. "Who are they?" he asked as he pointed under our umbrella. He hadn't shown an ounce of fear with James or me, yet suddenly, his trepidation was front and center.

"Those are your grandparents. Are you excited to meet them?" I'd raised the tone of my voice half an octave to try to convince him there was nothing to be afraid of. Clearly, it hadn't worked.

"I'm not supposed to talk to strangers, Cora." His generally wide eyes squinted in the sun as he stared up at me.

"They won't be strangers soon. They're your daddy's parents, and I promise, you'll love them as much as they do you."

He took a hesitant step in their direction. "They don't know me."

I squatted next to him and took his chin between my fingers. With a genuine smile, I said, "Remember how your mama told you about your daddy and me?" I continued talking when he nodded. "Your daddy told his parents all about you. And they can't wait to meet you."

"Do you think they have cake?"

I hoped like hell they did. I was also certain if they didn't, Susan would make a call and have one at our fingertips in thirty minutes. "Maybe, but if not, I bet we can make that happen. What's your favorite kind?"

We started walking with James on our heels.

"Carrot cake."

I ruffled his hair. Of course it was.

"Mine's red velvet."

"What about Daddy?" I realized there was so much none of us knew about each other and how much I enjoyed these simple questions.

"Vanilla."

"That's boring. Does he at least like it with sprinkles?"

"Nope. Just vanilla cake and vanilla icing. Maybe you can convince him otherwise. He has a birthday coming up, and I'm sure he'll like anything you pick out."

"You must be Legend," Susan exclaimed as she clapped her hands together and kneeled in front of him.

"Cora said my daddy has a birthday soon, and I can pick out his cake."

Susan grinned wide, and Brock burst out with laughter. "White on white. That's all your daddy likes, son."

"Wait, who said you could pick out my cake?" James grabbed

Legend, swung him into his arms, and dug his fingers into his son's sides.

He erupted into a fit of giggles and pointed at me. "Cora did."

"Oh, she did, huh? Then maybe we should get her." And suddenly the two of them were both after me, poking me every chance they could, trying to get me to laugh.

I finally collapsed on the towel under the umbrella, and Legend hopped in my lap.

"Grandma, did you bring us something to eat?" He hadn't been told what to call her, but she beamed with pride at his declaration and acceptance of who she was in his life. Only a child could get away with the innocent way he brought us into his world.

My arms circled his chest in a hug I hoped conveyed to Legend what words failed to say.

"I did, and Papa brought some chairs for us all to sit in so we don't get sandy."

"What's in your basket, Papa?" And just like that, we were all in Legend's fold.

The five of us sat under the umbrella eating roast beef sandwiches, potato salad, and grapes. Susan and Brock asked Legend so many questions I was afraid his jaw would get tired between chewing and talking, but he ate up the attention as quickly as he did his lunch. He was well-mannered and equally well-behaved. I wondered how Chelsea managed to raise such a well-rounded child while managing a life-threatening disease.

"You have a big house, Papa. Do lots of people live with you?"

"Just me and your grandma. Although right now, your daddy and Cora are staying with us, too. Maybe you can spend the night with us before you guys go home."

"Where do you live?" Legend asked James while looking to me for the answer.

"In New York. Do you know where that is?" I tried to remember just how young he was. He hadn't started school yet, and I wasn't sure he'd ever been out of Geneva Key.

"That's a long way away from my Dottie." His expression turned sour, and he didn't say anything else.

"Who's Dottie?" Susan asked, unsure of what was going on.

"She was my mama's best friend. And her mama's, too."

"That's who Chelsea and Legend lived with. Dottie took care of Legend until we could get here." James pleaded silently with his parents not to ask more questions. Unfortunately, his mother missed the clue.

"I've lived here all my life. There's no one named Dottie on the island." Her gaze went back and forth to James and me before landing firmly on me...waiting.

"Dottie is Gwendolyn Chase." I let those words hang in the air so his parents could fully absorb the weight of what we'd walked into upon arriving in Geneva Key.

"Your grandmo—"

I cut her off with a wave of my hand before she could complete that thought.

"I thought she moved after Owen passed away?"

"I wasn't aware she'd moved at all, so you have more information than I do at this point." I shook my head. "Dottie and I need to find some time to sit down and talk. Up 'til now, other things have been more important."

Brock appeared irritated...although, I couldn't figure out why. I should be the one who was irate, but Dottie, or Gwendolyn—whatever she went by these days—was the least of my concerns right now. Clearly, I wasn't the only one stunned by this turn of events or how all the pieces fit together. In time, I hoped to be able to answer his parents' questions because it would mean I had answers to my own.

"I don't want to go to New York, Daddy." He'd been stewing while we talked.

James stared at me, and I shrugged. Our home, our lives, our friends, James's business—it was all in New York. And Legend was in Geneva Key…the one place we both loathed.

"We don't have to figure that out right now. Let's just enjoy the day. Okay?"

"Do you have cake?" He turned toward Susan, and I couldn't stop the laugh that escaped realizing he had a one-track mind.

"Will cupcakes work? I have chocolate and vanilla."

"That's pretty good. You didn't know my favorite is carrot cake. But now you do." He eagerly picked up the little dessert. "Thank you." His eyes were bright and sparkled in the sun.

"You're most welcome. And I promise, next time, I'll have carrot cake just for you."

"Cora's favorite is red velvet. If you have two flavors."

"I'll remember that, too." She handed him a napkin to wipe the icing from his freckled cheeks.

He'd taken one big bite, determined he liked it, and stuffed the rest into his mouth at once. Before I could stop him, he bit down and went to town with a smile from ear to ear and chocolate cake crumbs falling from his lips.

"That's so gross." I giggled and scrunched up my nose.

When he finished, he begged James to take him back out to the water and make a sand castle on the shore. I waved the two of them off in favor of lying back under the shade of the umbrella in the chair Brock brought.

I had just shut my eyes when Susan asked, "How on earth did your grandmother end up with custody of our grandson, and none of us were aware of it?"

"That's the million-dollar question, Susan. And I don't have a clue."

"Sweetheart, I'm sure you're as confused as we are, but Gwendolyn owes you some answers. Don't leave here without them."

I didn't respond. I didn't want to have that discussion with

Gwendolyn, even if it was inevitable. I just worried how it would change my past and shape my future. Whatever pieces linked us all together were likely more than I'd be able to handle.

James's parents spent the rest of the afternoon with the three of us on the beach. We each took turns playing with Legend in the sun, lathering him in sunblock, and wrapping him in a towel. And just as soon as we thought he was done for the day, he'd take off to the water's edge to jump around in the waves and splash with childish delight. I couldn't remember the last time I'd smiled as much as I had today, and the same was true of James. Legend had brought something into all four of our lives that was unexpected yet greatly appreciated.

We finally called it a day as the sun started to set. Susan and Brock had brought enough food and snacks that we'd forgone dinner and grazed throughout the afternoon. I could tell James was reluctant to drop Legend off at Dottie's, even though we did it just the same. After making plans to get Legend in the morning, my grandmother stopped me.

"Cora, why don't you let James and Legend spend some time together tomorrow and the two of us meet for coffee at the diner on Main Street?"

"Sure, would nine o'clock work for you?"

"I'll see you then."

I could only imagine what information Gwendolyn was going to share or what she might reveal that she believed could explain away her involvement in Chelsea's life or lack of one in mine.

***

I walked to the coffee shop from the Carpenters' house. It was only a few blocks and helped to expel some of the nervous energy I'd accumulated since last night. I had zero desire to do this, but I was grateful she'd suggested a public place. It would force me to maintain my composure. I hadn't realized until I saw Gwendolyn just how much pent-up aggression I harbored for her. Somehow, I'd convinced myself over the years that I was as aloof as she was. I'd allowed myself to believe she wasn't capable of anything different. That's what my dad had told me all my life, so I didn't think it was me she avoided. Clearly, that wasn't the case—she *was* capable of loving someone besides my grandfather...just not me.

When she joined me promptly at nine, I had a cup of coffee in my hand. I waited to order breakfast in case I had to make a quick exit. I had enough cash for what was on the table and a tip, and if I ordered food, I'd have to use a card to pay. This seemed like the most logical plan, or irrational, I hadn't decided which.

"Thanks for coming. I'm sorry it's taken us so long to find time to talk."

The waitress welcomed her, and she ordered her own coffee before setting a napkin in her lap.

"Why didn't you tell me you moved?" I didn't give her a chance to lead into whatever she hoped to discuss, and I had no idea why that one tidbit was so important.

She sighed. "I tried, Cora. You haven't exactly been receptive to communication."

"So it's my fault?"

"No, it's not." She poured cream and sugar into the mug the waitress set in front of her. "I made a lot of mistakes along the way, especially when you were younger, but I've tried to stay in touch with you since you went to college."

"With monthly e-mails and bi-weekly calls?" My question was snotty and disrespectful.

"How else would you have had me reach you? If it hadn't been for occasional withdrawals from your trust fund, I wouldn't have had a clue what city you were in."

"You could have found a way," I spat my self-righteous opinion her direction.

"I suppose I could have. But I didn't know what else to do, Cora. I tried all through your childhood to reach out, to get your parents to visit or let me and your grandfather come see you. I mailed cards and presents, all of which were refused. Every attempt I made was turned down or returned to sender."

"I don't believe you. My dad never would have kept me from you." I didn't recognize my own voice it was so sinister and unforgiving. This was not who I was as a person and not someone I cared to become. Somehow, my mind justified my snarly disposition with years of hurt by the woman seated across from me.

"There's a lot you weren't privy to. Things I'd like to share with you. But you have to be in a place to open your eyes to the truth, and it might not be what you're expecting."

"If the version paints you as a saint and my dad as a sinner, you're right, it won't be what I'm expecting nor anything I'm interested in."

"I'm no saint, but your father wasn't, either. We both made mistakes—some I regret and others I cherish."

"Just tell me why you sold the house." I wasn't ready for a frontal attack on my father. It was the last thing I'd expected, and I couldn't defend against it. This was a safe place to start, one where I might begin to understand her better.

She stirred her coffee with a spoon and let out a long sigh. "The house was never important to me. Your grandfather was driven by image and how we were viewed, in this community and the business world as well. Everything always had to appear a certain way. How we dressed, the cars we drove, the house we lived in—in his mind, they all said something about our success. He worked hard to maintain that picture, and as his wife, I did my best to help him— that was my role. But when he passed away, it wasn't who I wanted to be or how I chose to live."

"Would you guys like to order anything for breakfast?" The waitress smiled, completely unaware she'd interrupted anything.

"I'd like a bowl of fruit. Cora, would you like anything?"

I shook my head. "Coffee's fine for now, thank you."

When she retreated, Gwendolyn returned to her story without skipping a beat. "The house was too much for one person, and I wasn't interested in managing a staff. When I sold it, I bought the cottage I live in now. I downsized just about everything in my life. The only traveling I did was in support of the Huntington Foundation and their fundraisers."

"Is that how you met Chelsea and her mom?"

"It's how I got to know them." Her eyes smiled at the memory, even if her lips didn't. "I dropped the designer suits in favor of more comfortable clothing I could breathe in and stopped wearing my hair so tight that it looked like I'd had a facelift. All in all, I just relaxed and began to enjoy the slower pace of life in Geneva Key."

"I didn't even know you'd moved, Gwendolyn."

"Please, call me Dottie. Maybe if I had been invited to your wedding, I could have told you then."

"Would you have come?"

"Of course. But in fairness, you didn't know that. Which is one of many things I regret. There was little I could do when your father refused to let me see you, then when you came here, after he passed away, I should have done something to bridge that gap."

"You could have started by not taking off the day after I got here," I muttered under my breath, although I didn't try to keep her from hearing what I'd said.

"Yes, that would have been a good place to start. I wish I could go back and change those days, Cora. I truly do. At this point, all I can do is move forward and learn from them. And that's what I've tried to do. I hope you'll find it in your heart to hear the whole story and find a way to forgive me."

"We're basically strangers, Gwe—Dottie. I'm not sure there's need."

"I can tell you the only reason that matters, and what you do with it is up to you."

"What's that?"

"Legend."

"He'll adjust to New York just like I was forced to adjust here."

"If I had it to do over again, I would have let you stay with Faith. But if I had, you never would have met your husband, and your life would be totally different. I hope you'll remember what it was like to be ripped away from the only person you felt safe with when your parents died as you and James consider taking Legend away from Geneva Key."

"You're not going to guilt me into staying here. This isn't my home. It never has been."

"No, but it is *his*. And when you start thinking like a mother, your stance will change."

"Oh, is that what you're doing? Thinking like a mother? I must have missed the part where mothers leave their kids with paid staff instead of holding and hugging them through their grief. It doesn't matter *where* he is as long as he's loved and has attention."

I threw my cash down on the table, thankful I hadn't bothered ordering more. Grabbing my purse, I slid from the booth and glared in Dottie's direction. "Make no mistake, you can't atone for your sins by living through someone else."

Her eyes brimmed with tears, and I ignored them as I stormed out of the diner and into the warm, Florida air.

CORA

I WALKED UNTIL MY FEET HURT. GENEVA KEY WASN'T HUGE, YET BY the time I'd made it from the diner to the edge of the island, I felt like I'd climbed Mt. Everest in sandals. She infuriated me; everything about her just rubbed me the wrong way. I should have figured she'd try to paint my dad out to be the villain when he wasn't here to defend himself.

When I finally removed my sandals and started to make my way back to the Carpenters' house—via the sand instead of the sidewalks —each step lessened the frustration I felt toward my grandmother and brought me a tad bit closer to understanding. She was my only option for answers. There was no one left who knew anything about my parents. I either gained what information I could from her, or when she passed away, it would be lost forever.

I tried to believe I'd be able to discern the truth from lies, but it had been a lot of years since I'd heard my father's voice or held my mother's hand. I wasn't sure I'd recognize the difference between her story and theirs, and no matter what happened, I didn't want to lose what my parents had given me. I clung to their memories like a safety net that would prevent me from ever falling.

Without sunscreen on, I feared my fair skin would cook in the

Florida heat. I'd already been outside too long in nothing other than a strapless dress, so when I got to the Carpenters', I went inside hoping no one was home. To my dismay, not only did I find James in the kitchen when I thought he'd be with Legend, but his parents were there as well.

"Where's Legend?" I asked as I rinsed the sand off my shoes in the kitchen sink.

"He's upstairs taking a nap."

I glanced at my watch and gathered it was almost three in the afternoon. "I didn't realize how late it was. He must have been really tired."

"He fell asleep in the car after we went to the playground and had lunch. I'm glad you're home, though. I was hoping we could all talk about our options." James was apprehensive. I wasn't sure if it was because he and I hadn't discussed this or because he worried about what his parents would think.

"Okay." I set my shoes on the rug near the door and took a seat at the bar with him and his parents. "What's on your mind?"

"We need to figure out what we're doing. How long are we staying in Geneva Key? What are we doing with Legend? How does Dottie fit into that picture? How do my parents fit into it? This is different than us having a baby, and I can't figure out which way is up. Right now, it's all new and fun, but at some point, life has to resume."

"What do you *want* to do?" I shouldn't feel like I was being hit upside the head with this. We'd both known it was coming; James had just been the first one to say it out loud.

"I think what I'd prefer and what Legend needs are vastly different scenarios."

"Son, Legend needs to be with his dad. The rest will work itself out." His father believed it was all cut and dry. I knew that wasn't true.

"Brock, don't make things so simplistic. There's more to

consider than James's presence in the boy's life. His home is here, the only family he's had his whole life is here, we're here. The thing missing is his mother who won't be back. If James and Cora take him away right now, that could be detrimental to his well-being and forever alter his personality."

"Cora?" The way James said my name told my input was far more valuable than anyone else's in this kitchen. "You're the only one who's been where Legend is. I need you to tell me what to do."

People always thought there was only one answer to every problem. Yet the truth was, I could see good and bad in what my grandparents had done with me. "I wished my grandparents had left me in New York after my parents died. That was where my friends were, my school, Faith—my life. I didn't know my grandparents, and Geneva Key was a lifetime away from the things that mattered."

"So you think Legend needs to stay here?"

I shook my head. "James, if my grandparents hadn't made the choices they did, I never would have met you. So looking back, I can't say their decision was wrong; it just hurt at the time they made it. I also think they could have been more involved and helped make the transition easier, which they didn't do."

"So you think we should go back to New York?" Confusion marred his face.

"No, I think we have to consider both sides, make the best decision we can, and hope we don't screw him up in the process." It wasn't any more of an answer than he'd had before he asked the question.

James pulled on his hair in frustration, and his blue eyes looked weary. I'd never seen him this way; decisions had always come easily for my husband. As long as I'd been by his side, he never hesitated.

Susan chimed in softly, "Where do you think Legend needs to be, James?"

I already knew this answer, but my husband had to come to it on his own. Working out the logistics afterward was just a matter of phone calls and paperwork. James's hesitation didn't come from what he believed was best for Legend—he worried about me.

"Geneva Key." His eyes cast down to the counter, and when he blinked, a tear slid down his cheek. He was afraid I'd leave him if he chose to stay.

I looked at Susan and Brock. "Can you guys give us a few minutes?"

I waited for them to leave before lifting his chin. "Why are you crying?"

"I know you hate it here. I just don't think we can move him… not right now."

My thumb stroked his cheek, and I got lost in my love for the man he'd grown in to. We'd come so far since we lived in this town, and nothing would ever hold us back. James was my world, and it wouldn't be long before Legend sat in the number one seat. I'd do whatever I had to in order to keep them both happy. And if that meant Geneva Key, then we were moving to Florida for the foreseeable future. I wasn't keen on selling our house in New York and had no clue what James would do about the business, but if we wanted it to, it would work itself out.

"If this is where we need to be, then this is where we stay." The words came out with more conviction than I felt, yet they were still true.

"God, I love you. I'm so sorry you're going through all this. It must be like reliving your own personal hell." His lips pressed against mine in an intimate apology that wasn't necessary, although, it felt good just the same.

"I love you, too. Maybe this is how my own demons will be laid to rest. You never know what's in store for us or what we might learn by putting someone else first. We both have to be open to whatever life throws our way in the next few months."

"You going to extend that same attitude toward Dottie?"

"Don't get crazy." I giggled and hugged his neck.

"Maybe you should hear her out. I get the impression by the blisters on your heels that you didn't spend much time talking to her this morning. It looks like you spent more of it pounding your aggression out on the pavement. How many miles did you run?"

"No running, just a lot of walking. And I will, in my time. I'm just not ready, yet."

"Don't wait too long, Cora."

"When did you go all carpe diem on me?"

"The day I gained a son and realized what all I stood to lose."

I couldn't handle much more of this; I needed levity but couldn't find one smartass thing to say or one snarky comment to make.

We sat in silence for several minutes before I finally asked, "Do you think your parents will let us stay here while we figure things out?"

"The better question is, do you *want* to stay here while we figure things out. It feels weird sleeping in the same bed with you under their roof, and I'm not sure how long I can go without having sex."

"Why can't we have sex?"

"What if they hear you? You're not exactly quiet when you scream my name."

"Last I recall, it was you begging me to bring you release, not the other way around."

"Just because you get off easier than I do doesn't mean you're not loud. My mother will get scared when she hears you wailing like a banshee. Even worse, what if she calls the cops because she thinks I'm hurting you?"

"You're far too full of your sexual abilities, Mr. Carpenter. I think I'll take my chances staying here. If you get the heebie-jeebies frolicking in your parents' house, then I guess we'll just have to get creative." I moved to stand between his legs and pulled him close.

He was so easy to arouse and fun to play with. There was no

doubt in my mind that if I tried to get him to play right here and now, James Carpenter wouldn't turn me down. Testing the theory, I cupped his balls in my hand and made love to his lips. And just as I thought, being in his parents' home, in their kitchen with them only feet away, had done nothing to his drive—he'd hardened in my hand and been as responsive as he always was.

I pulled away, breathless, only to find he had pitched a tent for all the world to see. Through my giggles I told him, "Put that thing away. You don't want your parents to see it."

"I'm pretty sure they assume I'm attracted to my wife. I'd be willing to guess they even think we have sex."

"No need for them to see the evidence." I winked and went to find his parents.

They hadn't gone far—just around the corner. There was little doubt remaining that they'd heard everything we said. Brock couldn't stifle his laughter, and Susan was seven shades of pink—all of which looked good on her.

***

It had taken a few days to iron out details with Neil about the business. Most of what he did was by phone and computer anyhow, so the clients weren't aware of the difference. The one who picked up the slack was Neil, although he hadn't hesitated to do what was needed. There were only a few weeks left before Legend started school, which also meant, we only had about a month to decide whether we were staying in Geneva Key or going back to New York. Neil couldn't manage the business this way forever.

"Hey, baby," my husband cooed into my ear just before he wrapped his solid arms around my waist and pulled me in close. "What are you looking at?"

I pointed at his mother and Dottie down on the beach with Legend. Never in a million years did I imagine I'd be standing on the island watching James's son play in the surf, much less with Susan and my grandmother. "Just thinking how ironic it is that she was never able to be a grandparent to me, yet she's so amazing with him."

"Maybe our being here is the universe's way of giving the two of you a second chance," he spoke with his mouth tucked next to my ear as we continued to watch from the kitchen.

"Then I guess the universe is a sadistic bitch because I don't see that happening before hell freezes over."

He stood straight and turned me in his arms, pressing my back against the counter. "Cora, she means a lot to Legend. We're going to have to find a way around your animosity."

My jaw dropped in shock. I understood where he was coming from, but the woman had basically abandoned me when my parents died after forcing me to move to Florida. He already faced enough with his job and child; adding my drama to the mix wasn't fair. I was an adult, and he was right…I needed to find a way around my disdain for Gwendolyn.

"I don't know how to do it. I want to get back to the woman I was a week ago—the fun one you adored."

"I still adore you. I just hate seeing you so torn."

"My emotions are all over the place. One part of me is head-over-heels in love with this fantastic child we get to keep. A child I had no desire for until he hung upside down on the monkey bars in the sand giggling. Another part is stuck on the animosity I feel for my grandmother. And then there's this part I wasn't expecting at all that wishes I'd met Chelsea, or at the very least, could thank her for *that*." I pointed out the window to Legend and tears gathered in my eyes.

"She must have been a great mom."

"Right? He's the poster child for perfect kids." I swallowed hard before continuing. "We have to keep Chelsea alive in his memories, James. She promised him we would love him, and it's our duty to remind him daily how much he loves her so his memories don't fade. My grandparents never did that for me—"

"I'm glad I found you both together," Brock's voice boomed from the other side of the kitchen, interrupting our conversation. "I wanted to talk to you about a proposition I have."

James groaned behind me. "This ought to be interesting."

I smacked him playfully, wondering why he didn't think he should be making the same effort to build bridges with his parents when I had to make concessions. If Legend was our priority, then that not only left me finding a way to close gaps—James had to as well.

"Hey, Brock. What's up?"

He took a stool in front of us, and for some reason, the large kitchen seemed to dwarf him where he was normally a captivating, or even intimidating, part of a room. I'd grown to really like both of James's parents in the week or so we'd been here—time had softened them greatly.

"I understand the two of you haven't made any final plans about whether you're going to stay in Geneva Key or go back to New York, but I wanted to offer you a job, James. I don't need you to give me an answer today; just be aware that the offer is on the table, so that it's not a consideration in your choice to stay in New York or move back to Florida." He sat there smiling as though he were proud to be able to provide his son a viable solution, not as though he held something over our heads.

James's silence indicated he was equally dumbfounded. Their relationship had grown leaps and bounds in the last few years, but neither of us expected this. While we hadn't figured out the best plan, having one major problem solved, if we chose to stay, was monumental.

"Thanks, Dad. I'm kind of speechless at the moment."

"If you stay in Geneva Key, your mother and I want to do everything we can to make the transition easier. Employment is hard to come by here—at least anything you could live on—and you don't need to face that burden. You could live off your trust fund while

251

you work things out, but based on how infrequently you've made any withdrawals, I assume you won't do that. And I don't think you should—a man should provide for his family. The two of you need to do what's best for you and not be forced into either place." He smacked his hands on his thighs just before he stood. "Just something to think about." And he turned and left as quickly as he'd joined us.

"That was unexpected," James said to no one in particular.

"Your parents are really trying."

If I planned to make the most of the opportunity for healing, that didn't just mean becoming friends with the Carpenters or accepting Legend—that also meant making peace with Gwendolyn and my past.

***

"Daddy, can we have a slumber party tonight?" Legend lay on a towel in the sun with his hands behind his head and his feet kicked out.

Other than his jabbering, the rest of us had been rather quiet. I was sure Gwendolyn and Susan were worn out having spent the day playing on the beach with a rambunctious boy, and I was just lost in my thoughts. I didn't have a clue what to say when my grandmother was around, and I didn't care to chance things erupting into an argument if one of us said something the other took offense to. Legend loved her, and I wouldn't do anything to tarnish that. Although, I had to admit, it was taking a toll on me and bringing me down. I wasn't the type to hold a grudge—or at least I never thought I was. I'd also never been put in the position I was in with Gwendolyn. In the long run, this emotional back and forth would do nothing other than hurt the people I loved.

"What do you think, Cora? Should we let the little monster crash the Carpenter pad?"

"I'm not a monster. I'm a superhero." Legend stood and flexed his muscles to show us his power.

I reached out and tickled his sides, turning him back to the giggly mush he normally was. "I think that would be wonderful." And then I realized, we hadn't mentioned it to Gwendolyn—just before it dawned on me, we didn't have to. James had custody and was Legend's legal guardian, not to mention, father. Yet out of courtesy, I asked, "Would that be okay with you, Gwendolyn?"

She seemed as surprised by my request as I was, but James offered me a gentle smile, knowing how hard it was for me to ask her for anything, let alone permission.

"I'm sure he'd love that." A tear glistened in her eye, and she turned away to remove the evidence before it fell.

"You hear that, buddy? You get to spend the night with us. What do you want to do?"

"Can we play hide-and-seek? I bet there's a ton of places to hide in that big house. Oh, can we get pizza? Dottie doesn't like pizza, and we haven't had it since my mama got sick. Or maybe ice cream for dinner? That would be cool."

"How about pizza for dinner and ice cream for dessert?" James tried to negotiate. Legend hadn't figured it out yet, but if he put up any sort of fight, James would concede.

"Hide-and-seek?" The kid was smart. He aimed to get everything he was after.

"Of course," James agreed.

"Can we go now? Dottie's baked like chicken and tough like a shoe. She needs a nap because she's old, too."

I couldn't stop my laughter. "You're just like your dad. I think you got a few similes mixed up."

He didn't have a clue what a simile was, but he beamed at being compared to his father. And I couldn't stop giggling at this little version of my husband. They looked nothing alike, but even at five, I saw so many of James's traits in him. The way he laughed, the way he thought, the way he pulled his hair when he was frustrated —it was like a miniature replica of the man I loved, and for the first time in my life, I wondered what our children would have been like.

"Why don't I run home and pack a bag for you?"

"Thanks, Dottie. That would be great." James grabbed Legend and ran toward the water with him under his arm like a football.

Gwendolyn gathered her things and shook out her towel. I'd noticed the more time we spent with Legend, the more subdued she became. And as she said goodbye with a promise to return with clothes for Legend after showering, it dawned on me what all she would lose if we took him to New York.

"Do you need help?" My offer came out before I could stop it.

"Thank you. I can manage. I'll see you both in a little while." She waved at me and then to Susan before walking up the boardwalk to her car.

Any thoughts I had earlier about the possibility of wanting children were squashed by the end of the night. I was too old to chase multiple kids around an enormous house. By the time we finally got Legend to sleep, I was exhausted, and James could barely move. Legend had so much energy even after being zapped by the sun for hours.

When I finally dropped my weary body onto the bed next to James, I didn't think I'd be able to keep my eyes open for five more minutes. "It's a good thing we don't have more kids. I don't have a clue how people do this."

I crawled under the covers with my husband. No matter what the day brought or how it ended, this was my favorite place to be— in his arms. It soothed any ailment and fought back demons. James had been my haven since the day we met. He kissed my forehead, and I closed my eyes. Although, it seemed as soon as I'd drifted off, I woke to frantic cries from the room next door.

Without thought, I threw the blankets back and dashed into the hall, never waking James. Bursting through Legend's door, I found him in a ball in the middle of the queen-sized bed. I couldn't understand anything he said over the crying, but whatever it was had destroyed him. He trembled when I turned the bedside lamp on, and the instant I sat on the mattress to pull him into my arms, my shorts were wet, and it only got worse when he made his way to my lap. Legend had wet the bed, though I wasn't sure he even realized it at this point.

It seemed more important to calm whatever had him upset than to change either of our clothes. So I rocked him in my arms and tried to quiet him with my touch before bothering him with my words.

"Did you have a bad dream?" I asked in a hushed voice after the tears eased up.

He nodded his little, red head against my chest and clung to my arm.

"Do you want to talk about it?" When he didn't answer, I kept talking. "I used to have really bad dreams after my parents passed away. They would keep me up for hours, but there was never anyone around to hold me or tell me it would be okay."

"I miss my mama," he whimpered.

I still missed mine every day, and she'd been gone for almost half my life, but I couldn't lie to him and tell him that would stop. It wouldn't—ever. Instead, I offered him the only truth I had. "I know you do, and you always will. I promise it will get easier. And you have your daddy now. And me. And I promise, we both love you very much." My hand stroked his hair absentmindedly, although I thought it comforted me as much as it did him. "Can I tell you what I miss most about my parents?"

He finally released the death grip he had on me and pulled back to see my face. "What?"

"My mom's hugs and the way my dad smelled. She gave the best hugs, and he always smelled like spice." My meek smile told him of the pain that still lingered from my loss, even if he couldn't

STEPHIE WALLS

verbalize what he saw—he grasped that I understood. "You give hugs just like my mom did."

He smiled, but it didn't quite reach his eyes.

"What do you miss most about your mama, Legend?" This was the start to never letting him forget.

He thought for a minute and when he finally answered, he said, "Her telling me she loves me. I want to tell her one more time—just to make sure she really knows until I see her again."

"You know you can talk to her? She can hear you as long as you carry her in your heart. And you can tell her every day how much you love her, and when you do, you'll feel it right here"—I pointed to his chest—"when she responds."

"Do you still talk to your mama?"

"Every single day." Not out loud but in my thoughts. Her and my dad. It kept them both close to me. "And you should, too." I gave him another squeeze. "How do you feel about a bath?" I didn't care to draw attention to his accident, but I needed to get him cleaned up.

"Will you make it really warm? And add bubbles?"

"I'll see what I can do. Come on." Susan and Brock didn't have bubble bath in the guest bathroom, but they did have shampoo, and I might have poured copious amounts of it under the faucet to give Legend a foam-filled tub.

I wasn't sure what the protocol was for little boys being naked in front of their stepmothers, but when I tried to give him privacy, he used my shoulder to steady himself while he pulled his wet pajamas off. Once I had him into the water, I asked, "You okay in here for a few minutes while I go clean up?"

"You're not supposed to leave kids alone in a bathtub. I could drown in an inch of water." He stared at me with innocent eyes just before he started laughing.

I exhaled loudly and shook my finger at him. "You think you're funny. I'll be back to check on you in just a few minutes. Keep your head out of the bubbles until then." I winked at him and left the bathroom door open, so I could see him while I stripped the sheets from the bed and grabbed a change of clothes for him. Without waking up the entire house, I couldn't find another set of linens to put on the mattress, so I grabbed a blanket from my room and quickly changed my own clothes while Legend dried off.

When he finally got back in bed, I pulled the covers up to his chin and kissed his forehead. I'd left the light on beside the bed in case he got scared. His little hand wrapped around my wrist, and I met his sweet, brown eyes.

"Cora, will you stay with me?"

I ruffled his hair and gave him a smirk. "Of course. Scoot over."

And that's where James found me the next morning, with Legend wrapped in my arms and owning my heart.

18

CORA

"How are things going?" I hadn't had much time to talk to Hannah since we'd left New York, and I missed my best friend.

"Status quo. The real question is how are you holding up?" The concern was evident in Hannah's tone.

"Honestly, I'm struggling, but not with what you'd expect."

"Oh yeah? Insta-mom has been a walk in the park?" She giggled.

"Hannah, he's awesome. You're going to love him. He looks nothing like James, but it's uncanny how similar the two are. I'm completely gone for him."

"Then what's the problem, are you jealous?"

"Of what?" I'd just told her how much I adored Legend. There was no reason to think I'd be jealous of his relationship with his dad.

"The *other* woman," she whispered as if Chelsea were a secret.

"You *are* aware she passed away, right?"

"Yeah, but she still had your husband's child. And I remember how you felt about her when you were in France. This has to be like a giant slap in the face—her parting gift to you."

"Oh God, no, Hannah. Not at all. Actually, quite the opposite. I think my jealousy over her relationship with James when I was gone was kind of petty. He never even saw her, yet somehow, it equated to more in my mind than it ever actually was. I didn't comprehend how much James actually told her about our relationship until I met Legend. Chelsea went out of her way to tell her son how much his dad loved me."

"*I'd* be jealous."

"No, you wouldn't." I dismissed her comment and waved my hand in front of me like she could actually see it through the phone. "I'm sure it's hard to imagine finding out your husband has a child, and I admit, I was shocked. And I struggled with my emotions on that issue alone for days—back and forth. Then once I met Legend, I realized what a blessing Chelsea gave to James, and indirectly, me."

"Then what are you struggling with? If it's not Legend, and it's not Chelsea, what does that leave?"

"Dottie. Gwendolyn. Whatever she goes by these days." Anger seeped through the line, clutching my words until they reached Hannah's ear.

"I'm lost. Who is that?"

"Dottie is the woman who has taken care of Legend until we got here. Gwendolyn is my grandmother." That was clear as mud. Even speaking about it brought out a side of me I didn't like.

"And they're connected, how?"

"They're one and the same."

"But you were never close to your grandmother, right?"

"Never. Yet she's this amazing, doting, caring figure in Legend's life. And while I appreciate what she's done for James's son, I resent her for not doing the same when I lost my parents."

"I thought Geneva Key was like the Beverly Hills of Florida; how did this twisted situation become your life?"

"Good question. I don't have answers. Every time I get close to getting any, my anger and resentment rear their ugly heads, and I ruin any attempt I make to talk to her."

"If she's this close to Legend, you have to fix it, Cora. That's not fair to him. Or James. And it's really unlike you. I could totally understand having resentment toward the woman who'd kept a child a secret for years, or even James indirectly. The only people you're hurting by not resolving whatever it is that's going on in your head, are you and Legend."

Hannah was right. I *knew* she was right. And somehow, I had to rectify, or at least minimize, the destruction my animosity created. The two of us talked for an hour about nothing—it was one of the things I loved most about her. She had an uncanny ability to sweep my thoughts from anything important and bring me back to a happy place. I hated not having her around and wondered how hard it would be if we made Geneva Key home again.

We'd spent the better part of the two weeks getting to know Legend. I never imagined James would be great with kids, and I surprised myself with how easily I'd fallen for him. Something clicked between us that night he'd woken up from a bad dream. Maybe it was that we both shared something most kids never experience, or maybe he was just easy to love—either way, he'd captured my heart, and now I had to make things right. For Legend's sake.

I hadn't called. Legend was with James, and I hoped Gwendolyn was home. I hesitated—feeling like an intruder—the brass knocker was the only thing I recognized. The weathered *C* had been on their front door at the beach house when I was in high school. I should have noticed it no longer adorned the beach house when I'd rapped on a stranger's door—somehow, I hadn't missed it then, yet I recognized it now. It made a rich thud with each bang I gave it, and after three, I stopped to wait.

My weight shifted from side to side, foot to foot. I didn't often get nervous, but whatever happened today would not only define my life, it would direct the path of James's and Legend's as well. I hadn't comprehended what a burden I'd carried until we came back to Geneva Key. And now, being here, with her, brought all of that resentment and anger to the surface. No matter how hard I tried, I hadn't been able to let it go.

When the door finally cracked open, I was met by a face I wanted to love but couldn't figure out how.

"I had hoped you'd come by at some point. Please, come in." She ushered me through and straight into her home. "Is everything all right with Legend?" Gwendolyn asked as she pointed me toward the couch.

"Oh yeah, he's fine. He and James went to the park."

"Would you like some coffee?"

Coffee indicated I'd be here a while. It would also give me something to do besides fidget with my hands and pick at my fingers. "That would be nice, thank you."

She made her way to the kitchen, leaving me on the couch. "Your father was a big coffee drinker, although, I don't recall your mother ever liking it much."

I smiled at the memory. My love of the drink had indeed come from my dad. "She didn't care for it, but I used to steal sips of his when he wasn't looking." It had slipped out before I realized I was being civil.

"Are you hungry? I have some muffins."

"No, thank you. Coffee is good."

She returned to the living room and sat in the chair facing me on the couch. Her long, slender fingers rested in her lap, and her eyes sparkled when she looked at me. "You look just like them both. A perfect mixture of their best qualities."

I'd heard that all my life, and it was true. "Thank you. They were amazing people."

"That they were. Your father loved your mother very much."

I didn't think I could handle the niceties for long. I was well

STEPHIE WALLS

aware of how great my parents were; I lived with them. I'd spent seventeen years with them that she hadn't been a part of so I didn't need her to preach to me about their greatness.

"I don't mean to be impolite, Gwendolyn, or ungrateful, because I can't tell you how much it means to James that you were there for Legend, but what happened?"

"Cora, there's a lot of years to account for—most of which no longer matter."

"Don't do that. Please. It took a lot for me to come here, and I need to make this work for Legend. If we're going to make peace, you're going to have to be honest with me. What was so wrong with me that you didn't love me the way you do him? What made Chelsea so special that when she needed a home, yours was available, yet you left me isolated after my parents died? I just need the truth, Gwendolyn."

"I can give you my version...although, I think it will raise more questions than it will answer."

Losing my patience wasn't going to get us anywhere. "I need you to give me something, please."

"Okay. Would you like me to start from the beginning?"

"Sure." I didn't care where she started.

She held up a finger and went to the kitchen when the timer for the coffee went off. A few minutes later, she returned with two mugs, creamer and sugar, and a carafe. I imagined if she brought the whole pot, she intended to be here a while. When she finished making a cup, she leaned back in the chair, and I felt like I was listening to Sophia from *The Golden Girls* tell me a story about Sicily.

"I wasn't a very good mother to Joey. I tried. I meant well. It was just a different time, and I allowed my life to be dictated by your grandfather. Don't get me wrong—he wasn't a bad person; he just had an image to uphold, and certain things were expected of

262

him being a Chase. The name comes with a lot of responsibility, Cora."

I rolled my eyes, having heard this same song and dance from my father. Not because he believed it, but rather because my grandparents had.

"Even when I was home—which wasn't a lot due to my obligations to charities and women's organizations—I wasn't very present in your dad's life. We had nannies who did the things mothers should. I didn't know any different—it's all I witnessed growing up. And by the time your dad graduated, we didn't have the type of bond that kept him coming home every chance he got. And that was my fault, not his."

So far, I hadn't learned anything I wasn't already aware of. "So why not fix it?"

"I didn't think much about it when he was in college. Your grandfather convinced me it was all part and parcel for a man when leaving the nest. He didn't need his mother coddling him. After graduation, I tried to reconnect with him. We still spent some holidays together. By that point, he and your mother were close to marriage and split their free time between her family and ours."

She broke to take a sip of her coffee.

"Your mother was brilliant, smart as a whip. There was no doubt she'd go far; I just didn't realize they'd end up in New York. Not that any of that mattered. I had a hard time trying to connect when they were so far away, and your grandfather thought I was coddling Joey by attempting to strengthen the tie. 'Cut the cord, Gwynnie.' I can't tell you how many times I heard that from Owen." She seemed lost in a time she hadn't thought about in ages.

I just stared at her, waiting for her to get to the point.

"It's hard to start being a mother when your son is in his twenties, Cora. And while your dad was never unkind, it was clear that he'd started his own life, one I wasn't an important part of. I kept trying. I called, sent cards, presents. At first, they were received and reciprocated. It wasn't until your mom found out she was pregnant with you that so much changed."

And there it was. My mother and I were the reason for the separation from her son. At least the final separation. "I just don't understand. If you longed for this relationship with him, then why didn't you try to have it with me when you had the chance?"

"I had made commitments I believed I couldn't get out of that coincided with your parents' death. Plain and simple, I made the wrong choice. At the time, I was heavily involved in the Huntington Foundation, and Chelsea's mom, Janie, was already showing symptoms. I didn't know how to be there for you without letting someone I'd loved like my own down."

"But I *was* your own."

"In a lot of ways, so was she. Cora, I admit I didn't handle things properly. I made mistakes. But it was never because I didn't love you—"

"No. Just that you loved someone else more." I set my cup on the coffee table. "I shouldn't have come here. I don't know what I had hoped to resolve." My voice remained calm and steady. If I stayed any longer, my emotions would get the best of me, and I wouldn't be able to restrain myself.

She leaned forward and put her hand on mine. "Please don't go. I can't take any of it back, although I desperately hope to fix whatever we have going forward."

I looked at the pictures she had around the house. It was hard not to notice that the few of my dad stopped in his late teens, and there were more of Legend—and the girl I assumed was Chelsea—than anyone else, including my grandfather. There wasn't a single one of me.

"It's like he ceased to exist in your world when he left Geneva Key. Funny how that happens, huh?" My heart tore in two at the thought of my dad experiencing this same pain with her. I'd never had anything other than loving parents, and having an absent grandparent was completely different than it being my mom or dad.

My grandmother had begun to cry, but her tears were meaningless. I grabbed my keys and headed for the door. With my fingers wrapped around the handle, I turned to face her again. "I deserved better, Gwendolyn."

And as I slammed the door behind me, I heard her say, "So did they."

***

I made it to the end of the driveway before curiosity got the better of me. I shouldn't care what she'd meant by *so did they*, yet each step I took got harder as the sentiment echoed in my mind. I stopped and stared at the sky, cursing God for giving me a heart that made me unable to let those three words go.

"Ugh," I groaned to no one. Nothing she could say would change anything. Still, for some reason, I couldn't walk away. It was like not picking up the next book after a major cliffhanger. I had to have the truth, even if the ending sucked.

My shoulders dropped in defeat, and I pivoted on the ball of my foot to head back to my grandmother's porch. Each time I lifted my foot, taking me closer to her front door, I cringed inside.

"Get the information. In and out. You don't have to make friends with her or even peace. Just find out her side and go." Talking to myself in my head was one thing; doing it out loud took my irritation to a whole new level. I sounded like an idiot having a conversation with no one around. Thankfully, there were no witnesses.

I took a deep breath and clanged the brass *C* before Gwendolyn answered again. I hated eating crow, it was sinewy and tough to swallow. Just as I was about to turn around and give up, she answered with a gracious smile on her face. There wasn't a hint of "I told you so" to be found. In fact, she looked relieved that I'd returned.

"What was that supposed to mean?" I quipped.

"Cora, this isn't a conversation for all of Geneva Key to take part in. You'll need to come inside."

I huffed before following her back to the seat I'd just vacated on her couch.

"I think it might be best if I just get to the heart of where the problems started. I need you to promise you'll stick this out and not walk off. There's too much history at stake for you not to hear it all. And a lot of it I didn't know until you and James arrived here."

"Fine." I had to drop the attitude and the wall. If my mind weren't open to what she had to say, I wouldn't hear or retain any of it. I'd be thinking of ways to retort instead of listening to the things that came out of her mouth.

She took a deep breath and let it out. "I met Janie after your father asked me to go speak with her."

"Janie? As in Chelsea's mother?" I really was confused.

"Yes. Every Chase signs iron-clad prenuptial agreements—well, prior to you, however, that's neither here nor there."

"What does that have to do with Janie?"

"Your father violated the agreement between himself and your mother with her."

My brows dipped. I wasn't sure I heard what she insinuated.

"Joey made mistakes. He traveled a lot, and unfortunately, never hearing the word no and always getting everything he wanted in life without consequences didn't set him up to turn down things he was after as an adult. Including another woman."

I cocked my head to the side, now wide-eyed as a thousand thoughts ran through my head. And I remained quiet.

She closed her eyes, and it appeared to hurt her to tell me whatever was on the tip of her tongue as much as it was going to pain me to hear it. Gwendolyn didn't reopen them when she started speaking, either. Somehow, I sensed she couldn't bear to see my face.

"Your father adored your mother. And you were less than a year old. That first year of your life was one of the best in mine. You had brought your dad back into my life, and I was determined not to let the opportunity slip away. Nevertheless, it all came crashing down the day he called me about Janie."

Her lids slowly parted and tears streamed down her cheeks. "He and Janie were pregnant. If your mother found out, she'd leave him and take you. Neither of which he could stomach, nor could I."

"My dad got another woman pregnant?"

She nodded.

"Did my mom ever find out?" I almost shrieked. My mother and father had the epitome of a perfect marriage. I had always hoped James and mine would be as strong—and they were so similar in my eyes.

I just didn't realize *how* similar their stories were.

"Not that I'm aware of."

My mother lived her entire married life with a man who'd cheated on her, and she'd never found out. That baffled me. However, as quickly as that thought entered my head, it fled to make room for another. I closed my eyes and shook my head, unable to fathom the weight of the reality I was about to acknowledge.

"Chelsea was my half sister?" Jesus, this was like a scene straight out of *Deliverance*. Not only was Chelsea my sister, she'd had a child with my husband making me her son's stepmother and aunt. There was nowhere in the world any of this was acceptable.

"Yes. But, Cora, I had no idea James was Legend's father. In all the years they lived with me, she never shared that piece of information because she knew how much he loved you. I begged her to tell him before he went to Paris, and she refused. James told her he planned to propose to the girl he loved, and that girl didn't want children."

"She didn't tell James because she thought I wouldn't accept his proposal if he had a child on the way?"

She nodded. "And had she ever said your name, I would have connected the dots. She held those secrets until she died. I didn't know whose house she worked at that night she met him. The only information I had was that he was in town for a few days and then went back to New York. Sadly, it was like reliving the nightmare I'd endured with your father."

Nothing she said made any sense. No one could be that selfless —or selfish, I wasn't sure which. Part of me was grateful I hadn't known, and part of me was angry as hell that James missed out on five years of his son's life.

"Was she sick when she got pregnant?"

"Yes. Although, I doubt James even realized it. She had tremors in her hands, and at that point, she wasn't comfortable driving because every once in a while, she'd get turned around. However, most of her symptoms were easily masked as fatigue or clumsiness. And she wasn't around James much before he left town. The disease didn't progress drastically until Legend was about three."

"How could she have ever thought she could raise a child alone?" The part of me that had been grateful to Chelsea for the gift she'd given us had turned to rage. "I can't imagine being so selfish knowing she was going to die and that child would have no one."

"He had me. The same way she always had. And in her eyes, that was a great life."

"Explain that to me. How did my dad go from knocking up her mom to you being the grandmother to her that you never were to me?"

"Would you like some more coffee, dear?"

I could tell that was her way of trying to rein in the conversation. She offered me a breather in the form of refreshments. My agitation had gotten out of control quickly, and I snapped at her. When in fact, the people I should be mad at were both dead. That word sobered me and calmed my stormy temper. *Dead.* They weren't here to defend themselves, and I hadn't been around when decisions were made. Instead of judging any of them, I needed to try to be compassionate—understanding.

I clenched my jaw and spoke through gritted teeth. "Yes, please."

With a fresh cup of coffee in hand, she finally put some pieces into the puzzle of my father's messed-up past. "When Joey called me, things had been going so well between us. Owen and I got to see you regularly, and something had finally changed your grandfather's priorities. He would rearrange his schedule a hundred times to fit in a trip to New York to visit you. If you believe nothing else I say, please trust your grandfather and I tried very hard to keep the relationship up, even though your father wouldn't have any part of it, and eventually, with enough time, your mother conceded."

"But why?" It broke my heart to think I'd had the love I'd seen Gwendolyn give to Legend and lost it.

"If your mother had found out Janie was pregnant, she would have been entitled to a large sum of money and likely would have divorced your father. I don't think he cared about the money, but he was terrified of losing the two of you. Your grandfather, on the other hand, was a different story."

With every word she spoke, it was as if she were reliving those days. The anguish visibly marked her expressions, and she appeared weary. Suddenly, she seemed older than she had minutes ago, and my heart hurt for her. Each sentence she uttered seeped into my soul, taking root.

"From the moment your dad called, Owen was convinced Janie was after the Chase money. He didn't believe she hadn't known Joey was married, even though Joey admitted to having kept it from her. In your grandfather's mind—which soon became your father's belief—Janie had intentionally gotten pregnant to ensure herself a paycheck."

This was not the man who loved me until I was seventeen. My

father had been affectionate and gentle and kind. He was gracious and generous to a fault. Most of all, he cherished my mother.

"Since the two men were such hotheads, I was sent to Chicago to negotiate a deal with Janie."

"Like hush money?" I was mortified, and my jaw hung loosely in shock and dismay. "Are you kidding me?"

"Cora, sweetheart, one of the things that come with privilege is image. And that was very big to the Chase name and reputation. No Chase man could afford to be associated with infidelity. They'd kept their noses clean for generations, and neither your grandfather nor your father were willing to stake their character on a woman your dad had a fling with."

"Is that what Janie was? Just a fling?" I agonized for the woman I'd never met. Even if she had been insignificant to my dad, someone paying her off was demoralizing.

"I wasn't sure until I met her. She cared for your father, although they were never serious. The two of them met up when he was in town. However, once she told him she was pregnant, and he wasn't interested in the child, she never spoke to him again."

"He wouldn't talk to her?"

"She never tried. He assumed she had gotten an attorney, which was why I was brought in. The family needed to settle the matter out of court to keep it out of the papers and off the news. Honestly, I don't believe she would have ever breathed a word of it to anyone. She refused the settlements I offered her every time I went to Chicago during the pregnancy."

I shook my head. "She didn't take a penny?" Here was a woman sitting on a goldmine who was about to be a single parent, and she didn't take anything.

"Not one."

"And that's how you got to know her?"

Her head bobbed slowly. "She was a wonderful woman. We became good friends—best friends, even. Nevertheless, your father resented my relationship with her and insisted I cut ties. He was afraid your mother would find out, and he'd lose everything."

"You wouldn't do that?" It wasn't really a question, because I already had the answer.

"Had he made the request before Chelsea had been born, it might have been a possibility. She was my grandchild just as much as you were. And I loved her. It just wasn't that easy."

"Then why did you stop seeing *me*?"

"It wasn't by choice, Cora. Joey quit answering my calls and found excuses why visits didn't work with your family's schedule. And over time, the divide had gotten so great there was no coming back from it. Right or wrong, I devoted my time to the grandchild I could see—the one whose mother welcomed me into their lives. I became very active in the Huntington Foundation because of the two of them, and the rest is history."

"Did Chelsea know?" I prayed to God she hadn't known we were related. That would take this whole situation from redneck to weird.

"No, sweetheart. It wasn't until she had lost the ability to talk that I told her the truth. Her mother had never wanted her to know, and I'd made a promise not to tell her. Although, when I faced Chelsea's passing away, it didn't seem right for her not to have *her* truth."

"How'd she take it?" I couldn't imagine finding out who my father was that late in life, much less after he'd passed away. Or knowing I was related to the wife of the father of my child—Jesus, it made my head spin. I had a hard time accepting it, I couldn't fathom hearing it on my death bed.

"I'm not sure she even understood, Cora. There's a lot doctors don't know about Huntingtons. Some believe the cognitive function is still good and the brain works normally, and the body has malfunctioned. While others believe that the brain suffers from something like dementia. Add in that she was young and how quickly the disease progressed, and there's no telling."

"So they're the reason you have devoted all your time to fundraising?"

"Them and hundreds of others I've met along the way. There's no cure, and I've lost two people I love to the disease. If I can be part of helping to find a cure, then I will have done something with my life that I'm proud of."

I stared at the grain in the wood of the coffee table without a clue as to how to process the years of deception my grandmother had unloaded on me. While I was desperate to cling to the anger I'd come in the room holding, all I felt was sadness and remorse. And I wondered how different our worlds would have been had my father let us all be a part of the other's lives. As much as I wanted to call Gwendolyn a liar, poke holes in her story, and refuse to believe my father had ever been anything different than the man I adored, something told me every bit of it was true.

"Cora..." My name hung in the air, and her tone wasn't warm.

I shifted my eyes to her and saw something that resembled fear.

"You and James need to have Legend tested."

***

I wandered aimlessly across the island. Although, the years of blame and weeks of turmoil with Gwendolyn at the forefront subsided. Eventually, I had to end up back at the Carpenters', nevertheless my mind was a disaster. The farther I walked, the more muddled I became. I'd cried more in the last two hours than I could remember in the last two years. Tears didn't bring clarity, only a headache.

I couldn't imagine how I'd tell James that Legend had a fifty percent chance of having Huntingtons, much less suggest having him tested. Moreover, I couldn't figure out why we would want a death sentence for a child we'd just met. If there wasn't a cure, then why live with that looming overhead. It made no sense to me, but it wasn't my choice to make. Legend wasn't my son—not biologically anyway. James and Gwendolyn would need to be the ones to make that decision. I didn't envy either in that choice and wished I could fix it with a hug, since that was about all I had to offer.

When the sun started to set, and I had no clearer understanding of anything I'd learned, I finally made my way up the beach and inside.

"Cora, where have you been? I've been worried sick. I tried calling your cell, but you left it here." Panic laced James's voice. And once he pulled me into the light and saw my puffy eyes, red from crying, he grabbed my cheeks. "Baby, what's wrong? Talk to me."

I was lost about where to start or how to unravel the tale I'd been told. There were too many moving pieces and parts I wasn't familiar with to paint an accurate picture. While rationally, I should have been more careful with my word choice, what flew out at the moment was less than eloquent.

"Gwendolyn thinks you need to have Legend tested."

His face contorted with confusion. "Tested? For what? He seems healthy as a horse."

"Huntingtons. It's hereditary." And just like that, the cat was out of the bag, and the weight began to lift from my shoulders. It wasn't fair to James, yet anytime I needed to unload, he'd always helped me carry my burden—this was no different.

"W-what?"

I nodded.

"Like what are the chances he has it?"

"Fifty-fifty." And I broke down in tears again. I'd done nothing other than cry since I'd left my grandmother's house.

"There's no way it's that high," he said in disbelief.

"My grandmother is as close to an expert on the disease as one can get without being a doctor. And that's what she told me." I'd learned far more than I'd ever cared to about what had taken

Legend's mother—my sister—so early in life. It was easy to see how she'd become completely engrossed in the charity. Just the idea that Legend might be afflicted made me want to join her plight.

"What else did she tell you? Have you been there all day?"

"Pretty much. Although, you probably should to sit down to hear all I have to say. Where's Legend?"

"My mom is putting him to bed. He was worn out from an afternoon in the sun. I swear I don't know where he gets all that energy from."

"Oh, he's staying tonight?"

"Is that a problem?"

"No." I smiled through my tears and touched his arm. "It's perfect." And somehow it was. That little boy was a piece of my husband and the sister I'd never met, and I refused to ever let him go.

When I finished telling James everything Gwendolyn had imparted on me, he struggled to comfort me while appreciating all she'd done for Chelsea, and in turn, Legend. I didn't have it in me to be jealous that she'd been there for the Airys. The truth was, had Chelsea told James about the baby, I wasn't sure I would have said yes when he proposed, and our lives would have been much more complicated. I hesitated to admit she'd done us a favor by not involving herself in our relationship, because that made me selfish as hell, however, I couldn't deny that thought or the truth in the reality.

"James, I don't think we can leave Geneva Key."

"You hate it here."

"I hated it for reasons that didn't really exist...at least not in the light I thought they had. I don't want to look back and have regrets. There's still time to get close to Gwendolyn, and Legend needs her. She's the only connection he has to his mom. I need her to help me to help him remember her—share things with him to keep Chelsea's memory alive."

"So you think we should what? Sell our house? What about the business in New York?"

"I don't have all the answers. I don't have *any* of the answers, nonetheless, I think with a decision, the rest will fall into place." We had long since moved to the couch, and sitting in the moonlight, I rested my hand on his forearm. "Legend should be in Geneva Key —where we have a support system, and so does he."

"You're sure about this?"

"Your dad already said he had a job for you. We have a place to stay until our house sells. The only detail to iron out is Neil. So yeah, I'm sure."

"Then I guess we need to talk to my parents, get Neil's input, and do what's necessary to take custody of Legend. I hate bouncing him around. He needs a home—whether that's in this house, one of our own, or New York. He needs to feel secure."

There was a long stretch of silence while the two of us pondered what lay ahead.

James kissed my temple and whispered into my ear, "I knew you'd find your way." My husband wasn't referring to clarity; he'd waited for me to shed the weight of anger to find the path we needed to walk as a family of three instead of two.

We talked late into the night, and when we finally went to bed, we'd made a decision not to have Legend tested along with having ironed out aspects of our lives that didn't exist on this island. I felt more confident than I had since James had shown me the letter from Clary, White, & Boyd. It would take getting used to, but both of us were about to have something we'd never dreamed of.

A family.

19

CORA

"SO YOUR FATHER WAS CHELSEA'S DAD, BUT SHE NEVER MET HIM, which makes you Legend's aunt and stepmother? And Gwendolyn, or Dottie, is not only your grandmother; she's my son's great-grand-mother? For a Chase, that sounds awfully reprehensible and totally preposterous—not to mention, a tad trashy."

I couldn't tell if he didn't buy it or he was so dumbfounded that reality hadn't quite hit him. So I stood there with my arms crossed over my chest, my hip cocked to the side against the dresser, and a death glare on my face while I blinked slowly in his direction. He continued to move about our room getting ready for bed, and still, I said nothing—waiting for it to register. When he finally stopped, presumably because I hadn't made a peep, I pursed my lips and raised my brow, daring him to make another joke.

"Baby, what do you want me to say?" He patted the mattress next to him, but I remained firmly planted. "I can't begin to wrap my mind around any of the twisted pieces in the puzzle or how none of the wires ever crossed in thirty-plus years. It's like a perfectly played game of Operation."

My arms dropped to my sides, and my fists balled in agitation as I pushed off the dresser. "You don't even seem to care. Like it's just another day in Geneva Key." I threw my hands in the air, exasperated by his indifference.

"That's not true. I just don't have a clue what to do with the information. It's like you found out your entire life was a lie, and the people who could answer questions aren't around anymore. I know you're struggling with letting go of the contempt for Gwendolyn, so I'm stuck mentally as to how to give you any advice."

I finally joined him on the bed and leaned against his shoulder. "That's not true. I think after everything she told me, that portion of my story doesn't warrant grasping much less clinging to as the gospel. If everything Gwendolyn says is true, then I haven't been fair to her. Unfortunately, I'm reluctant to believe what she said about my dad, either. He can't defend himself; he can't justify his actions—he was a good man, James. I just can't make heads or tails out of any of this. And worst of all, my grandmother has taken the fall for so many years, and we now have a son that we will have to explain this mess to."

He kissed the top of my head and wrapped his arm around my waist. "You know what's great?"

I shook my head.

"He's not going to ask anytime soon, and we have time to figure that part out. However, we're coming down to the wire on making a decision about staying here or going back to New York."

"I thought we'd made the decision." I didn't bother looking up, I just drew circles on his knee with my fingers absentmindedly.

"I wasn't sure if this stuff with Gwendolyn changed anything for you."

"If anything, it solidified my resolve to stay." I pulled back to meet my husband's gaze. "I've wasted a lot of years believing she was something she wasn't. I get that she still made mistakes, but she's the only Chase I have left in my life. I think I owe it to her to give her a chance, and maybe the two of us could be friends."

His brows came together and three little creases formed between them. I loved how he looked when he was thinking about something. "I'm surprised you're not more upset than this."

"I was." My shoulders rose in a half-hearted shrug. "But all the tears I cried didn't change my past or Chelsea's or Legend's...or even Gwendolyn's. And no matter how far I walked, the only solution I came up with was giving her the chance to prove my dad wrong."

"Never in a million years did I envision our life this way." He fell to the mattress on his back with his arms spread out.

I followed suit and then curled onto my side with his forearm under my neck. "You and me both. If it's the hand we have to play, might as well go for broke."

"That's entirely possibly moving to Geneva Key, but I'm all in." He winked at me and chuckled.

It was a scary truth. We had a house to sell and a business to deal with. Not to mention, our two best friends lived in New York and had followed us there. I dreaded telling Hannah we weren't coming back to live.

"Have you thought about what you're going to tell Neil?"

He turned to me, straight-faced, and said, "I assumed you'd tell Hannah, and she could break it to Neil." The humor danced in his eyes, and I playfully swatted at his chest.

"So I get to be the bad guy?"

"Girls are way more forgiving."

"Hardly, they hold a grudge forever. Guys slap each other on the ass and forget what was said in the previous sentence. This one's on you."

He sat straight up and leaned over to the nightstand to grab his phone. "No time like the present."

"You can't call him now. James, it's ten thirty at night."

"Yeah, and he probably just got home from the office."

"Oh, that makes it so much better. I'm not having any part of this."

"Where are you going? I thought this was for better or worse? In sickness and in health?" He was incorrigible.

"I'm going to take a shower. You can tell me how things go with Neil when I get out. I'll call Hannah tomorrow at a respectable time of day." And I sauntered off to the bathroom, closing the door just as Neil answered.

I couldn't stand the thought of losing our friends, even if it was just distance—they'd been our family when we thought we had no one else. And now it seemed we were abandoning them. Regardless, no matter how I worked the scenario in my head, doing what was best for Legend remained our greatest responsibility...I just hoped they understood.

I'd have to wait until tomorrow to find out. When I emerged from the shower turned bubble bath, my husband was fast asleep on top of the comforter. It was the only time I usually saw the boy I'd fallen in love with. When his features weren't marred with stress or the pressure of a day, the years fell away, and the James of our youth was there. And while I wanted to run my thumb over his eyebrow and caress his jaw, I simply kissed his forehead and covered him with a blanket. And silently thanked God for delivering me my own piece of perfection when I'd so desperately needed him.

***

Having joint custody of a young child was exhausting. We weren't obligated by court order to give Gwendolyn any time, but Legend loved her, and it gave me an excuse to spend time with her out of perceived obligation. I didn't have to admit I was anxious to get to know her or that I had questions. I didn't have to tell her I'd done nothing besides think about all the ways I'd missed out over the years. I got to use Legend as an excuse to have lunch with her during an exchange or walk on the beach while he played in the waves, or sit on a park bench when he climbed on a jungle gym like a monkey. And each opportunity opened the door to a relationship I'd never imagined I'd have, much less crave. Day by day, I realized what I would have missed out on had I not given her the chance. And I tried not to dwell on all I'd lost in favor of all I had to gain.

"I'm going to miss you tonight, buddy." Legend was tall and lanky, much like the pictures I'd seen of James at his age, and he gave the best hugs in the world. "You be good for Dottie tonight, okay?"

He gave me a look to indicate I had nothing to worry about, and it dawned on me, I was acting like a mother. Not just any mother, but Legend's. I ruffled his sunny, red hair, and then popped him playfully on the bottom as I stood. I handed Gwendolyn his bag as though he was her guest instead of ours, yet she took it graciously and didn't point out that he had everything he needed at her house.

"You two have fun."

"Bye, Cora." He turned to wave over his shoulder, as did Gwendolyn.

I just stood there, wondering why his departure left a gaping hole in my chest. I'd see him the next day—my grandmother, too. His absence suddenly seemed unfamiliar, and I wondered if this was how all mothers felt when their children were away—just before it dawned on me that I wasn't really his mother.

Although I wanted to be.

I stood on the pier, basking in the sunshine and watched the two of them walk into the distance. When I couldn't see them anymore, I finally turned around and went home.

"Where have you been?" James's panicked voice worried me.

"Legend and I had lunch with Gwendolyn, remember?" My brow furrowed, and I wondered how he could've forgotten.

"I didn't think you'd be gone this long. When did you stop carrying your cell phone with you?" He held up the device in question like I was being interrogated.

I shrugged and stepped past him to get water from the kitchen. "When we relocated to an island I can scream across, and I no longer had a job." I couldn't fathom what had him in an uproar.

Even with the chaos of finding out he had a son, meeting him, and staying at his parents' house, I hadn't felt so stress-free in years.

"Cora, we needed to leave for the airport fifteen minutes ago."

I glanced at the clock and realized just how late it was. "Okay, so let's go. I'll apologize when we get there."

"To them or me?"

I lifted up on my toes and placed a kiss on his jaw since it was the only thing I could reach. "Them of course. You already know I love you."

His inability to stay irritated with me always played in my favor —not that I took advantage of it. As I lowered my feet, his arm snuck around my waist, and his face nestled into the crook of my neck when he bent down. His whiskers were rough on my skin, although coupled with his fingers tickling my side, I broke out in gales of laughter. The harder I tried to escape, the more brutal his assault became until I wasn't convinced I'd walk away without peeing in my pants. "James—" His name was a breathless syllable between two giggles.

"Say it." The humor in his voice only spurred my silliness.

"Uncle."

"Try again."

"I surrender."

"Uh-huh."

"I love you?" I knew what he wanted, but this was so much more fun. Even if it just made us later to pick up our friends.

"Nice, but no."

As my back arched and he didn't relent, I finally gave him what he silently demanded. "I'm sorry."

He immediately ceased fire and secured me in his embrace. With a quick peck to the nose, he let me go and grabbed my hand to pull me out the door. "I love you, too."

The smile hadn't left my lips since the first poke in the ribs, still, hearing those three words from James Carpenter's mouth never ceased to make me feel like a teenager falling for the first time. I'd keep that goofy, love-struck grin plastered to my face until my cheeks hurt and the muscle refused to maintain it.

It didn't take all that long to get to the airport. Thankfully, traffic was light, so there would be no more apologizing. Neil and Hannah had no idea we'd been late since their plane hadn't landed, and we now waited on them.

"Are you excited to see Hannah?" We sat on a bench near the baggage claim.

I loved airports. People from all over the world moved seamlessly through space and time going from one destination to another, completely oblivious they were being watched. I could see people from all walks of life, countries I'd never been to, who spoke languages I didn't understand, and all had a purpose and a destination.

"Of course. It's only been a few weeks, but I haven't talked to her much. It'll be good to have a few days with them. Are you sad about the business?" I'd asked this question repeatedly and kept getting the same answer, yet I worried James had made a decision he'd regret just to please me. I had to continually remind myself that he made it for Legend.

His mouth twitched just before it opened. "Not really. I mean, I hate that I'm just dumping it on Neil, but a lot's happened, and it's just not where we're meant to be right now. That might change down the road, unfortunately, I have to focus on today."

"Do you ever think about how odd it is that your story and my dad's could have been so similar?"

"No, do you?"

The cart carrying elderly people flew past us, honking its horn, and a late passenger was called over the intercom, derailing my thoughts momentarily.

"Yeah." And it bothered me. My dad, not James.

The man who'd left Chelsea's mom alone wasn't the same guy

who'd raised me or been the husband to my mother. I hadn't fathomed any of these things when he was alive and had never even met my half-sister. I couldn't stop thinking about how odd it was that he'd left a child who ended up having a child who never met him to be raised by my grandmother. And had James decided not to be a part of Legend's life, Legend would have met the same fate his mother had. Somehow, Gwendolyn was left holding the hands of all those involved.

"Cora!"

Down the escalator came my best friend and her boyfriend. I jumped up, not bothering to elaborate on the topic James and I were discussing, and took off toward them. We met in the middle of baggage claim in an embrace. When she finally pulled back, her hands remained on my forearms like she was appraising me.

"Unemployment looks fantastic on you, and so does that tan. Are you living in the sand and sun?"

When she took my hands in hers, the light bounced off her finger and the giant diamond perched on the fourth one. "Oh. My. God. *When* did this happen?" I let go of her to use all ten of my fingers to inspect the engagement ring she'd waited so long for.

When I could finally focus on something other than the blinding sparkle from the two carats set in platinum, I glanced at James to show him her hand before meeting her eyes. They glistened with tears of happiness.

"He proposed two days ago. I was going to call you, I swear. Neil thought it would be better to tell you in person so we could all celebrate. Don't be mad." She poked out her bottom lip just slightly. I couldn't have cared less that she hadn't called—I was just grateful she was here.

James clapped Neil on the shoulder. "It's about damn time. You're lucky she waited. How many years has it been? Nine? Ten?"

"Eleven. Eleven years," Hannah answered for Neil with a chortle. Even if he'd never proposed, she wouldn't have left. They were as right together as James and I were.

"At least my girl didn't take a two-year, international hiatus." This was an ongoing ribbing between James and Neil, and thankfully, they usually left me out of it—even though I was the one who'd left.

"I hate to tell you, Mr. Carpenter, your stats aren't much better. We had a decade under our belt when you finally got serious." I loved to jab him.

"High school hardly counts, and again, you left for two years—so by default, those two things take off three and half years. I should get credit for having the ring even if it wasn't on your finger."

"Hard to wear a rock without a setting." Hannah giggled, clearly proud of her smartass insertion into the conversation.

"I'm wounded, Hannah. Here I thought we were pals, amigos, compadres—the first chance you get, you throw me to the wolves." James was so melodramatic.

However, it all felt so normal. The four of us. Together. I'd have a hard time when they left, but I was determined to enjoy them while they were here.

By the time we'd grabbed their bags and driven back to Geneva Key, the afternoon had gotten away from us. Together, with our best friends, we strolled the beach and picked up shells. We had dinner on the patio of a restaurant I didn't know existed even though I'd walked by a dozen times. With dessert and drinks, we ended the perfect evening listening to the waves crash against the shore and the few lone gulls cry into the night. As the breeze blew strands of hair against my face, I watched the tiny flame in the centerpiece flicker, yet never go out. The sounds of friendship lingered around the table, and my heart was full.

The next day, James sold his half of the company to Neil. They'd spent the morning with the Carpenters' attorney, and we hadn't heard from them. I worried what frame of mind James would be in when he and Neil got back. Although, I had to admit I hadn't been prepared for the smiles and overall joy that lit up his features.

When I got a second to pull him aside, I whispered, "Are you really all right with this?"

He kissed my lips and smacked my ass. "Baby, I'm thrilled. Life is good." And the truth was written on his face.

***

"So when do we get to meet the little urchin?" Neil was excited to meet his best friend's son.

"Cora's grandmother is bringing him home around lunch."

"How's that going, Cora?" The concern on Neil's face was endearing.

"Really well. It's not going to fix itself overnight, even so, I think we're both trying. And that's about all we can do right now. Legend makes it a lot easier."

"Does anyone have any idea why his mom gave him such an... odd name?" Hannah had chosen her words carefully as not to offend James, but he'd wondered the same thing.

"We haven't asked." I wanted to. However, with everything else going on, it seemed to be at the bottom of the list of things to question.

Before the conversation of namesakes could continue, the front door flew open as the doorbell rang. Gwendolyn tried to respect the Carpenters, while Legend had already made himself at home.

"Daddy, look what Dottie got me." He flew through the foyer and into the breakfast area where the four of us sat, bypassing Neil, Hannah, and me, in favor of launching himself into his father's lap.

I realized when I saw Neil's expression change how odd it must be for other people to hear Legend call James "Daddy," but it didn't sound foreign to my ears—it sounded like magic.

"What is it?" James stared at the toy as though he'd never seen one before, playing into the wonder of his son's amazement.

"A Nerf gun!"

Before anyone could warn him not to shoot it in the house, he popped off three right in a row, one of which bounced off my chair.

He bowed his head as though he were ashamed. "I'm sorry, Cora." He wasn't able to hide the grin that made his cheeks round, and I could tell he was trying to disguise his amusement.

It was easier to laugh and see him smile than to try to scold him when he was so cute. Thankfully, Gwendolyn had joined us, and she had no problems telling him not to shoot the gun at anyone or in the house. I mouthed, "Thank you," in her direction, and she waved me off as though it was nothing.

Remembering my manners, I jumped from my seat. "Hannah, Neil, this is my grandmother, Gwendolyn Chase—affectionately referred to as Dottie." The words had come out before I realized who bore witness to them.

No one else noticed, except Legend. "Hey," he dragged out the word the way only kids could. "I didn't know my Dottie is your grandma. That means you're in my family." And as quickly as he'd considered it, he'd moved on to another subject. "Is my grandma here? I wanna show her my gun."

"She's upstairs, Legend," I said, trying to lead him away from the conversation we weren't ready to have, and he took off in compliance.

"It was nice to meet you both. I hope you enjoy your stay."

I showed Gwendolyn out with an unexpected hug and returned to the table to a conversation already underway.

"He doesn't look anything like you. Other than the fact he clearly got your height and weight issues." Neil and James had been friends their entire lives, and he apparently remembered him as a child. "You look way better as a redhead," he joked.

"You just said he didn't look a thing like me. Make up your mind, man."

"Well, DNA doesn't lie."

James threw a dish towel at his friend while Hannah and I

merely observed their stupidity. We'd all known each other for a lot of years, and some things never changed—I wouldn't have it any other way. When I'd been in Paris, Hannah had painted a mental picture of a James I never cared to see, and I'd feared that was who I would find when he came to France. Thankfully, we'd healed, and their friendships had mended.

FOUR DAYS HADN'T BEEN NEARLY ENOUGH TIME TO SOAK IN EACH other's company. They were completely enamored with Legend by the time they left and begged us to bring him with us when we sold the house. I never thought I'd see a day when any of us had wanted to spend time with kids. Life had a funny way of throwing curve-balls that ended up being the perfect pitch.

When the three of us said goodbye to Neil and Hannah at the airport, it was with the assumption we'd see them again soon, nevertheless, the pain was still staggering. We only had one more thing to do before our lives had come full circle—and that was sell our house. I refused to consider that we needed to buy one here or pack or move—those were all chores for another day. I had a hard enough time saying goodbye to the only girlfriend I had. I loved James and Legend both, but Geneva Key was a far cry from New York City, and making friends would be a challenge.

Maybe the portal down on Main near the grocery store would spit out some of the girls it had swallowed after high school and shoot them in my direction. It'd be great if one of them had managed to have a kid during their time in the black hole that existed in the population here. James had joked about it for years, and now that I was back, I realized just how truthful he'd been. We'd spent so little time here after graduation that it hadn't occurred to me that people left and never returned or that there was a genera-tion consistently missing from the census in Geneva Key.

Now that we were here, I had to find a way to make it a home. I couldn't count the days until I left for college or the number of weeks before I turned eighteen. We'd made a commitment for Legend, and this was our new life. Geneva Key, not the bright lights of the city.

Standing in the airport, watching our friends go through security, James put his arm around my waist, and Legend stood in front of us waving. It wasn't the life I pictured, yet now, I couldn't imagine a world without that little boy in it. James bent down and kissed the top of my head.

"You ready?" he asked me.

And I was—for whatever came next.

EPILOGUE

LEGEND

I missed my mama every day. She told me she'd have to go to heaven first, but I hadn't really believed her. Or maybe I didn't understand what that meant. Everything she told me had been true. My daddy came to take his turn when hers was over, and he brought Cora. My mama hadn't been able to tell me much about her except that she would love me. And she'd been right.

Daddy and I played when he'd get home from work, but Cora was my best friend. We made scrapbooks together and told stories about our mamas, and when I wanted to cry, she didn't treat me like a baby. She held me, and she cried, too. I knew she was sad here, even if she never told me, so I took her out every day looking for a friend—not for me, for Cora. And every time I saw a shooting star, I gave Cora my wish.

When I started school, I met lots of kids. My teacher said they were friends—but I didn't think if someone bit you or hit someone else that made them a friend. I thought it made them mean. Maybe Cora should tell Mrs. White what a friend *really* is.

"Legend, are you ready?" Cora cracked open my door to peek around it.

"Yep." I only had to go to school until lunch, then Cora and I got to play until Daddy came home.

I grabbed her hand after she slid the glass door closed on the porch. Our new house wasn't as big as Grandma and Papa's. I had my own room, and Daddy and Cora were right across the hall. There were two more rooms, one for Hannah and Neil, and one that didn't have anything in it—it needed a little brother, but when I asked Cora for one, she laughed.

That room was still empty.

"It's hot today." Cora put a baseball hat on my head.

I hated hats. Still, I loved Cora, so I left it.

She grabbed my bag of toys and our towels, and I ran down the path behind our house to the shore.

"Wait for me, Legend," she called.

One day, I'd be big enough not to have to stop in the sand. One day, I'd be able to run straight into the water and dive in the waves just like my daddy did. Today, as I bound toward the sand and jumped over piles and dodged holes, I almost ran into a little girl who was walking in circles, talking on the phone. When I looked around, her mama wasn't far away, and then before I could say anything, Cora did.

"She's cute."

"Thank you." The lady smiled at Cora. "I'm Jade, and that's my daughter, Aria."

They shook hands, which I thought was silly; I didn't know why grownups did that—seemed like a fast way to pass germs.

"I'm Cora, and this is Legend. He's five. How old is your little girl?"

"Oh, she's two and a half."

Aria walked in a big eight on the sand going back to her mom and then gave her the phone before running over to me. I thought she was going to tackle me like a football player. Instead, she grabbed my hand and pulled me toward the wet sand.

Cora waved at me when I looked back to make sure she was close by, and she pointed at the bag of toys. I ran back to get them, leaving Aria on her bottom in a puddle. When I grabbed the handles of the bag, Cora smiled while she talked to the lady she'd met.

I'd done my job—Cora had found a friend, and I hadn't wasted all my wishes on shooting stars.

Later that night, after Cora had read me stories, my daddy came in to kiss me goodnight. Instead of messing up my hair and hugging me like he always did, he kneeled on the floor, and Cora sat up. Both of them took my hands, and I wondered what horrible thing they were going to tell me. My mama and Dottie always did this when something bad happened, and I immediately started to cry. I got five years with my mama; there was no way Daddy and Cora's turn was up already.

"What's wrong, little man?" My daddy was worried, but I had to put on a brave face. If he was sick, I'd be a big boy and put on my superhero cape—my mama told me I was a warrior. "Why are you crying?"

I shook my head, unwilling to answer until they told me.

Cora took my chin and turned my head in her direction. Her smile was sweet like my mama's. "Your daddy and I have something to tell you."

My chest puffed out as I took a deep breath, and I waited for how bad it would hurt to hear. My eyes squeezed shut, and I heard my mama tell me she loved me in my heart, just as Cora brushed her finger on my cheek and wiped away a tear.

"Don't cry." She laughed, and I opened my eyes. "We hope this is something you'll be happy about."

I fought my frown, and even as I opened my mouth, I could tell I wasn't doing a good job of hiding it. "W-what?" I hiccupped.

My dad stood and picked me up before setting me in his lap on the bed. He had big arms, and no one could hurt me when they were around me...but Cora needed to be inside them, so she was safe, too. I pulled on her hand until she landed in the middle of our hug. Once everyone adjusted, my daddy finally told me their secret.

"You know how you asked for a brother for that room next door?"

"You got me a brother?" I practically screamed in my daddy's ear. "Where is he?" I tried to get out from the pile, but neither of them let me go.

"He's not here just yet, Legend." Cora's eyes were happy when she pointed to her belly. "He's still in here. He'll be here in a few months, and you'll get to meet him then."

My shoulders slumped. I hated waiting, but I really wanted a little brother...until I realized he would be theirs—and I wasn't. "Will you love him more than me?"

Daddy turned me in his lap. "Never. That's a promise."

"Can I name him? My mama said names are important. That's why she named me Legend."

"They are." Cora looked confused. "Do you *know* why your mom picked Legend?"

I nodded my head and smiled like I would if I said, "cheese"— big and happy. "Because a legend is as powerful as a dream but as fragile as a thought."

I didn't know what that meant, but it had been important to my mama, so I made sure to remember it. And whatever it was, it meant something to Cora, too, because she started to cry like girls do when they watch a silly movie.

When the baby finally came, I was already six, so Daddy and Cora let me name her. It wasn't a brother like they'd said, but she wasn't so bad. They'd made me a promise never to love her more than they did me, so that's what we named her—as a reminder.

And Promise Carpenter was my favorite girl in the whole world...next to Cora.

THE END

ACKNOWLEDGMENTS

My peeps...

Linda—Lucky number seven. Thank you for all you do. There aren't words.

Jason—There are days I'm not sure why you put up with this whole writing/author gig, but I'm grateful you do. My dream is always your top priority. Not if, but when.

Magoo—just...you!

Readers, bloggers, editors, proofreaders, cover designers, and anyone else who had a hand in this coming to fruition, being read, or even being love...without you, my words just letters on a page. Thank you!

ABOUT THE AUTHOR

Stephie Walls is a lover of words—the more poetic the better. She lives on the outskirts of Greenville, South Carolina in her own veritable zoo with two dogs, three cats, the Mister, and Magoo (in no preferential order).

She would live on coffee, books, and Charlie Hunnam if it were possible, but since it's not, add in some Chinese food or sushi and she's one happy girl.

For more information:
www.stephiewalls.com
stephie@stephiewalls.com

Made in the USA
Middletown, DE
24 October 2020